... Roth and
Don Gannon Novel

CHEROKEE EMERALD

3rd Coast Books, LLC
19790 Hwy. 105 W. Ste. 1318
Montgomery, Texas 77356

R. M. MORGAN

Other Harriett Roth and Don Gannon Novels
By R. M. Morgan

CROWN HUNT
LAST TRAIN TO DANVILLE

Cherokee Emerald

A Novel

by

R. M. Morgan

3rd Coast Books, LLC
19790 Hwy. 105 W. Ste. 1318
Montgomery, Texas 77356

3rd Coast Books, LLC
19790 Hwy. 105 W. Ste. 1318
Montgomery, TX 77356

www.3rd CoastBooks.com

ISBNs
Perfect Binding (Print) 978-1-946743-54-1
eBook/Mobi 978-1-946743-55-8
eBook/ePub 978-1-946743-56-5

Project Coordinator - Ian W. Gorman, Co-Publisher
Editor - Ian W. Gorman
Cover Artist - Fiona Jayde
Cover Coordinator- Theo Viggers
Text Designer - Theo Viggers

Printed in the United States of America

READER TESTIMONIALS

"R.M. Morgan has done it yet again! After giving us the *Crown Hunt and Last Train to Danville*, he offers us a third helping of a gripping mystery begging to be solved. As always, he incites us to sleuth for the truth!"

— Leonard Szymczak,
bestselling author of
The Roadmap Home: Your GPS to Inner Peace
and award-winning author of *Kookaburra's Last Laugh.*

"In *Cherokee Emerald*, Morgan cleverly develops his characters and plot into an intriguing, kick-ass whodunnit. It reveals an intriguing premise, engaging characters and the kinds of twists and suspense mystery readers love. This real page-turner captivates from the beginning and satisfies to the end."

— Craig Wells

"As with the previous two books, I like how the story travels through time. Events in the past sit dormant, and then come back to affect the present. I also like the word imagery, there are many, many examples throughout the book. Comparison of gunfire to popcorn slowly bursting in a microwave, description of Sandford as a muskrat, and his black, lifeless eyes."

— Barbara Hennessey

"What I liked about the book, was the setting in Cherokee country, and the history about the Cherokees and the fact that there were gems and gold in the East. Who knew? I also liked the way the story flowed so easily after I got started. It was a page-turner."

— Linda Rosenberg

"*Cherokee Emerald* is the latest mystery from R. M. Morgan. It combines page-turning action with a history tale reminiscent of Clive Cussler's method of weaving a little-known historical story with an action-packed mystery. His characters have a warm, homey feeling that pulls the reader through the story. The who-dun-it aspect keeps the reader anticipating the conclusion."

— Richard Hoff

CONTENTS

ACKNOWLEDGMENTS

This tale of events connected to the Cherokee Nation and the Trail of Tears is fiction. In researching the episodes underlying this story, I read many books. For readers wishing to peruse historical fact, I suggest the following books as a starting point:

The Cherokees vs. Andrew Jackson. Brian Hicks (Editor). March 2011. Smithsonian Institute. October 16, 2020.

The Cherokee Nation and the Trail of Tears. Theda Perdue and Michael D. Green. Penguin Group, New York, 2008.

Medicine of the Cherokee: The Way of Right Relationship. J. T. Garrett and Michael Tlanusta Garrett. Bear and Company, Santa Fe, NW 87504, 1996.

Blood Moon: An American Epic of War and Splendor in the Cherokee Nation. John Sedgwick. Simon and Schuster, New York, 2018.

My writing coach, Leonard Szymczak, continues to guide my writing growth and increase my enjoyment of composing fiction.

Special thanks go to the Morgan kinfolk (Travis, Tyler, Debbie, and Ida), who encouraged me and hypothesized with me on the story. I profited from the reviews of Mel Zimmerman, Craig Wells, Dirk Sayers, Mary Keown-Watkins, and Dick Hoff. Mary Harris performed a manuscript critique and edit.

Ron Mumford and Ian Gorman at 3rd Coast Books rooted for me and supported me in so many ways. Fiona Jayde did another marvelous job with the cover design.

"The proud heart feels not terror nor turns to run
and it is his own courage that kills him."
— Homer, The Iliad

1

THE TRAIL OF TEARS – THE YEAR EIGHTEEN-THIRTY-EIGHT

The first death on the hunt occurred on the road to Oklahoma. It happened on a freezing, misty day in December 1838 when Waya was exhausted and shaky. Weak from throwing up, he stumbled off the trail, his entrails straining to hold back a loose, watery bowel movement. Relieved, he slumbered, sprawling close to a leafless maple tree. After waking in the bitter cold, he rose, braced himself against the tree, and glanced up the muddy dirt road. His body felt a sudden iciness. Just visible through the snow squalls, three men on horseback approached. They disappeared for a second in a flurry, before reappearing closer.

They moved without haste toward the sick man. The first rider, his eyes blue and lifeless, wore a long tan coat and a wide-brimmed black hat. The second rider was a shorter Indian brave in a drab brown jacket and pants. The third rider was also an Indian brave, carrying a lance and wearing a red coat hand-sewn from a blanket. The man in the wide-brimmed hat bumped Waya off the road with his horse. Sprawled on the ground, the unwell brave searched the mud-covered way for help, but it was empty, no one was nearby to rescue him.

The three dismounted and surrounded him. Their leader stood in front of the brave. "My name's Sandford. Been looking for you. Give me the gem."

Waya stood and shoved the man backward, knocking his wide-brimmed hat off his head, and turned to plod up the road. In his weakened state, the three thieves caught him and dragged him back to the tree. The brave lowered his head and butted Sanford to the ground. His remaining strength faded, and Sandford's two comrades held him tight and pushed him toward their leader, who asked, "Where is it?"

The sickly man clamped his jaws tight and didn't speak.

In a vicious response, Sandford pounded the brave with his fists and kicked him in the stomach. Waya was unable to protect himself and vomited on the ground. The three thieves laughed.

Waya heard a sucking noise from the mud out on the road. A woman in a blanket, carrying a small child on her back in a shawl, tottered by. She appeared exhausted, ignored the four of them, and kept staggering down the road.

Sandford opened his coat. On his belt, he had a long knife in a leather sheath. The three held the brave and went through his garments, searching for the gem. Sandford discovered a folded-up sheet of paper in Waya's pants pocket.

He took the fake map, Waya thought. He'll let me go.

Sandford used his hat to keep the snowflakes off the map. He studied the sheet of paper for a minute and slowly smiled and shook his head in satisfaction. After folding the sheet and fixing it in his coat, he pulled out his steel knife with a blade long as his forearm. "I got what I came for." After scanning the road to ensure no one watched, he drove the nasty knife into Waya's stomach before slowly pulling it out. "That's for making me ride so far."

The other two released the brave. Waya fell rearward against the tree and slumped to the ground with his back against the trunk.

The three thieves mounted their horses and rode back east, disappearing once again into the falling snow.

Oh, Great One, it hurts. It hurts so bad, Waya thought. His injury, a deep penetrating puncture, caused him to bend forward from the hurt. The Indian brave pushed his hand against his belly to hold back the stream of blood and sat in the twilight with his back against the maple tree. To lessen his agony, he tried pressing both hands against his stomach. His fuzzy vision looked through flurries and off to his left side. He thought of his arrival on Mother Earth, heard the ghosts, lots of them, from long ago.

Years before, he had been born into the Indian Nation, arriving in the hut of his mother. He spent much of his childhood in that shelter, his Cherokee culture being a matriarchal society. The lodging of Waya's mother was one of several in a half-circle pattern, all surrounded by a large field cultivated by the women. The shelters and grounds were handed down mother to daughter. While the women hoed in the meadows, the men hunted for food, including rabbit and venison. He remembered weeding in his mother's small garden, where she talked with the herbs and plants.

As Waya sprawled under the tree and the dark-gray, gloomy sky, he groaned and watched the blood leaking through his fingers. An Indian woman, slouching and holding an army blanket around her, slogged past him. She was another helpless victim of the Native American *removal* termed 'The Trail of Tears.' The US Army had gathered masses of the Native Americans by force and took them without allowing time to pick provisions. It hurt Waya to move, and he felt too exhausted to cry out to the woman walking past him down the trail. Soon, he was alone again and falling asleep. But the constant hurt kept rousing him from slumber.

Years before, the Elders had trained him to hunt. They taught him Nature had been here before the Cherokee, and he must honor

Her. And he must accept his ancestors, who realized the critical balance the Indian had with all things. Waya had learned that to slay an animal required individual songs and prayers for the slain beast, and he was to use as much of the animal as possible. Among the Native Americans, the Cherokees had always hunted and farmed.

He recalled how things changed when the white men came, how they wanted to swap for the deer's skin. The white man's traders exchanged cheap goods—inferior muskets, low-grade rifles, Colonial-style clothing, gunpowder, pots, and pans—for the hides. Waya dropped out of the mission school he had attended and joined the Native American men in the hunt for deer hides to trade with the white man. The Cherokee Elders had spoken—when the hunter was hungry and needed warmth, permission had been given by the deer to be killed. However, the hunters were slaying when their bellies were full, and their bodies warm. In time, the deer grew scarce until there were so few that many hunting parties came back without a kill.

The injured brave blinked, and the images in his head changed. During this period, he had returned from a hunt and saw a beautiful young woman, just growing out of childhood. With skin so smooth and slightly tan, black flowing hair, and doe-like eyes. The two of them became closer, and Waya had begun to dream of a day he would provide for her. But the traders and the American Indians had decimated the deer population. Without venison, what would he bring to her hut to nourish them? He was strong, and one of the Elders taught him to search for gems. He unearthed feldspar—used for glass and ceramics—for trade. Over time, he dug a deep trench in an area where he had found a few small gems on the surface.

Despite his pain, he smiled at the memory of finding a large green emerald, a six-sided crystal about seven inches long—a stroke of luck. It was a dark green. Mother Earth had given him a treasure.

The graceful woman had grown and hoed in her field. Her name was Awinita. They married; in their wedding ceremony he gave her venison and she gave him corn. He moved into her hut.

Waya leaned against the tree, remembering those wondrous times. He groaned; the relentless ache stayed. In marching on the road to Oklahoma, many of his Native American brothers and sisters had perished. As the march had dragged on, the movement of the people grew slower, and the line began to lengthen and spread out. He continued to feel groggy, only his agony keeping him awake.

His image changed again. A branch of the white men, the Scotch-Irish, valued the independence of living in the high mountains of Appalachia and the isolation from government control and bureaucracy. They tended to coexist with the Indians, trading and marrying. Waya's sister married a Scotch-Irish farmer named Ian McDonald. His farm sat in a section of Cherokee land within the white man's state of North Carolina. Waya often visited McDonald and showed him the green gem. Because Waya had shown the emerald to friends, rumors of its existence spread and caught the attention of thieves. Three men attempted to break into McDonald's house. He held a rifle on the robbers and chased them off. The leader of the three was a white man named Sandford.

The Indian brave decided to hide the emerald. One night, McDonald and Waya buried the stone in a deep hole near McDonald's house; at the same time, they drew two identical diagrams on sheets of paper describing its location.

In 1829, catastrophe fell on his Cherokees like a biblical plague. The state of Georgia discovered gold in the land of the Cherokee. As a result, white prospectors swarmed into the Native American Nation, burning villages, and hunting for wealth. Greedy for gold and land, the men of Georgia voided all treaties between the Indian Nation and the federal government. In the same year, Andrew

Jackson, the man nicknamed "Indian Killer," began eight years as President of the United States. Disagreeing with the State of Georgia, the Supreme Court ruled the Cherokees had a clear title to the lands they occupied.

Ignoring the law and federal-Indian treaties, Andrew Jackson used political and military action to remove the Indians from their land. In 1838 and 1839, the Cherokees east of the Mississippi River were run off and went by steamboat, wagon, and walking to Oklahoma. Because the water levels along the route to the west were at a historical low, most of his people didn't travel by steamship but hiked. An estimated four thousand of the original seventeen thousand people would die on their journey, called 'The Trail of Tears.'

Before Waya and Awinita set out for Oklahoma, Ian McDonald, the Scotch-Irish man married to Awinita's sister, agreed to keep the giant emerald hidden and safe until Waya's return. To mislead any aspiring thieves, Waya carried a false map of the gem's burial site.

Heartbroken, the brave and Awinita left their beautiful Smoky Mountains with ridge after ridge of peaks up to the sky. They would miss the bluish haze emitted by the forest in the early morning. Gone would be the blissful rains that fell and ran off in mountain streams and waterfalls.

Waya remembered many of the Indians had few garments, and the lousy weather hurt them. Often, they went hungry. In time, they suffered disease. Measles, cholera, dysentery, and fever appeared among the column of the displaced. Waya's wife became sick and couldn't walk; he had to put her on one of the provision wagons. The only women who could ride were ill and couldn't walk.

As he marched with the column, Waya grew shakier with dysentery. He struggled to walk fast enough to keep his beloved Awinita's wagon in his sight.

Then the horrible three had caught up with him. Now, two hours had passed, and he grew light-headed, dizzy, and faint from pain and internal bleeding from the knife's lesion. He was thankful he had loved the doe-eyed woman and lived in her hut. He prayed she would survive her sickness. *I'm dying, but the Great One will watch over her*, he thought. *I leave the plants, the animals, and my friends.*

What he couldn't possibly have known at the arrival of his death was more than a hundred years would pass before the hunt for the long-lost gem would begin.

2

ROTH'S MANSION, ASHEVILLE – KENTUCKY DERBY DAY, SATURDAY

I remember the gathering for the Kentucky Derby in 2001. Throughout that morning in the mansion, my boss, Harriett Roth, had grown furious with me. She shouted at me when I knocked my highball glass onto the floor. "Behave yourself!"

I picked up the glass and wiped the floor with a napkin. "It wasss . . . an accident. Relax."

I had embarrassed myself in front of my friends. Taylor, our chef, served her potent mint juleps. She kept scurrying in and out of the kitchen and the media room. I realized my vision was off when I began seeing two of her. My impaired eyesight proved she had not skimped on the bourbon.

Roth barked at me, "Why are you closing one of your eyes?"

"It . . . it itches."

Roth had on a full-length black dress but had covered her head with a vast curved-brimmed red hat to celebrate Derby Day. I had upset her to the extent the color of her face matched her hat. "You're blind drunk."

I protested because Bruce, my partner and our computer whiz, had gulped just as many drinks. "Dis is a party."

"You're slurring your words, talking in a raucous outdoor voice." She turned to Taylor. "Not another mint julep for Bruce or Don."

Clad in a black tux with a red tie and red straw hat for Kentucky Derby Day, Bruce protested, "But, Boss, I didn't knock no glass over."

I grinned foolishly at her. "I ammm . . . Don Gannon, sleuth ex–ex–extraordinaire, and I promise I be quieter."

After my tongue-lashing, I'd kept my head down, waiting for the start of the Kentucky Derby Race. Roth urged me to be more grownup. I've been to college and traveled the world—served in the army's military police. But she thought me adolescent. I had let Roth down, and I felt a hollow feeling. She had planned carefully for this party, and I was spoiling it.

Taylor bent to hand me a cup of steaming black coffee. She shook her head as she straightened. "Engine's runnin', but nobody's drivin'."

When the house-phone rang, Mickey, our muscle man, slightly drunk but not blotto, went to the hall to answer it. He had a genuinely festive outfit, looked like a blurry leprechaun. His costume included a wide-brimmed hat, full lapel sports jacket, knitted jersey, and clip-on bow tie, all in dazzling green. He returned with the cordless handset for Roth. "Your favorite history professor, Angela Lightfoot."

My boss didn't down the more potent drink. She sipped a Biltmore House wine. After greeting Angela, Roth asked, "Where are you?"

I felt myself getting a little drowsy. In a flood of green clothes, Mickey went to mute the TV. Roth put down her wine glass and settled back on the couch to listen to Angela. "Say again. You are researching a farmhouse in Macon County. A building from the Early Republic period?"

My eyes tried to focus on the two Roths as they talked on the phone. "Your research may have led you into a dangerous situation—possibly requiring protection from criminals."

Roth picked up her glass, sipped, and continued listening. She frowned at me. "Yes, my right-hand man is here." I closed my left eye to see her correctly. "He's functioning, but barely. He's drunk as a skunk."

She listened a little longer. "Can you stop by the mansion now?"

Roth finished the call and handed the phone to Mickey and studied me. Taylor, in a lime green dress with a wide-brimmed yellow hat, looking like a showy flower, stood beside me. My boss said, "Taylor, bring Don and Bruce more coffee. Professor Lightfoot is on her way to see us."

My bladder felt tight to bursting. I needed a toilet soon, but what if I walked across the room swaying like a drunken elephant? Roth would go ballistic. My boss had admired me when we solved Digger Harper's murder. Now I had undercut my standing. When my eyes closed and opened again, the room spun. But detectives don't pee in their pants, and I had screwed up. I rose and lurched toward the door.

# # #

Angela arrived thirty minutes later. Monarchos had won the Kentucky Derby, Taylor had started clearing away empty glasses and snack trays, and I had begun to sober up. I saw a double of Angela enter the media room and take a seat on a couch. But by narrowing my eyes, the two history professors, the Angelas, became one. Roth had caught me squinting as she stared straight at me, pursing her lips. I opened both eyes and smiled in my disarming way.

Her white teeth complementing her ebony skin, Professor Lightfoot brightened the room with her smile. Turning in my direction, she said, "My, you dressed brightly for the Derby."

Clad in a tan shirt and pants with a red, white, and blue floral jacket, I smiled at the Angelas and nodded a thank you. My tongue felt a little thick.

The professor placed her briefcase beside her. "After we searched for the gold from the Confederate train, you said we might work together again."

Roth extended both her hands toward the history professor. "I found your assistance gratifying." She laid an index finger on her lower lip as if reflecting. "We could work together again, but our collaboration will function best if we investigate something of value to Roth Security."

Bruce spoke up. "Cos, you're a cool chick, but my boss worries 'bout payin' her operatives." Angela didn't say anything but returned a smile. Even though she was older and taller than Bruce, they had something going. I had seen them together in downtown Asheville.

Angela held up a palm to reject a mint julep from Taylor. I drank black coffee, which Taylor kept bringing me. "Several nights ago, intruders attacked a grandmother and burglarized her old farmhouse."

Roth cocked her head toward Angela. "This is a farm in Macon County, North Carolina?"

The history professor bobbed her Afro at Roth. "It is."

"Located roughly where?"

"About seventy miles southwest of Asheville, in the mountains."

Bruce interrupted. "Sounds like a routine burglary. Why we get involved?"

Angela wiggled her finger at Bruce. "The break-in is not routine in any way."

Bruce lifted his chin. "How so?"

"They took old family photographs off the wall and broke into a hidden room under the stairs."

I butted in, trying not to slur my words. "I bet there's more."

"The next night, intruders dug a deep hole on the farmland."

Bruce paused, glancing at Angela. "Don't gets involved. Cos, have the farm people call the police."

Angela shook her head. "The police came to the farm, but the diggers had vanished."

I was sobering up from the mint juleps and tried to organize my faltering thoughts. "Wait, how badly did the burglars hurt the grandmother?"

"She spent two days in the hospital, but she's okay now."

Roth sipped her wine. "Will the police keep a lookout at the farm?"

Angela shook her head. "The sheriff's deputy advised hiring private security."

"And?" Roth asked.

"Family's dirt poor."

Bruce gave a half shrug. "Bet dey could pay a rent-a-cop. They wants a freebie."

Our professor smiled at him. "I don't know. That farm's seen better days."

I swallowed more coffee. Roth asked a question. "You said the burglars took old photographs off the wall?"

"Ancient photographs."

Roth appeared puzzled. "Explain how you got involved?"

"The thieves scattered old journals and papers on the floor at the farmhouse."

Roth put down her glass. "And?"

"The family, name of McDonald, called my college, at the Asheville campus, exploring for a historian."

Roth stared at Angela. "Why did they think to call a college?"

"The grandmother thought the college would help for free—because of the age of the documents."

"How did you get involved?"

"Our department secretary passed their call to me. I drove to the farm to review the papers."

"What did you find?" Roth asked.

"A grandson, who lives there, walked me around a pond to the holes. The trespassers excavated another pit last night."

"You inspected the dug-up ground?" Roth asked.

"I wore my wellies, my Wellington boots. Stood next to the holes."

My boss leaned forward, focusing on Angela. "Tell me about their size, their dimensions."

Angela reached in her briefcase and took out photographs she had taken of the excavations. "The diggers made each pit roughly the size of a park bench. Three holes in three nights."

Roth turned to me and asked, "Could one person dig such a hole in a night?"

I thought a second about my answer. "I am guessing two men dug and kept to a procedure: One digs while the other watches, and every fifteen minutes, they switch roles."

Roth cupped her chin and gave me a steely stare. "But couldn't there have been more than two people?"

"Maybe, but then wouldn't they dig more holes each night?"

Angela seemed to consider what I had said and then continued recalling her visit to the farmhouse. "Inside, I gathered the papers off the floor. I held archaic documents, journals, and papers, over a hundred years old."

I suspected Angela hadn't told us everything. "Why tell us?"

"I took the papers back to my campus office to study—and decided to discuss safety with you."

My boss held up an index finger. "But what's in it for Roth Security?"

Roth had lost her husband and all the family wealth except for her estate house. I understood this calamity caused her fear of poverty. I was maybe the only person who knew. She said, every day, she swore she wouldn't allow extreme poverty to drag her down again.

Angela smirked. "When I read the journals, I found something that might interest you."

Reaching again into her briefcase, she pulled out a battered ledger with a gray cardboard cover. "The journals were mostly day-to-day accounts of farming life: raining, plowing a field, and sowing grain. But portions were like a diary and described life in the McDonald family." Angela paused as if for dramatic effect. "The family has lived on the farm since the early 1800s."

Professor Lightfoot moved to sit beside Roth on her couch, angling the tattered journal so they could read the yellow pages together. I walked behind the sofa to glance over Angela's shoulder.

"Great-great-great-Grandfather McDonald—first name Ian—wrote these pages from 1837 to 1838. He married a Cherokee woman."

Being a history buff, I was fascinated by Angela's tale, but Bruce raised his eyebrows in frustration. He cleared his throat. "If Great-great-great-grandfather McDonald is going to keep coming up, could we agree to call him Ian?"

Angela chuckled. "Ian's entries in the summer and fall of 1838 are remarkable."

She read directly from the journal:

> June 15, 1838 - Waya came to our home this morning. Brought two rabbits and several squash for us. We talked and walked the fields.

We all interrupted in a chorus. "Who's Waya?"

Angela glanced up from the journal. "A Cherokee brave. More about him later."

She continued reading:

> At night Waya and I smoked tobacco and talked. He spoke bad words about Andrew Jackson stealing the Cherokee Nation's lands. Waya does not want to leave these beautiful mountains.

Bruce interrupted, "We know dis story. A treaty wid the US protected the Cherokee Nation."

My boss twisted to him and said, "Hush. Let Angela finish."

Professor Lightfoot turned pages and continued reading from the journal:

> August 2, 1838 - Waya came to visit. Said some of the Cherokees applied for and became citizens of North Carolina. They may be allowed to live here and not forced to move to the western lands. Waya plans to apply for citizenship. If he must leave, he will come back later.

I didn't understand what she read. "The journal says some of the Cherokees had become US citizens?"

Angela took a moment before answering. "Some Cherokees purchased land along the Oconaluftee River. It was a land trust in North Carolina. It was like those Cherokees were part of the state in which they lived."

Roth brushed her palms together. "When do we get to the part in which you think I might be interested?"

Angela continued reading:

> August 4, 1838 - Waya feared army would force him to travel to western land. He asked would I guard his valuables until his return. I told him he was my brother. I would faithfully guard his treasure. He showed me a gem, an emerald, the size of a goose egg, with almost no flaws.

Roth's eyes gleamed. "Ahh, this part interests me."

Bruce snickered. "Dis reminds me of our case of the buried Confederate gold. What if we hunt an emerald, and it ain't there?"

Our professor didn't respond but continued reading:

> August 6, 1838 - Tonight, my brother and I took a wooden cask, tarred on the outside, to a field on the far side of the pond, away from the house. We put the large green stone in the barrel and buried it three feet down. I drew a treasure map of the location of the jewel. Whoever has this paper can find the cask.

We all began jabbering remarks at Angela.

"Guys, this is a fairy tale," Bruce said.

"Stone is long gone," Mickey said.

"Not again!" I said.

When we grew silent, she continued. "In the papers at the farmhouse, I didn't find a diagram to the hiding place."

Roth emptied the last of the red wine into her glass. "You mentioned Grandma McDonald. Did you ask her if she had heard about this gem?"

"Grandma McDonald said the family lore is Waya left on the Trail of Tears without the gem. She thinks the family journals were stacked under the stairs, sealed in by time, and forgotten."

The journal told an exciting tale. An emerald big as a goose egg. Could Ian, aka Great-great-great-grandfather McDonald, have stolen the big jewel? "Sounds like someone recently remembered the journals," I said.

Roth took another sip from her wine glass. She could nurse a drink better than anyone. "How much might such a stone be worth today?"

"The journal said it had few imperfections," Angela said. "So, my guess is millions of dollars."

"Why didn't you bring Grandma with you?"

"She wouldn't come because she feared you would want her to pay."

Mickey, usually a sphinx, spoke up. "Why should we believe the journal? Did anyone other than Ian see this stone?"

Angela nodded. "Good point. I'll ask Grandma if any other family member saw the green gem."

Bruce shifted on the couch where he sat. "And why would such a gemstone exist in North Carolina? It's fantasy made up to pass a cold night on de frontier."

Bruce's remark summoned the full weight of Roth's wrath; after all, she expected her investigators to know what they were saying. "Bruce, you know nothing about the natural resources in these mountains."

She rose, left the room, and returned with a book from her office. "The Appalachian Mountains used to be part of South Africa, where many valuable minerals are found."

She thumbed through pages until she found what she sought. "In 1799, twelve-year-old Conrad Reed found a seventeen-pound rock of gold in a North Carolina stream. This state was the leading gold-producing state in Colonial America until 1848 when the California Gold Rush began. The Crabtree Emerald Mine in North Carolina mined emerald crystals."

Roth stopped frowning at Bruce and turned to Angela. "How do we proceed?"

"I'll search for additional information on Waya, Ian McDonald, and a paper map. I suspect there may be more trespassing by unknown parties and possibly additional attacks."

Angela hesitated. "Would you be willing to help?"

I doubted Roth would get involved if she didn't get paid. On the other hand, she liked Professor Lightfoot and probably didn't want her in danger. After a short faltering, Roth said, "I'll send Don to inspect the farm. You say they lack funding?"

"They're poor."

Roth stood. "Our initial investigation around the farm and consultation is free. If Don and you decide the Cherokee Emerald might exist, we can offer the McDonald family a salvage-recovery agreement."

Angela also stood up. "How would that work?"

"We wouldn't charge them anything, but we'd get half the recovered value if we find the gemstone."

Angela stroked her chin as if thinking. "The McDonalds are desperate for money. They might agree to a split."

Before we closed our Kentucky Derby Party, Roth shared one final thought. "Please remember one salient fact about detectives: while the gumshoe constantly searches for an answer to a question, they search as well for new sources of payment."

Professor Lightfoot packed the journal away in her case, and we arranged to drive to the farmhouse the following day.

"Sober up," Roth said to me, "you have a long drive tomorrow."

I saw Angela out the front door and quietly slipped upstairs to sleep off the drunk. I didn't know then that the farmhouse's situation would introduce a profound mystery—a few of them.

3

GRANDMA'S FARM, MACON COUNTY – SUNDAY

In the early morning, I was on my way to the farmhouse in Macon County, North Carolina, a region surrounded by stunning elevated mountains. Angela guided Bruce, who was driving us through a maze of narrow two-lane roads surrounded by red spruce forest. I viewed dense woods that would provide cover for anyone digging holes in the ground without being seen. She led us farther back into the woodland, steering us through an area perhaps unchanged from the early 1800s.

Bruce slowed to go around a curve. "Yeah, my Jeep's de ideal vehicle for this bumpy driving."

Ever since Bruce got his all-wheel-drive vehicle in 1999, I had to listen to him brag about his purchase. "Bruce, ninety-nine percent of the time, you drive this box on paved roads and parking lots."

"That's right, good buddy, bite the hand that feeds you. Next time, I'll let you wreck the suspension on your toy."

"By toy, do you refer to my Mustang GT, a wolf not in sheep's clothing?"

"Toy! A bauble in sleek clothing."

Angela spoke from the right-front passenger seat. "You're a crabby pair. Do you dislike each other so much?"

Bruce rotated his head to stare at me, which was unnerving because he drove down a twisting road with trees abutting the narrow lane.

I leaned forward from the rear seat and explained to Angela. "We've been close friends since elementary school."

"We're as close as two penned-up hogs," Bruce said.

"Our life was hard, but Bruce and I lifted each other."

Bruce glanced at Angela and then switched his view back to the road. "I remember my dear old mother on her death bed."

I followed his lead. "I went to Bruce's home to draw the drapes and light candles."

Bruce picked up the yarn. "Don was a godsend, a blessing."

I carried on after sniffling and drying my eyes. "'Lord have mercy,' Bruce's mother said. 'Someone gotta care for my poor, simple-minded boy after I'm gone.'"

Angela steadied herself on the door handle, as the vehicle bumped along. She maintained a poker-player face.

"Bruce's mother took my hand and spoke her final words. 'Promise me you'll help him carry his burden—'"

"She passed away, clutched in Don's arms. That scene tore out my heart." Bruce gave Angela a pitiful expression and pressed his right hand against his chest.

Angela did an exaggerated eye roll and tilted her head back. "She was a truly amazing woman."

Bruce shot Angela a puzzled glance. "How do you mean?"

"I recall she called you last week. She must have called from heaven, which would make her truly amazing."

Angela studied the landscape as if searching for a turnoff. "You prattle at each other like a puppet show."

I rested my rump on a cushioned section of the rear seat in Bruce's Jeep. Going on a field trip with Bruce and Angela was diverting, but it was going to kill my morning. Apart from the attack on the grandmother, I suspected kids were messing around on the farm.

The vehicle's wheels hit a rut in the road. "Ouch, that smarted."

Why had Roth sent me to investigate? She must have seen something I hadn't. Her methods were a mystery to me; it irked me that she almost always seemed to be right.

Angela pointed out a white mailbox at the entrance to a road partially hidden by tall grass. The mailbox had block letters spelling McDonald, and the dirt road had a constricted width allowing one pickup or two cars to pass by hugging the shoulders of the lane. The way opened onto a vista of fields, a small pond and stream, trees bordering the areas, and a two-story, bleached-white farmhouse.

Bruce parked on the scraggly grass in front of the building, which appeared slightly lop-sided as if the owners had hammered additions onto the original farmhouse. We exited the vehicle and approached the structure.

A man with a full black beard answered the door. Dressed in dusty blue overalls held up by only one strap over his shoulders, he held a can of Mountain Dew and glanced at Angela. "Ms. Lightfoot."

Angela introduced Bruce and me. "Meet Ashley McDonald. His grandmother owns this farm."

Ashley stepped back to let us enter. "Them the gumshoes you told me about?"

I corrected him. "Gumshoes extraordinaire."

He didn't blink. "I ain't got money to pay you."

The dull *thunk* of metal on wood startled me. I turned. An undersized woman with white hair, which was partially covered by a white gauze bandage, whacked a doorframe with an aluminum crutch. "I see we got guests. Why wasn't I notified?"

We had found the matriarch of the McDonald Clan. She leaned against the doorframe and polished her glasses. "We heard digging again last night. Tell them, Ashley."

When he was slow to respond, she said, "Four nights in a row. Them trashy people were out there."

She moved from the doorframe into the room, and Ashley assisted his grandmother onto a couch.

I coughed to get her attention. "Did the sheriff's deputy come to arrest the intruders?"

She smiled at me as if I were a slow student showing promise. "That they didn't. They're worthless."

"They won't help," Ashley said. "The deputy covers a large area and don't come a-runnin' every time a digger pops up."

Grandma settled herself on the couch and pointed the end of the crutch at her grandson. "Them thieves search for Waya's gem."

"Grandma, we don't know that's true."

"Fiddlesticks, why else dig up our yard? Sometimes, you don't have the brains of a donkey."

Grandma again took off her glasses and wiped them with a cloth. Ashley remained quiet and sucked on his Dew as if their outbursts were commonplace. The old woman adjusted her glasses on her prominent nose and turned to Angela. "Why am I talkin' to these two young pups? Need to talk with their boss lady."

Angela spoke up. "I've worked with Mr. Gannon. He's a tenacious investigator."

The grandmother stared at me. "Humph! See de scar on the big one's face. Can't even protect hisself."

The slash to the left side of my face had been a little over five months ago. I had picked up the trauma in an unfortunate encounter with a machete-twirling gardener. The wound was no longer red but a pale color. When I realized I had been touching it, I dropped my hand. "The man who cut my face—he had to stay in the hospital."

Angela continued. "Ms. Roth, their boss, doesn't leave her mansion on investigations. She sends her right-hand men, Mr. Gannon and Mr. Seeker."

Grandma appeared skeptical. "Why don't she come here?"

Angela took a deep breath as if gathering her thoughts. "For medical reasons, she remains at her mansion."

"He doesn't appear like a right-hand man to me," the grandmother said. "Isn't he going to take a peek at them holes?"

I got a kick out of Grandma McDonald. She was long in the tooth, but no one was going to push her around. She reminded me of my grandmother. When I was a toddler and Nana pushed me in a stroller in downtown Asheville, a woman, walking in the opposite direction, spat toward the street, missed, and splattered my face. My grandmother raged and stormed at the woman. I wish Nana were still with me.

Bruce's voice broke through my reverie. "Don, you're daydreaming."

Everyone stared at me. "What? Oh, just thinking."

The old lady began to get off the couch. "If you ain't goin' to listen to me, I'm gonna go take a nap."

Ashley tried to calm his grandmother and help her stand up.

I butted in. "Wait, could I talk to you?"

The grandson frowned but let her stay. Bruce stood behind the couch. I pulled a chair in front of the old lady and asked my questions. She had a bruised right arm, probably from her assault. I would ask her about the attack later. "It's Mrs. McDonald, isn't it?"

Her mouth twitched. Might have been a smile. "You can call me Grandma McDonald."

"We'll study the holes shortly. Let me ask you something first."

She waited for my question. Ashley went out of the room and returned with another can of Mountain Dew.

"Angela read in your family's journal that Waya found a large gem? Tell me about him and your family."

The old lady leaned back on the couch. She stared straight at me with pale blue eyes and began her story. "My family goes back to Colonial days. We had Scotch-Irish and Cherokee ancestors."

Angela pulled up a chair and sat across from Grandma. "Was your ancient ancestor, Great-great-great-great-grandfather McDonald, Scotch-Irish?"

Grandma McDonald spoke without hesitation. "He were. He married a Cherokee woman who was Waya's sister. Our family was like a Cherokee extended family."

I wrote down what I heard. "Where is the Cherokee branch of the family?"

"The removal took many of 'em to the western lands."

Bruce spoke from behind the couch. "The Trail of Tears?"

"Yes. The Army forced Waya and his kin to Oklahoma."

I scribbled away. "And you think Waya left a large gem for safekeeping at this farm?"

"Yes."

"And you think that is what the thieves are looking for?" Angela asked.

Grandma grimaced. "You see anything else worth anything around dis old beaten-down farm? What in tarnation can it be but Waya's stone?"

"Did it exist?" I asked. "Did anyone other than Great-great-great-grandfather McDonald see this gem?"

She set her jaw, and her eyes stared straight at me as if ready to fight. She believed in the emerald. "His wife lived to her mid-nineties. Our family lore holds she saw the gem Waya and her husband hid."

I scribbled.

"There, you ain't so smart-alecky now, are you?" The old lady wasn't going to accept any guff from the pups.

"Did the wife mention the size of the gem?"

"Big as her clenched fist."

"Did she see where they buried the gem?"

"She said they went out on a moonlit night."

I thought for a second. Was this the same guy who wrote the diary? "What was the husband's first name, his given name?"

"Ian . . . Now, Mr. Investigator, investigate dem holes."

I flipped my notepad shut.

# # #

Bruce, Angela, and I accompanied Ashley down the front steps and around a small pond in front of the farmhouse. A cluster of four holes lay a long distance in front of the house. Each hole went down about four feet. Angela had a point—you could probably drop a park bench into each hole.

Before turning back to the farmhouse, Ashley warned us again. "Observe as much as you want. I'm not paying you anything."

Bruce kneeled and fingered the earth around the excavations. "I'm looking at a boot imprint. Want to take a cast?"

I glanced at him. "Hardly seems necessary. We could come back tonight and take the boots off the fella's feet."

Bruce paused as if considering what I had said. "You think Roth will take dis case?"

I didn't answer but scrunched up my mouth.

Bruce went from one hole to another. "Did you notice where they dug?"

I didn't see what he meant. "Where?"

"Each hole is about four to five feet offset from that oak tree."

I checked, and he was correct. "How long do oak trees live?"

Angela broke in. "Long time. Two hundred to four hundred years,"

Where we stood, the tree was old. Maybe it had grown back in the time period Professor Lightfoot termed the Early Republic, a time when Ian McDonald and Waya might have buried a barrel.

When we returned to the farmhouse, I slipped away into a neglected garden at the rear and phoned Roth. I gave a word-by-word report of what I'd heard and seen.

When I finished, Roth grilled me. "So, Mrs. McDonald confirmed other family members saw the stone many years ago?"

"Yeah."

"Big stone?"

"Yeah."

"The intruders sank the holes near an ancient oak?"

"The tree is at a distance in front of the farmhouse."

A minute passed. Two minutes. Roth was taking her time. I held the phone while I studied the garden behind the farmhouse. Dilapidation was everywhere: a scraggly evergreen bush at my feet, a brown and dead bush next in line, a weather-beaten wooden bench, and tall grass crowding out the remaining garden plants. Roth finally replied. "I want to ask Grandma McDonald two questions. Bring her to the mansion."

"Getting the old lady to travel might be difficult."

"Just do it. Once she's here, I'll offer to identify the intruders and hunt for the Cherokee Emerald, absorbing all costs."

"And if the gem exists?"

"If the stone exists, we split the salvage with the McDonald family fifty-fifty."

"What if she balks?"

"Just get her here."

I moved the mobile to my other ear. "What's the second question?"

"How was she attacked? I need to learn what happened that night."

I ended the conversation and entered the farmhouse and spoke to Grandma. "Ms. Roth asks you to come to her mansion and talk with her."

"No," Ashley said to the old lady.

"You don't tell me what to do, young pup."

After an Ashley versus Grandma argument, which sounded like bellowing hippos, she agreed to meet my boss the next afternoon. Roth and I had started on a new and treacherous path, a path of planned viciousness, the outcome of which I did not and could not see.

4

ROTH'S MANSION – MONDAY

Grandma McDonald arrived at Roth's mansion shortly after noon and settled herself in a wrought-iron chair at the patio table. She stared cautiously at my boss as if she were examining a deli menu. Standing beside her, Ashley, her grandson, blustered, "We oughta leave. We can't pay anyone to guard the farm."

Grandma smirked at him. "Ashley, I'm here to listen. Stick food in your mouth."

Taylor, holding a tray bearing two wine bottles, stepped through the kitchen door and out onto the flagstone courtyard, which the afternoon sun had warmed. She asked Grandma, "Red or white?"

"Wet." She accepted her glass of red and downed half in a guzzle.

Both the short, reed-like Grandma and the tall, sturdy Roth had dressed warmly for the luncheon meeting. The former came in a coarse, beige coat with a red knitted scarf wrapped around her head and neck. The latter had on her maroon, full-length tunic with a black silk scarf covering her shoulder-length white hair. Angela and I wore balmy-weather garments as the May day was uncommonly mild with a 65-degree Fahrenheit temperature.

Taylor served lunch on two black wrought-iron tables. She had pushed them together on the blue flagstone patio on the right side of the mansion. Short, slender, red hair in a braid, and everyone's buddy, she glided around and served sautéed trout with cucumber salad and boiled potatoes. Ashley—in his blue overalls and a long-sleeved white shirt buttoned at the collar—got a Mountain Dew from her.

Sitting across the table from me, Grandma acknowledged my existence. "Stop a-gawkin' at me and pass them potatoes."

Afterward, when we had eaten the trout, the air was calm and pleasant, and the Asheville sun continued to shine on the patio. The old lady—who possessed hollow legs worthy of legend—waved her glass at Taylor, who winked at Roth and filled the wineglass halfway. Grandma swirled her drink around, indicating she wished it topped off.

Ashley pushed back his chair. "We ought to be a-gettin' home."

The old lady ignored him and spoke to Roth. "Can you keep them thieving scoundrels off ma farm?"

"I can. The thing is, you and I need to come to an agreement."

The old lady nodded her head at my boss and waited.

"I'll find out who is invading your farm and why they are doing what they're doing. And I'll pay my costs while investigating."

Grandma continued to sip wine and stare at the vast blue above us. "What would you'ns get out of this?"

"If I can recover the Cherokee Emerald, I take my expense off its worth and split what's left with you, fifty-fifty."

Ashley lowered his Mountain Dew and said, "Hell no. It's ours."

Grandma's eyes dilated as if she was fuming mad. "Be quiet. Let the grownups talk. What if we don't find de gem?"

"I'll assume that risk and you'll owe me nothing."

Putting her wine glass down, Grandma took a moment to think. "Ma problem are I don't got money, and your problem are you'ns want money. Your agreement solves both problems. I accept it."

Somehow, Roth had gained the old lady's agreement. It wasn't their age; Roth was closer to my age than Grandma's. My boss could be blunt and rude, but she was loyal and truthful. The two might have recognized these similar traits in each other.

Roth rubbed the tip of her nose as if considering. "Tell us about your night mugging?"

"Why?"

"I'm exploring for clues, to the identity of the thieves and what they are seeking."

"What you want to know?"

Taylor waited with the bottle of red, occasionally checking the old lady had a full glass.

Roth said, "What do you remember?"

I took out my notepad to jot down the old lady's words. Didn't want to miss a pointer to the crooks.

She thought before beginning. "I had to pee. Fixin' to pop. I curse old age with its need to go frequently at night."

She held a forefinger against her lips as if remembering. "Didn't turn on a lamp—a bright light keeps me awake later in de night."

At our table and the adjacent table, everyone listened. I continued taking notes.

"Thar, I heard a strange noise. My old house creaks and groans, like a jazz band using freed springs, bending boards, and shaking windows. Dat unfamiliar swish sounded like masonry sliding over masonry."

Ashley broke in. "She didn't wake me."

"Shut up. I'm tellin' my story."

She took another swallow and looked to Taylor for a top-up. "I done found the commode in the dark, relieved myself, and catnapped on the seat."

Her story had everyone's ears. Even Taylor moved closer to hear better.

"That noise—sliding stonework—came again. I had to explore downstairs. I reckoned I'd find a small animal intruder."

I stared at that small woman. "Weren't you scared?"

She smirked at me. "Heavens no, I weren't scared. I had my pistol with me."

Grandma took off her glasses and cleaned them on a napkin. "I picked de Colt Navy 1851 off de wall fer protection. I started downstairs. Had to be careful on dem slick wood stairs."

It took me several seconds to sort out what the old lady had said. "Hold on. You went below carrying a gun?"

"Yep. It were an old revolver been in the family fer years. Ashley always a-cleanin' it."

I was stunned. "Wasn't that heavy for you?"

Grandma hesitated a second. "No. Weighs about the same as a bottle of wine."

Roth listened with her hands forming a steeple. "The house was still dark?"

"No light. I gripped the banister with one of my hands. Thar were a musty odor as if someone had turned over dirt."

I pictured this thin, petite woman gliding through the shadows with a long pistol, hunting an odd sound. She was made of stern stuff.

"Near the bottom rung, my feet slid out from under me, and I stumbled onto a throw rug in the front living room. Me and the rug slid until we bumped against an upright pair of legs. I whacked de leg with ma gun."

Ashley spoke up. "I woke. Heard hollering downstairs."

Grandma continued, waving her wine glass in the air. "A hard object hit ma head. I was ate up with an ache."

"I got myself out of bed," Ashley said. "Turned on lights."

Grandma paused to lay her empty glass on the patio table. She led my boss in draining her wine glass. The guzzler always beats the sipper.

"I heard a man say, 'Get out.' Next, I heard footsteps going out the rear of de house."

Roth held up her hand to signal *whoa*. "In the days before your attack, did you see a stranger on your property?"

Ashley and Grandma shook their heads.

"I were in a bed at de medical center when I got back my senses. I had them IV tubes hooked up to me and flashing lights from a monitor over ma head."

Roth asked Ashley, "You were with her at the hospital?"

He nodded. "Grandma's head were bandaged. She were right woozy."

"Who hit her?"

"Don't know. Them robbers escaped before I got downstairs. Called an ambulance. It come and got her."

Grandma held up her wineglass for a refill. "My chest pained me."

"The doc found she had three fractured ribs." Ashley drank his Mountain Dew. "He kept her under observation. Took scans of her head. Said she had a head injury, but she should recover completely."

"I didn't like de hospital. I wanted to go home."

Roth switched her approach to search for clues. "What were the intruders doing?"

Ashley lifted his shoulder in a half shrug. "Don't know."

My boss frowned. "Where were they?"

"In the den and the cubbyhole under the stairs," the grandson said.

Roth leaned forward in a pose reminiscent of Rodin's *The Thinker*. "Describe the room under the stairs."

Grandma answered. "That moldy old room. Ian McDonald, our long-dead relative, built it as part of the original farmhouse—early eighteen-hundreds."

"Was the current house built up around that room?"

She nodded. "The stone wall are in dat room."

"The stone wall?"

"The stones are big uns."

Roth rubbed her chin. "I don't understand you, Mrs. McDonald?"

"One of the stones is only a surface plate, about an inch thick."

Roth's eyes went to slits. "Ahh. One of the stones in the wall was a veneer. Were you aware this hidey-hole existed?"

"It were a surprise to me. Dat hole held old family papers."

Roth glanced at Ashley. "The thieves knew this? How?"

His face went blank.

My boss tightened her lips. "We need to think about how they knew."

She had found something odd. I scribbled away.

"What happened next?"

"When I got downstairs, the burglars had dropped the papers in the hidden room. My grandmother must have startled them."

The old lady narrowed her eyes. "Why didn't I know about that hole in de wall?"

Angela had a suggestion. "Maybe when the family built up the rest of the house over the wall, the knowledge faded away."

Roth turned to the grandson and asked, "How many robbers entered your house?"

"Police think two."

"What did the intruders do in the den?"

"Took two pictures off the wall."

Roth stared at Ashley. "Were these the only two pictures on the den wall?"

"Naw. Thar are about two dozen. Most real old."

"Describe the stolen pictures?"

"Don't know. Can't remember what was there."

Roth switched to Grandma. "Do you remember?"

After emptying her wine glass, she took off her clear-framed glasses and wiped the lenses. "I couldn't recollect de two missing pictures at first. When I awoke in the morning, both popped up in ma head."

Taylor stepped to the table and filled Grandma's glass again.

"Describe them," Roth said.

"Photos. One were taken looking outward from the front door and showed a wide area in front of de house."

"And the other."

"It were shot at a far piece away and showed the front of de house. The family took the photographs back in the eighteen-nineties."

"Why steal those particular photographs?"

Grandma shrugged. "Ain't got no idea."

Roth and I locked eyes for an instant. I scribbled in the notepad.

"What were the papers on the floor?" Roth asked.

The old lady responded. "Old and brittle, turned out to be diaries."

"And?"

"Ma family wrote them journals in the early eighteen-hundreds. All about the sale of crops and livestock back in the eighteen-thirties to eighteen-forties. Why would intruders want them pages?"

Roth shook her head. "I don't know. Maybe they were just after the photos. What happened next?"

The grandson continued. "The second night Grandma were still in the hospital, I heard scraping outside, in the distance."

Likely the group who attacked Grandma had returned. "Did you call the police?"

Ashley finished his Mountain Dew and crushed the empty can. "No. Decided I'd wait till mornin'. See what they was a-doin'."

Roth's wrought-iron chair squeaked as she pulled it closer to the table. "What happened next?"

"Just before dawn, the outdoor noise stopped."

"What did you find?"

Ashley leaned over the table toward Roth. "Whopping hole in the ground—dirt piled up aside it."

Ashley paused and then continued. "Da pictures stolen in the night must a-been connected to the hole in the ground. Them two intrusions occurred pert-near the same time."

"When I were a child, my ma told me old Ian McDonald buried treasure on de farm," Grandma said. "Ian and Waya made two duplicate maps dat showed where they hid de gem."

"We know," Angela said. "The documents on the floor told us about the hidden gem."

I paused my notetaking. It's a farm—with acres and acres. I would have to have a map to know where to excavate. Couldn't dig up the whole farm.

"Did you call the sheriff in the morning?" Roth asked.

"Yep," Ashley said. "They told us to call if the digging continued."

The old lady took off her glasses, wiped them clean, and adjusted them on her nose. "Ta next night, after the hospital released me, I done heard the digging begin across the pond. Ma grandson phoned the sheriff's office."

"And did they come?" I asked.

She gave me an appalled glance. "Don't be so impatient. I'm gonna tell you."

She continued disclosing what happened her first night back from the hospital. "Later, the beams of headlights appeared in the distance, followed by a sheriff's car driving up to our farmhouse."

Roth mumbled. "At least they came."

"The deputy came to the house and said, 'We found a fresh hole, but they left before we could corral them. Guess they had a lookout.'"

The old lady finished the last of the wine in her glass. Her eyelids had begun to droop. "Da deputy left. We sat in da living room and fussed about what to do."

"Before they started digging holes in the ground, the thieves searched through the old documents in the farmhouse," Angela said. "Maybe there's something in those old records to tell us why they're digging where they are."

Ashley took up the story once more. "Dat's when I called the history department at the Asheville campus. Got in touch with Professor Lightfoot." He jerked his thumb toward Angela.

Grandma spoke up. "I told her intruders done left old papers all over da floor."

Angela spoke from the next table. "I found your journals authentic. Also, I was worried about the invasions onto your property."

The old lady's head had been sagging, and now her chin met her chest. She needed a lie-down.

Roth turned to Angela. "Continue reading the Ian McDonald papers and investigate the area in front of the farmhouse."

Angela nodded.

Roth glanced sideways at me. "Find out who's digging at the farm. Use Bruce and Mickey, as needed."

"Yeah, Boss."

Roth closed the meeting by serving up another of her aphorisms. "Discovery is the core of the human life force. Tomorrow, you step off into the undiscovered. Choose your steps carefully."

5

GRANDMA'S FARM — TUESDAY

"Stop what you're doing," Roth said, standing at my office door. "Angela made a discovery."

I jerked my head up. What's gotten my boss in an uproar?

Roth pushed a button on her mobile phone. "I'm here with Bruce and Don. You're on speakerphone."

I raised my eyebrows at Bruce, who shrugged. Angela's voice came from the mobile phone. "Grandma didn't tell us everything. Waya never returned from The Trail of Tears."

My mind sorted out her meaning. "You're saying Waya never came back for his emerald?"

"I read through the McDonald Family journals," Angela said. "Nowhere does it say he took back the gem."

Bruce shifted closer to the speakerphone. "Maybe Ian stole de gem?"

Angela sucked in air. "Ian McDonald went off to the California Gold Rush in 1849. He left his entire family and the emerald behind in North Carolina."

Roth sat in one of my chairs and spoke into the speakerphone. "Is it still where Waya and Ian buried it?"

Angela paused. "I can't say. Probably."

Bruce chimed in with a skeptic's view. "If the gem exists at all."

My body settled in my chair, so I could view Roth and browse out the windows behind my desk. On the mature oak tree, the buds were leafing out. A gray squirrel hung upside down to pull itself along a horizontal wire. The animal's focus was on a bird feeder hanging from the line. I was confident the gray animal would reach the bird feeder but not as convinced the emerald still lay buried on the McDonald farm.

Roth glanced at the ceiling as if reflecting. "Who wound up with the two diagrams showing the emerald's location?"

Angela took her time answering. "The journals say Ian took one map to California."

"Are you sure?" Bruce asked. "Did you look for a diagram among de papers scattered over the floor?"

"I did. No map there."

Roth covered her eyes with her hands as if thinking. "Maybe the thieves had the map. Could they have been after the photographs to decipher the diagram?"

"I don't know," Angela said.

Across the desk from me, Roth pursed her lips. "Is Ian always the writer in the journals?"

"No. After he left for California, the handwriting changes."

Roth stared at the phone. "So, we don't have access to anything Ian wrote after 1849?" She leaned forward in her chair and addressed Angela over the speakerphone. "I assume he continued writing in 1849 and after. Please ask Grandma McDonald where to find Ian's later journals."

I could hear scratching as Angela wrote in her notebook. "Okay, you want to know if there are later writings by Ian discussing the gem's hiding place."

Appearing to reflect, Roth tapped on my desk with her left hand. "Oh! And Angela, gather the family photographs showing the front of the farmhouse and bring them to me."

"Got it. You want photos shot in the area forward of the farmhouse."

Roth snapped her fingers. "Ask Grandma to date the photographs." Roth continued speaking to Angela. "The McDonald family viewed those snapshots for years. We, as outsiders, possess the perspective of fresh eyes."

She ended the call with Angela, turned to leave my office, but stopped at the door to face Bruce and me. "Find the diggers."

The quickest way to identify the intruders would be to drive to the farm late at night and catch them shoveling. Bruce and I went to the McDonald's mailbox when it got dark and parked. Under a partial cloud cover, sometimes revealing the moon and occasionally overcast, the grandson was there, as arranged, to meet us. He had heard digging in the direction of the existing holes. We sent him back to the farmhouse while we set out to surprise the intruders.

Bruce and I wore black pants, black long-sleeve turtleneck jerseys, and laced-up boots. I had smeared black grease on my face. Our approach took us along one side of the lane from the mailbox onto the farm, into a right turn at the lane's end, and through woods bordering the fields, pond, and farmhouse. Above the constant chirp of crickets, a distant *thump* of spade and pick carried through the night. "We'll be an unpleasant surprise for someone," Bruce said.

We did a stealthy walk in the dark, avoiding using our flashlights with black tape covering the lenses, designed to emit a narrow beam of illumination. Traveling along what appeared to be a narrow path through the woods, we increased our pace. I led with Bruce right behind me. When I rammed my shin into the dark cord strung across the path, the impulse passed to steel cans containing pebbles, creating a loud metallic sound. My leg had activated a simple warning device, one I had seen before in our army.

In a rage behind me, Bruce added to the din. "Crap. Get out of my way." He brushed past me, heading down the path with the diminished beam of his flashlight leading. I heard escape-and-pursuit sounds: branches snapping ahead of us and soft-soled boots slapping the ground.

We broke free of the woods. With the moon behind a cloud, we pursued the sounds of running. We lagged the intruders. Whoever they were, they had grabbed their digging tools and scampered.

We rushed close to the craters, which the intruders had gouged into the ground. Ahead of me, Bruce said, "Watch those open holes."

I clicked on my flashlight, revealing a pit. As I stepped around it, Bruce shouted from my left, "This way."

The intruders ran toward the stream, where we stopped when we reached it.

"Where'd they go?" Bruce asked.

I flashed the light over the water, which was deep here. No one swam in it to escape. "Follow the stream."

As we ran, the moon poked through a break in the clouds. The stream lay at an even more profound depth; trees rose out of the water.

Clouds blurred the moon again, and I listened for footfalls, hearing nothing but insects, especially the—*ch-ch . . . ch-ch-ch*—of the crickets. Perhaps the intruders had hidden nearby, hoping we'd run past them in the gloom. Nothing. All was still.

Seconds passed and the clouds receded from the moon, permitting its full radiance to highlight the scene. I sensed no movement of the fleeing prowlers and scanned farther down the stream. Beside me, Bruce jerked. "Tere's a house in the middle of the water."

Sure enough, a trailer house stood on stilts in the water. I made out a man in light-brown pants and dark-brown coat by the moonlight, sitting on the roof in a folding chair. "I think he got a rifle," Bruce said.

The man watched me, as motionless as a mantis.

The setting stunned me, pinning me like an insect on a display board. Was he our digger? Had he had time to cross the stream and climb up to the roof while we chased him? I found that hard to believe. Or had he been perched on the top the entire time we ran after the intruders?

The clouds cleared further; objects took on a blue color if in the moonshine or stayed black in shadow. A small boat floated at the front door of the trailer. Were the house—on stilts and five feet off the stream's bottom—to shift, it could flip over into the water.

I felt vulnerable. Who was this rooftop man? "Did some men run past here?" I shouted across the stream at the man on the roof.

He didn't seem eager to talk to me. Finally, he withdrew his pipe from his mouth and shouted back. "Yep."

"Where'd they go?"

Again, he hesitated. "Down da stream."

The intruders had escaped, showing skill and strength as they ran away lugging their digging gear. I looked back at the man on the roof, making out he smoked a pipe and wore a flat hat with a short brim, a porkpie hat. "Who are you?" I asked.

He waited before answering. "Who you?"

"I'm a guard . . . for the McDonald farm. Name's Gannon, Don Gannon."

"McDonald property's upstream," he said. "Dis is my land."

"What do I call you?"

"Name's Connor Sandford."

Sandford stood up and folded his chair. Next, he climbed a ladder from the trailer roof and slipped inside through a window on the side. We waited, but he didn't reappear.

The cloud cover rolled over the moon and turned the forest black. Bruce and I walked back upstream to the McDonald farmhouse, told the grandson we had chased away the diggers, and drove back to the mansion—our tails between our legs. This failure reminded me that to catch a baddie, one must genuinely know them.

6

SANDFORD'S TRAILER IN THE STREAM, MACON COUNTY — WEDNESDAY

In Roth's office the next morning, I reported—word for word and with every detail—the particulars of our chase through the woods to find Mr. Sandford sitting atop his house in the stream. When I finished, Roth resembled a Buddha statue thinking. "Go earlier to the excavation site next time, hide, and wait for the diggers to come to you."

I nodded at her. That was the approach I had already chosen. Her micromanaging was getting old but there was no way I could tell her that.

She continued, "Who's Connor Sandford? What does Grandma McDonald know about him?"

"I'll find out this morning when I'm at the farmhouse. Any reason for your interest?"

"His story doesn't sound right. See if you can extract something insightful."

"Will do. Anything else?"

Roth stared at her fireplace for a moment. "Angela researched Waya's travel to Oklahoma in 1838."

She had already told us the Indian brave didn't come back to claim his emerald. "And?"

"Angela discovered Waya had followed John Ross, the Cherokee Nation's principal chief on the Trail of Tears. When the travelers reached Oklahoma in June 1839, Ross insisted the old Cherokee government continue in the new site."

Why was she dragging me into a history lesson? Had she gone mysterious on me? Too much wine? I blinked rapidly and then openly stared.

"Of importance to us is Ross's government recorded every citizen of the Cherokee Nation who arrived in Oklahoma. It turns out Waya didn't reach this new land. If he didn't get there, we have no way to learn what happened to his copy of the map."

I gave a crisp nod. "Nowhere to pick up his trail. Close to two hundred years have passed. We aren't going to find Waya's map."

"That's right." Roth picked up a novel sitting on her desk. She had dismissed me.

I crossed my arms and didn't move.

She bookmarked her novel and laid it back down. "What is it?"

I raised my eyebrows. "May I suggest a different tactic?"

She sighed heavily. "What do you want?"

She annoyed me, triggering me to open my mouth to criticize, but shutting it. After a few moments, I said, "We don't have a useful clue. Hunting this emerald is costly and frustrating. We should withdraw now and cut our losses."

"What if I told you that continuing has a low cost and a high benefit?"

"Hmm, you're saying there's a high benefit in continuing?"

My boss rocked in her chair. "A superior emerald is a truly breathtaking sight and deserves its placement among the traditional big-four gems, along with diamond, ruby, and sapphire."

"But it's a single gem. Why would someone pay a fortune?"

Roth shook her head. "Emeralds have enthralled us since prehistoric ages. Tales of famous emeralds have enchanted people for centuries."

I had heard stories of Cleopatra's emeralds, but the folks I knew didn't have one. "I'm not that familiar with emeralds."

"Most emeralds are found outside North America, in Colombia, Russia, Brazil, and Afghanistan. Our state has the lone noteworthy emerald deposit in North America."

"Do most emeralds have the same appearance as our Cherokee one?"

"They do. The majority happen naturally as six-sided prisms, usually elongated with smooth sides."

"You're not interested in my suggestion?"

She picked up her novel. "Go solve your case."

# # #

I talked with the grandson and Grandma McDonald in the impoverished garden behind the farmhouse. Rarely had I seen so complete a ruin. I sat on a faded wood bench, which lay beside a grass-covered brick pathway through the shabby remains of hedges and recounted the late-night chase.

Grandma snickered at me. "That there's classic clumsy."

"Umm, what can you tell me about this Sandford guy?"

Her grandson, Ashley, shuddered and then remarked, "You've met our local oddball, the old guy in the porkpie hat. Scary."

"Tell me about him."

"Well, he hunts a lot . . . and trades game for our vegetables."

Turning back to Grandma, I asked, "Is he local?"

Before talking, she repeated her nervous habit of taking off her glasses and wiping them. "The Sandford family done lived next door to our farm forever. Mountain stock from way back."

"Could Sandford be the intruder?"

She put her glasses back on her nose. "He do get around in these woods. He might be a little old to be digging holes all night by hisself."

"Would he know about the tale of the hidden gem?"

Before speaking, she studied the beaten-down hedges with frustration. "Connor, our mountain man, has been sneaking around in dis region forever. Did he find something about de emerald recently? Don't know if he did, but I think somebody did."

"Is Sandford dangerous?"

Grandma smirked. "He always carries a rifle. You figure it out, Mr. Detective."

My moments with Grandma continued to carry me back in time. *She's a dead ringer for my grandmother, sharp tongue and all.* I switched topics to keep us focused. "I want to go talk with Sandford. Professor Lightfoot wants to discuss the journals with you."

"Good luck," the old woman said. "If he don't want you to see him, you won't see him."

"Oh, one last question," I said.

Grandma was taken aback, her mouth falling open. "What'd y'all forget?"

"When Ian got to California, did he keep a journal there?"

"Yes. He kept a-writin'."

I left the garden and walked to last night's dig but learned nothing new. I confirmed the trespassers had taken their spades when they ran.

My walk took me to Sandford's trailer in the stream. A boat floated at the front door. Before long, he opened his door and looked across the water at me, pulling on his pipe, his porkpie hat on his head. He had long, white, shaggy hair and a lengthy, white, unkempt, Vandyke beard. "You're back."

"Could I talk with you?"

He paused, not speaking for a minute.

I pointed at the stream bank under my feet. "Over here."

He went back in the trailer to get his rifle and paddled his boat about twenty yards across the water to me. I noticed he picked up his weapon when he got out of his rowboat.

I faced him. "Interesting place for a house."

The skin on his forehead constricted, and he gave me an insincere, thin-lipped smile. "When the stream rose, my neighbors abandoned their homes. They're farther downstream in several feet of water."

"Doesn't seem to bother you."

"If you'd learned to live off the land, you'd be okay.'

"What if the stream rises higher?"

"I'll get out."

"How do you get supplies?"

"Once I get onshore, I walk a mile to a general store. Lots of animals have swum by my trailer, searching for higher ground—I shoot snakes."

He sat down on the bank. I sat beside him.

"I'll shoot dead anyone who threatens me in my trailer. What did you want ta ask me?"

"Did you dig a hole in McDonald's land last night?"

"Nope."

"See anything?"

"Saw two people running, just ahead of you and your partner."

"Seen them before?"

"Same two people in da woods. They're huntin' for something."

"Know who they are?"

"Nope."

"They see you?"

"Nope."

"You chase them off?"

"Nope."

"What do they do?

He spoke through his teeth with forced restraint. "I told you—they search."

"For what?"

"Don't know." He seemed to pause, perhaps to enjoy the effect of his words. "Maybe that Cherokee Emerald."

Did everyone in Macon County know that old tale?

Sandford grinned and stood. "You ask a lot of questions. I ain't your information service."

"What do you mean?"

"Next time you come, bring a bottle of moonshine nectar for me." Carrying his rifle, he got back in his boat and paddled to his trailer on stilts.

This mountain man, always still, like a snake. Lifeless dark pupils staring as if ready to strike, like a snake. Who was he, an actor or a poisonous snake?

7

GRANDMA'S FARM — THURSDAY

The next night, the rain did a pour-down on my waterproof Boonie Hat, half the time obscuring my vision of the recently dug holes on the McDonald Farm. I stood close to a tree to stay out of the shower. Around the tree trunk from me, Bruce ranted and fumed in a muffled mumble, which occasionally grew noisy. "Would you shut up?"

"You had to tell da boss we was running around in circles chasing da diggers. See where you got us."

A sheen of water covered my dark-olive rain jacket, with its water–repellent finish. The tree pushed against my coat and jammed my holstered pistol into my side, adding to my misery. Why wouldn't my partner shut up? "It's pouring down water buckets. Nothing we can do. You're complaining like a dog baying at the moon."

"Dog. You got dat right. This water-soaked hound's wantin' to get inside out of de rain."

At least my feet weren't squishing in water. I had duct-taped the bottom hem of my jeans to my boot tops. "How was I to know the diggers wouldn't show up?"

Bruce snuffled. "Cos, the diggers read the weather forecast."

I guessed my partner wasn't going to let up until I agreed to get back into the car. "Bruce, I admit I got us into a shower. Cut me some slack."

"Can't catch the diggers. Can't find where da gem got hid. You da Fumbler."

Fumbler! I would catch the diggers, eventually, though I had made no progress finding the gem's hidey-hole. When Ian got gold fever in 1849 and left for California, he had a copy of the map. He left his wife and five children behind in North Carolina and never returned. If I could get that drawing, maybe I could crack this case wide open.

The rain surge let up. Bruce broke into my reverie. "Let's leave yo' tree and start runnin' for the Jeep?"

"Stop prattling and give me a minute to think." Because Ian ran off, the McDonald family didn't have his journals after 1848. Maybe Ian's later writings told where he put the map? Could I find the documents he wrote in California?

I sheltered my eyes with my right palm and studied the sky. The rain would continue. No digging tonight. "Yeah. Let's head for your Jeep."

"Finally."

We plodded through the thick woods to the lane entering the farm and jumped in Bruce's yellow Jeep. He started the engine and wipers. "Ain't ready yet. Let it warm up."

As we waited, I glanced at the two-lane rural road leading into the farm. A figure in a black rain suit powered past on a red and white motorcycle. Bet he was eager to get out of the rain.

# # #

As soon as I got back to the mansion, I dumped my wet clothes in the bathroom, collapsed in bed, and fell into a deep sleep. I suppose the rain pounded on the building all night but, if it did, the noise didn't wake me. In the morning, bright stripes of sunlight streaked under my window shades and stirred me from a sound sleep. Tottering to the window and peering under the blinds, my half-open eyes saw the rain had ceased, and the dark-gray rain blanket had broken down into white clouds scattered over an azure sky. I groaned and swayed back to bed, pulling the covers over my head. But I couldn't lapse back into sleep, my mind alert and thinking about the case.

I got beneath my warm shower and lathered soapsuds over my body. Gradually turning the water temperature colder, my body came alive, moving fluidly, my eyes dancing around the bathroom. I pulled on casual garments, blue jeans, a crew-neck sweater, and loafers. Down at the breakfast table, Taylor fixed eggs and grits. She told me Roth had read a novel until late the previous evening and hadn't yet come down to eat. I had to wait until she got up.

I passed the time in my office for the boss to appear, annoyance creeping over my body, my jaw clenching, and my fingers tapping on the desktop. My brain wouldn't focus on the case but did mental fidgets. I needed a peaceful place to refresh my head, a space to walk and muse about the gem-hunt puzzle.

# # #

My silver Mustang GT took me to Weaver Park in North Asheville, a well-mowed grassy area of seven acres, a childhood stomping ground dear to me. The park was unoccupied this morning and tranquil, with tall trees along one side and two-lane Murdock Avenue along another side.

My head down, contemplating, I strolled along the stream to a wooden bench on a wooden bridge over the creek and sat. My body loosened up, and my brain churned through everything I knew about the Cherokee emerald. After a while, I raised my head and took a deep breath. If we caught the diggers, would the case be over? Bruce and I would grab those guys, sooner or later, but would they be the bosses or some goons hired to dig? Might not answer why the digging was occurring. Catching the excavators might not crack the case or find the emerald.

Other paths of rummaging for clues didn't appear helpful. Common sense and intuition told me Waya's trail was stone cold. I had mixed feelings about the usefulness of searching for what Ian did with his map. A California search would probably lead me up a blind alley. But if I didn't try, I'd never know. I stood up and strolled into open space around a baseball diamond. Years ago, during my summer vacations, I had laughed and yelled, and hit baseballs at this playground. Workers had relocated the baseball field from the upper end of the park to this lower area. I saw the authorities had installed lights for nighttime play.

I continued strolling. Searching in California for Ian's map wouldn't succeed without Grandma's intervention, using her connections. She would be difficult for me to handle alone. The thought of being the single person going with Grandma caused me uneasiness, as a headache started at the reflection. To take her to the Golden State, I'd need Angela's aid—and Roth's approval and money.

I had no reason to guide my next step. My logical wild-ass guess was to search for a clue on the West Coast. I pulled out my mobile phone and rang Angela. "If we went to California, do you think we could find the map?"

She didn't miss a beat. "I think we'd need Grandma."

"Would you go with me?"

"I'd help you hunt."

"Can you get away?"

"My teaching assistant can cover classes for me."

"Let's go talk to Grandma?"

"Pick me up."

"On my way."

As I walked to my car in the parking lot, I glanced up at Murdock Avenue, with houses perched across the hillside above the park. A person wearing black clothes and a helmet with a shield sat on a red and white motorcycle.

# # #

At Grandma's farmhouse, Angela and I sat in Adirondack chairs on Grandma's screened-in side porch, while Grandma sipped her ever-present glass of wine and talked about her great-great-great-grandfather. "Ian met a woman in California, and plumb stayed wid her. When he died in eighteen-eighty, I heared he had lived with dat branch of his family."

"Where are they?" Angela asked.

"They're in Coloma, California, where Ian had mined for gold."

Grandma fiddled with her glasses before continuing. "Back when I were a young'un, I visited Coloma twice. There were a stack of Ian journals he wrote in California."

A gush of adrenalin pricked through my body. "Did you go through the journals?"

Grandma shook her head. "I didn't read them. I never saw anyone in the family glance at them."

I rubbed my chin. Hopefully, no one had tossed out those papers. "Where did you see them?"

"On a shelf in the old Coloma house."

What was she talking about? "Did you say old Coloma house?"

Grandma waved a dismissive hand in the air. "Ian stayed in a shack while he panned fer gold."

I raised my eyebrows to Grandma, encouraging her to continue.

"The journals sat on a shelf, with a lot of old tools, bottles, and rags."

"Did you see an eighteen-forty-nine journal?" I asked.

Grandma shook her head again. "Don't remember."

I was curious about Ian's stay in the gold-rush country. "Did Ian find gold?"

"He did. When he died, he left everything he earned in California to that branch of our family."

"Was the woman in California a McDonald?"

"She were. Ian done married her."

As I mulled over my next move, I leaned back on my chair and asked Angela. "What do you think?"

Angela leaned forward. "I want to go through those Coloma journals."

"Yeah. Me too." I turned to the old lady. "When were you last in Coloma?"

"Ain't been for a coon's age."

"Come to California with us. Could you show me the journals?"

"Might-could. Way too spendy for me."

I stood up. "We should talk to Roth."

Angela stood up with me. "I've got the time."

At first, Grandma didn't want to leave the farmhouse to go to the mansion with Angela and me. Luckily, her grandson—who had been out of the house working on the farm—returned for a Mountain Dew. When he had his drink, he took a breather to listen to our conversation. As Grandma took a moment to adjust her glasses, Ashley whispered into my ear, "Say you'll stop for lunch and wine on the way. Buy her two glasses of wine—no more."

# # #

I got her to Roth's office in a talkative but conscious state. My boss and the old woman chatted like childhood friends who hadn't seen each other since elementary school.

Sitting at her desk, Roth rubbed her hands together. "I need your help unraveling the mystery. I believe you know what Ian did in the mid-eighteen-hundreds."

Grandma smiled at my boss. "From the get-go, I figured I ought to talk with you instead of them boys."

Roth smirked at me, then turned back to Grandma and nodded. "I want to ask, other than looking for a big emerald, was there any other reason to burglarize your farmhouse?"

"We got an old TV set and beat-up silverware, but no one would want dem things."

Taylor brought in glasses and a bottle of Merlot. Grandma took her drink with a nod toward Taylor.

Reaching for her glass, Roth asked, "Where is the map Waya and Ian drew, their diagram?"

Grandma lifted her Merlot. "After Ian skedaddled, the family searched but found no map. It weren't in the farmhouse."

"But it might have been in the hole in the stone wall?"

Grandma shrugged. "I think de family—back in de mid-eighteen-hundreds—knew where to search. Dat map wasn't in the house."

Roth raised her wine glass and paused before she drank. "The intruders either had the map, or they didn't. If they had the map, why did they search in your house? If they didn't, why the sudden interest after a hundred and fifty-plus years?"

Grandma took off her glasses and cleaned them. "It's a mystery."

The old lady kept wiping her spectacles. I wondered if she had cataracts instead of soiled lenses.

I stood. "Are we wasting time? Better Bruce and I grab the diggers and find out what they know?"

Roth wagged her index finger at me. "Don't be hasty. They'll answer our questions with all sorts of mendacities. We might get nowhere with a brute-force approach."

I wiggled my index finger back at her. "What other way do we have?"

Roth pursed her lips before answering. "A further way is to garner more information." Roth peered at Grandma McDonald. "You saw copies of Ian's journal in California?"

Grandma McDonald had drained her wine glass and now looked longingly for Taylor. "Ian's offspring in Coloma and Placerville had some of his papers."

Roth turned to Angela. "Have you communicated with them?"

Angela shook her head. "I called the McDonald relatives in Coloma, but they refused to talk with me."

"Give me the number."

Roth called a number in Placerville and began speaking with Grandma's cousin, Gertrude Johnson. "Mrs. Johnson, I am phoning on behalf of your cousin, Mrs. McDonald, in Macon County, North Carolina."

I heard a shout from the phone in Roth's hand. "I'll tell you the same thing I told that other woman 'I don't want to talk with you.' "

My boss's lips curled. "You could protect your relatives. Intruders have invaded their farm."

"I don't know anything about invaders. Go away."

Roth placed the phone against her chest, expelled air from her lungs, and put the phone to her ear again. "Mrs. Johnson, the burglars may have learned something from the old journals of Ian McDonald. Allowing us to see them would greatly expedite our identifying the culprits."

"We don't x-pee-dot, and we don't have journals. Wouldn't let you see them if I did. I'm hanging up."

Grandma McDonald—carefully setting down her wineglass, rising out of her chair, wobbling a little—grabbed the phone out of Roth's hand, and shouted, "Gertie, I'm coming to see you now," before disconnecting the call.

8

OLD GOLD-RUSH CABIN, COLOMA, CALIFORNIA – FRIDAY

The next morning, I rose early and picked up Angela from her house and then the old lady. I gulped when I spotted her standing there with three suitcases. I got the luggage and my passengers to the Asheville Regional Airport, nine miles south of downtown Asheville.

The airline charged Grandma for excessive baggage, which I paid. She whined about airport security as they seized her long tweezers. "Ain't nobody can steal a plane with tweezers?" The old lady fidgeted in the window seat. The stewardess came down the aisle, and Grandma asked her to open the window. "Reckon you could let some fresh air in?" It turned out this was her first flight. She kept asking when the food service would start and exchanged her window seat with my aisle seat. She took two wines and asked Angela and me for our other wine. Grandma asked the whereabouts of the lavatory and went down the row of seats. I settled back in my place. The old lady yelled from the back of the plane, "Where am I? Am I on da right flight?" She was drunk. I hurried down the aisle to pull her back to her seat.

After a landing and short stay at the connector airport in Chicago, during which Grandma groused, we took off and disembarked in San Francisco. While my partner and I gathered the old lady's luggage, she slipped away. It took us over an hour, but Angela finally hunted her down in a VIP lounge, watching TV and killing small bottles of wine. Somehow, she had sneaked past the check-in desk.

She wouldn't tell me how she evaded the attendant at the entrance. "You ain't got to be a detective to find a watering hole." Feeling a sudden release of pent-up tensions, I was glad Angela had come along to help watch the old lady.

On the shuttle bus to get our rental car, I thought about Roth's parting words. "If this Gertrude person lets you see the journals, fine. However, refuse any offer she makes to split the gem's value." Angela and I got Grandma and her luggage settled in the hatch and rear seat of our rented Ford Focus. She wasn't happy. "There ain't no room back here." I drove northeast toward Coloma and Placerville.

From the back seat, Grandma whined, "I'm hungry."

I twisted my head toward her. "We'll stop and get you some chips."

"I want to et food at a restaurant."

We pulled into an IHOP. Grandma ordered hot coffee and filled the cup to the brim with cold cream. She called the server over and complained, "My coffee's cold."

It went like that until we got to a motel in Placerville, near Coloma, where we took three rooms. I left my luggage in my bedroom and got back into the rental car. No Grandma. Angela went to fetch her from her accommodation. Angela returned and slid into the right-front passenger seat. "Where's Grandma?" I asked.

"She purchased a bottle of wine at the airport."

I groaned. "She's asleep?"

Angela held her fists to her temples as if exasperated. "A trip to California . . . wasted."

# # #

When Grandma awoke two hours later, we drove to a one-story wood house in Placerville and parked in the driveway.

She spoke from the rear seat. "They has two homes."

Why hadn't I found that out before now? "Why two homes?"

"After Ian made a little money prospecting, he built his first house, a small one, in Coloma."

"What's the population of Coloma?" Angela asked.

"Four to five hundred people live thar tops."

Gertie, an older, stouter woman, opened the front door greeting us with a pout. She wore a filthy apron over a shapeless dress. Before she could close the door, Grandma pushed her way into the house.

Gertie cranked up her loud voice and said to Grandma. "I told you not to come."

Grandma displayed a tight-lipped smile to her cousin. "I'm glad to see you, too, Gertie."

A skinny male, in his early twenties, stood behind Gertie, who said, "Ask what you want and then get out."

While the relatives quarreled, I peeked around the room, a living room. It was crowded. Angela and I stood in silence. Grandma and Gertie went nose to nose. A mousy woman stood beside the thin youth. Six people were present.

The front room was messy, with magazines and plates and pillows strewn about. I eased along the wall to peer into a bedroom, seeing nothing resembling a work area or bookshelves. Most eyes in the front room focused on the battling cousins. The youth was an exception, staring at me with dead eyes, set in a face devoid of emotion.

Grandma had lost every sign of her inebriation and was in full battle mode. She boomed at her cousin. "Stop your shouting! We done come to read Ian's journals." To show their disinclination to reach an agreement, Gertrude and Grandma positioned their faces about six inches apart. Creeping as a rabbit, I kept my head down and edged toward the kitchen. I spied trash bags, plates, cups, and a full sink of dirty dishes; I saw no books or study area. A shotgun stood in a corner.

Gertie kept up her harangue. “Doesn’t make sense to me.”

Grandma shouted back. “What don’t?”

“How can reading old journals keep invaders out of your home?”

Grandma lowered her head and mumbled to herself. Then she spoke. “Just let us see them.”

Gertie fired back. “Does this have anything to do with that old legend about a hidden jewel?”

I gawked at her. Everyone knew about the emerald.

The two cousins continued to circle like roosters, keeping their faces way too close. As they rotated in a loop, I sneaked a peek at the other bedroom: nothing, no books, no work areas, and no documents or journal sheets. The youth—pimply-faced and clad in a gray sweatshirt with hoodie—watched me. At first, I had thought him harmless, but now I wasn’t so sure.

Gertie kept pushing. “Give up half the gem, and I’ll help.”

Grandma scrunched up her face before replying. “Like my side of the family got half the gold Ian mined?”

Gertie’s face turned so red; it didn’t seem healthy. “Get out! Get out now!”

“You can’t do that.”

“It’s my place.”

“I’m your relative.”

“Well, relative, go to hell and take your two toadies with you.”

My eye caught the rumpled blue pants of canvas and dirty-white running shoes worn by the young man. He was moving toward the kitchen. We needed to leave. Besides, I doubted this house held Ian's old papers.

Grandma surprised me with her next question. "Where are my cousin Jeremiah? Let me jaw with him."

Gertie shook her head. "Haven't seen him for a while."

"What you mean? You ain't seed him?"

Gertie turned to the skinny man. "Son, get the shotgun."

Time to go. I darted across the room, grabbed Grandma, and pulled her out the front door. Behind us, Gertie ranted. "We'll shoot you. Don't come back."

Angela got into the passenger seat. "Did you see any old papers, journals, anything?"

I started the rental and drove off. "Didn't see them in that house. It's a jumble like the grounds around a Fourth of July celebration."

Angela rubbed her chin. "What do we do now?"

I headed back to our motel. "Don't know."

From the back seat, Grandma grumbled. "Talking with Gertie, I remembered what a horse's ass she is."

Angela's head turned toward the old lady. "What about Ian's documents?"

"Back when I visited my cousins in Placerville, the journals wasn't in dat house. I remember dem in Ian's old Coloma building."

I slowed the car and turned my head around to Grandma. "Do you remember how to get to his Coloma place?"

She dug through her purse. "No, but I knowed to write down the address."

I stopped at a convenience store for directions to Ian's ancient dwelling. I bought two packages: a couple of flashlights and six small bottles of wine to keep the old lady occupied. We arrived in Coloma, the town that originated the California Gold Rush of 1849 and changed the history of California and the nation. The township seemed all but hidden within a densely forested section of the American River Canyon. The woods consisted of native California oaks. As we drove, turkeys appeared on the side of the road.

Our history professor glanced at Coloma with excitement. "This was the epicenter of the California Gold Rush. It was here, on the South Fork American River, that a carpenter initially discovered a gold nugget. A gold camp sprung up and was named Coloma after the valley around it."

I slowed to read a road sign. "Did Coloma boom and bust?"

Angela studied our travel map, trying to pinpoint Ian's old house. "At one point, Coloma had three hundred buildings. By 1870, it had only two hundred inhabitants."

"What do the people do for a living?"

"Agriculture and tourism."

Ian's old house stood alone, a dark gray, weathered, one-story building of wood.

"I remember de ancient journals in dis house," Grandma said. "That Ian were a writing fool."

By grabbing my right arm, Angela signaled me to stop. "But we can't go in. We'd be trespassing, and the son has a shotgun. I'd be scared to death."

Grandma disagreed. "We came dis far. Don't stop now." She had gumption.

"Grandma's right," I said. "I'll come back tonight when it's dark."

Angela pursed her lips. "I'd be trespassing, but I ought to come with you."

I wanted Angela to stay behind with the old lady. "Don't see why."

Angela smirked at me. "You'd take too long reading the documents. I'm a historian, and I need to be there."

"I'm coming," Grandma said. "I remember de room with shelves of papers at de rear of this shabby shack."

# # #

At dusk, we drove back to the gold-rush cabin, parked the car at the edge of some woods, and walked to Ian's house, which was quiet and dark. Angela and I had flashlights.

I stepped up on the front porch. The door was locked. Stepping off the porch, I tried to push up the window to the right of the door but found it wouldn't open either. I had crept around to the right side of the building when I heard glass breaking. In the still country air, the breakage sounded as loud as a leaf-blower starting up.

At the window in the front, Angela stood holding a hand over her mouth, and Grandma held her big purse.

"Why'd you do that?" I asked in a whisper.

"Saw it on TV," the old lady said in a raised voice.

I shook my head. "Use your whisper voice."

I went in through the window, searched for and found no electronic security, and opened the front door. It made a loud *screeching* sound that could have woken the dead.

Grandma shook her finger at me. "Silly boy. Why tell me to be quiet when you gonna make all dat noise?"

Angela took Grandma to the rear room and looked for the journals. Partially to keep a lookout in front of the house, I remained in the front office and combed the room.

I found bills and correspondence on a desk, with all these documents addressed to Jeremiah McDonald. Much of the mail was overdue notices for unpaid bills. Picking up a coffee cup from a counter, I saw a mass of crud at the bottom; this cup hadn't held fresh coffee for a month. On the right side of the desk, I viewed a picture of American soldiers with a jungle in the background, like a Vietnam War-era scene. The backdrop was mostly spindly trees without an overabundance of vegetation. The picture framed three soldiers, one draped in ammo belts of shells and holding an M60 machine gun, one was standing in the background, and another held an M79 grenade launcher. An inscription, "Jeremiah – Your buddy, Talk," was penned next to the trooper holding the launcher.

A pile of mail had grown on the desk and spilled onto the floor. The postmarked dates told me the envelopes began stacking up a month ago. I found a credit card bill, saw Jeremiah gassed up at Shell, and guessed he had a car. I pulled out my notepad and wrote down much of the information on the statement.

I moved to the rear room, where I found Angela under a table reading journals with her flashlight. Shielded by the tabletop, she emitted little light, keeping the room in darkness. I knelt under the table. "Find anything?"

She held a ledger in her hands. "This is the 1850 journal. Ian writes about the gem. He states he folded a diagram—describing its hiding place—between two pages of this journal."

"It's gone? Isn't it?"

She sighed and nodded.

I raked my fingers through my hair. "Gertie's brother, Jeremiah McDonald, hasn't lived here for at least a month."

Angela flipped through the other journals, checking if Ian had mislaid the map in a different diary. Angela pointed at the shelves around the room. "Dust all over this room, but the ledgers are spotless. Someone's been reading them."

I glanced at Grandma, who sat on a chair, noiselessly for a change. Next, I turned back to Angela. "We're too late."

She kept her head down and carried on reading. "I'm going through every one of the Ian journals. As I finish one, you check to see if I missed anything."

We read in silence. As I grew familiar with Ian's handwriting, my reading speed increased. We went through every page; someone had taken the map.

Angela grasped her hands in frustration. "My guess would be Jeremiah McDonald read the journals and found the map."

I tried to visualize his situation. "Just as Jeremiah found himself with inadequate funds and reduced to reading old work journals, he turns a page and wealth crashes into his lap."

I dialed Bruce on my mobile phone.

"Guy, what's happenin'?"

"I broke into Ian McDonald's old shack. Need you to check out a suspect."

"No can do. You owe me fer my last appraisal."

"Bruce, I don't have time to argue. Help me, and I'll pay you back."

"You get to go to California, an' I get to do your dirty work. Does dat seem fair to you?"

"What's it going to cost me?"

"Guy, on our next visit to the Blazer Tavern, you pay for every beer pitcher we get."

"That's your deal, and I'm stuck with it?"

"Yep."

I gave him the information on Jeremiah McDonald and hung up.

A *screech* made me jump.

Angela whispered. "Put the journals back."

"Someone's at the door," Grandma said in a whisper.

My brain exploded, causing images of what could be to flash through my mind. Was it the kid with the shotgun? My lizard brain screamed, *Hide or die.*

9

TRAPPED IN IAN'S COLOMA SHACK – SATURDAY

I had let down my guard; someone had come in through the front door. Who was at the entrance? Was it the pimply-faced kid with a shotgun? I needed to get us out of here, but I figured Grandma would slow us down if we went out of the rear window.

I slid into the back room, shutting the door. Under it, I saw the sudden glow of light in the front chamber as someone flipped the light switch. I could wait behind the door and jump the intruder when they entered, but what if they anticipated me being there? Angela stood, motionless and staring, white showing around all sides of her irises. She was a scholar, not an Indiana Jones fighter.

I heard a noise, a *squeak* of wheels as if someone sat down at the desk as I had a few minutes before.

Behind me, Grandma opened the window on the back wall. If the three of us tried to squirm through the window and the man opened the door, he would snare us. "Stop, he'll catch us if—"

Grandma pressed a finger against my lips. "Hush your mouth, Sonny." She bent down in front of the window and fidgeted with the molding along the bottom of the wall.

She pulled up a two-foot square section of the rough floor and stepped down the resulting void. As she descended, she turned her head to whisper, "Y'all hurry now."

Jeezus Cripes, she was sober.

Angela slipped down into the emptiness, trailing her flashlight beam. I followed, sticking my foot down, finding support, a step.

As slipping a square peg into a round hole, I wedged my husky body down a small pit. Grandma realized my difficulty and pulled on my pants and belt. "Suck your gut in, Mr. Bigshot."

My body popped down the hole like a cork bursting out of a bottle of bubbly. Grandma pulled the section of the floor back down to cover the void into our pit. She was rail-thin and white-haired, but she could still think fast. I sat on a dirt floor with shelves poking my back. I was Gulliver in the land of the Lilliputians, now a vault of pitch-black darkness.

On the floor above, footsteps sounded. The footfalls stopped on the section of the flooring above us. It could be the kid with the shotgun. I felt helpless; my heart raced. There was nothing for me to do but wait. The steps resumed, and I heard them moving toward the front of the shack.

Silence and darkness encased me; my heartbeat slowed. I smelled rotten vegetables. "Grandma, where are we?"

"Keep your voice down," she said. "It's a root cellar. Back when we'd play hide-and-seek, I'd sneak down here."

"Root cellar?"

Angela's voice came out of the darkness. "Before refrigeration."

The area was chilly. "Like a storage area?"

"People used the root cellar to keep stuff," Grandma said, "carrots, turnips, and potatoes, fresh in the winter."

I listened but heard no movement above my head. Shifting my back to keep the shelves from digging into me, I experienced a breeze. "I feel air moving."

Grandma whispered. "Boy, didn't your parents teach you 'bout root cellars?"

How did she do that? She made me feel like a small child. The slightest noise startled me, but Grandma and Angela's whispered comments calmed me by blocking the dread of discovery.

Grandma continued speaking in a low voice. "Root cellars done let fresh air in from de outside and stale air to vent."

I shifted my thighs, which had fallen asleep. "Are these underground rooms damp?"

Grandma continued. "Water drains out down de slope behind dis house."

We sat in silence for about ten minutes. My heart rate, which had jumped when the intruder had appeared, subsided. Presently, I heard the footsteps return, and I tried to slow my breathing to remain calm. I caught the sound of someone closing the open window. After a minute, footfalls grew faint and then vanished.

An hour passed with silence everywhere. My body had grown numb. Eventually, with Angela pulling me from above and Grandma pushing from below, I squeezed back through the small opening into the cabin's rear room. We snuck our way back to the rental Ford and slipped away into the night. As I drove back to the motel, I grinned. A window of opportunity had opened to our investigation, giving it a clear-cut way.

I intended for us to get a few hours of sleep and in the morning head for San Francisco Airport and our flight back to Asheville. My soft spot for Grandma had swelled. She had thought quickly: leaving the window open to make it appear we had gone out that way and hiding us in the root cellar.

10

REPORTING OUR PROGRESS, ROTH'S MANSION — SUNDAY

I woke later than usual that Sunday morning. The flight back from California had been uneventful except for Grandma wandering off in search of wine again while we were waiting for our flight to be called. Angela tracked her down, so we made our plane. On arriving in Asheville, Angela and I put Grandma and her luggage into a cab and sent her on her way to her farmhouse.

Once washed and dressed, I made my way downstairs when I heard the front doorbell ring. It was Angela, looking far more rested than I felt. Bruce, attired in white pants, tee shirt, and sport coat, met us in the front hallway with a big smile. "Guys. You're back."

Angela stared at Bruce's clothing and smiled. "My, aren't you something?"

He returned her beam. "Think of me as your white knight, Miss Lightfoot."

She presented him with a closed-mouth smile.

"Where's Roth?" I asked my grinning partner.

"Guys, da Boss done took a thermos of coffee out to da shade garden."

I led Angela out the back and along a path of gray flagstones through low-lying green plants, which border gave way to tall oaks with their spirally arranged leaves and acorns. The trees blocked and diffused the sunlight along that section of the footpath. Ahead, the trail passed a small clearing, upon which a patio of gray pea gravel had been laid. Roth sat on a light-brown wicker chair with white cushions. She put down a book.

I reclined on a wicker couch to her side. "What are you reading?"

She wore a black, wide-weave veil over her hair and pulled on a lock of her straight, white hair. "*Skipping Christmas* by John Grisham. Tell me about California."

Angela reviewed our Coloma findings for Roth. She concluded with, "Ian's journals lay in that back room maybe a hundred and fifty years but were dust-free. Someone had been reading them."

My boss turned to me. "Naturally, you have an idea who read the ledgers."

I felt a chill as the sun went behind a cloud. I zipped up the front of my black leather bomber jacket. "Jeremiah McDonald, Gertie's brother, lived in the house until a month ago when he vanished."

Roth stared at me. "You're progressing. Someone found Ian's old map, which caused the burglary. You suspect this Jeremiah fellow."

She tipped her head back and closed her eyes for a moment. "What do you know about Mr. McDonald?"

"He fought in the Vietnam War and is maybe sixty years old. Gertie didn't know where he went."

"What did the authorities tell you about Mr. McDonald?"

I shook my head. "We broke into a Coloma house. Police weren't going to help us."

My boss raised her eyebrows. "What do you plan to do?"

"Find Jeremiah."

My boss nodded. "Ask Bruce to join us."

While she and Angela discussed the garden, I called Bruce on my mobile phone. "We need you. We're out back on the patio."

After my partner joined us, Roth summarized the story of Coloma and the missing man. "Have you started getting particulars on Jeremiah McDonald in Coloma, or possibly Placerville?"

Bruce glanced up from where he sat in one of the wicker chairs. "I'm already on it, Boss."

Roth stared at the surrounding woods as if thinking. She does that a lot. "Tell Donnell and Angela about your stakeout last night."

"Guys, last night, while you were getting back from California, Mickey and I waited in de woods at the farm. We hid until dawn."

"And?"

"No one dug a hole on de farm." He shrugged and held his hands up in the air as if surrendering.

I waited.

"Some fricking lowlife punctured all four tires on my Jeep though."

"Sorry, my friend. Any clues?"

He frowned. "A message on my windshield."

"A message?"

"Dey wrote in block letters on a sheet of lined paper. Asked if I thought dey were stupid."

I shook my head.

Bruce bowed his head and stood up. "I'll continue working on Jeremiah McDonald." He left the patio.

Roth brushed a leaf off the arm of her black dress and glanced at Angela. "What else did Grandma McDonald say about Jeremiah?"

"When he returned from the war, he did odd jobs; cutting grass and moving trash. When Grandma visited the family, he was always hanging about."

My boss straightened her veil. "This Jeremiah had time on his hands. He read Ian McDonald's journals. Is that what you envision?"

"I read Ian's journals at the Coloma house," Angela said. "He wrote he put the diagram in the leaves of his ledger."

"But you didn't find a map?"

Angela blew out her cheeks and shook her head.

Roth folded her napkin and placed it on her plate. "Tell me if this is what you think. Mr. Johnson drove cross-country to North Carolina. He's in Macon County with the map searching for the Cherokee Emerald."

I felt tired and realized I suffered jet lag. I relaxed on this mild day, about sixty degrees Fahrenheit with a few clouds and a clear blue sky. My boss continued. "Donnell, you intuit two people dug the holes?"

I shook my head to revive myself. "That's right."

Roth leaned back and made a steeple of her fingers. "If Jeremiah came to North Carolina, did he bring a second person with him?"

Oops. I remembered the old Vietnam War photograph in the front room at Coloma. The inscription said—what was it?

"Did you recall something?" Angela asked.

I formed an image of the picture. In my mind, I made out the words. The writing stated, 'To Jere. Wherever you lead, I'll follow. Talk.'

"I think I know who he could be. An old Army buddy named Talk."

Angela gave me a stony stare. "How do you know?"

"I saw an inscription on a photograph on Jeremiah's desk."

"When were you going to tell me? I thought we worked together."

I should have told her. Just didn't think. "Sorry, Angela. My bad." Silence.

My boss twisted toward me. "Inform Bruce we suspect a second person, nicknamed Talk, is with Jeremiah."

She paused to study the sunlight diffusing through the tall oak trees. "If Jeremiah got to the farm with the map, it makes sense he would be digging up the ground. But, why would he burglarize the farmhouse to snatch photographs off the wall?"

Roth glared at us as if seeking an answer, appearing like a praying mantis waiting for something to eat. "I have three thoughts."

We waited.

"Is he hunting in the wrong location? Is the lost-gem story a hoax? Did someone already dig up the emerald?"

"I don't know." Sounded weak even to me.

# # #

A few hours later, I was in Roth's office, going over my expense report for the trip to California. Suddenly, she peered up from my receipts, "Three hundred dollars to fly Grandma's overweight luggage to and from California? What was she thinking?"

"She doesn't travel much."

My boss shook my expense report at me. "And what were you thinking? Why didn't you tell her she could take one suitcase?"

Bruce entered the room, flipping through his notepad. "Guys, Jeremiah drives a 1990 white Ford Ranger. He was arrested three times for drunkenness wid an old army buddy, Samuel Talkowski, nicknamed Talk because he keeps his mouth shut."

I snapped my fingers. "You found the second man."

Bruce gave me a superior stare, his head tilted back and his eyes staring into mine. "Guy, I'm lookin' at every information source. I covered tax records, real estate dealings, birth and death records—"

"I get it. That's enough."

Bruce's eyes gleamed, and he continued. "Court records, business licenses, DMV records, warrants, arrests, convictions—"

I raised both arms in surrender. "Okay. You're the best. Stop."

"The army gave Jeremiah an honorable discharge after his Vietnam tour," Bruce said.

"A white Ford Ranger pickup describes many vehicles driving around Macon County," I said. "Does Talk have a vehicle?"

"No, and he doesn't have a driver's license. Jeremiah does and here," Bruce laid down a photograph of Jeremiah, "are the picture on his license."

Back in Coloma, I had glanced over Jeremiah's credit card record. "His lack of credit card activity implied he used cash," I said.

My boss studied Jeremiah's photograph and handed it to me. The picture showed the face of a chubby man, bald on top with medium-length white hair on the sides, with an open, gaping mouth. He was average-looking. She leaned toward Bruce. "Well done."

Roth tapped on her desk as if she were considering what to make of our investigation. "I accept Jeremiah read an old diary, written by his ancient relative, Ian McDonald. And he found the map."

She turned to me. "Find Jeremiah and Talk."

# # #

I drove to the farmhouse in Macon County and showed Jeremiah's picture to the grandson and Grandma McDonald. Ashley hadn't seen the man, and she hadn't seen him lately but remembered him from when she visited Coloma years ago.

The grandson phoned the Corporal, Clay Hallowell, the officer who had first responded to the burglary and intrusion at the farm. He met us at a convenience store along his patrol route. Wearing the black trousers and long-sleeve shirt uniform for cooler weather, he repeated he couldn't respond to each intrusion in the area.

Hallowell appeared frustrated, rubbing the back of his neck. "It's getting to where I don't have enough time for my duties. I see more unlawful drugs than ever before."

I told Hallowell I suspected Jeremiah McDonald had burglarized the McDonald farm. I provided Jeremiah's picture and Ford Ranger license plate number to the officer. Using the sheriff's office dispatch, he checked his county records and found nothing on Jeremiah or his pickup. Hallowell put out a BOLO (be on the lookout) for Jeremiah in Macon and surrounding counties. He said he would be in touch and started to leave.

I called after him. "Wait, Clay, you can't just walk away."

"I wish I could help more, but I've got rounds to do."

"Attacking an aged woman and repeated trespassing doesn't deserve your attention?"

The officer spread his arms wide. "No can do. All our sheriff's office is on the watch for this Jeremiah." He returned to his vehicle.

# # #

Arriving back at the mansion, I found Angela in my boss's office and reported my activity with the McDonald family and Corporal Hallowell.

When I finished, my boss made a steeple of her fingers, a gesture she employed when she analyzed a knotty problem. "You recall I asked Angela to find out why the burglars stole the two photographs they did?"

Maybe Angela had a clue. "Yeah."

Angela reached down and pulled her briefcase off the floor. "I gathered Grandma's photographs, some old and some contemporary." Angela reached into her document case to extract a manila file, which contained a thick stack of pictures. "We know the burglars took two framed pictures. They showed the region in front of the farmhouse taken from different angles. Grandma gathered similar photos, going through old albums at the McDonald house."

Angela carried her stack of photographs to Roth and covered her desk with them. "Also, I took shots in front of the farmhouse from different distances and directions."

Roth and I viewed the photos and arranged them roughly by similar orientation to the house. Angela sat back to wait while my boss and I rummaged through all the images.

"Tell me again. For the photos stolen, what was the orientation to the farmhouse?" Roth asked.

"If you recall, the burglars stole one photograph oriented away from the front door and a second view at a great distance from the house and showing its front," Angela said.

Angela had gathered numerous views. They varied by year, the existence of the pond, with and without mountains, crops, and woods. For photos of the area in front of the house, the McDonalds had cleared the land, and the original trees were small, with trees growing taller in later photos and more numerous. The pond was bigger at times and sometimes more modest, with crops occasionally in front of the house.

Roth would group the photos one way, and next rearrange them in other ways. After half an hour of reshuffling, she smiled, pushed her chair back from the desk, and stood. "Gratifying, Angela. I now know what Jeremiah wanted."

I crept forward, so my rump was on the edge of the chair, eager to hear my boss utter the reason Jeremiah and Talk invaded Grandma's farmhouse.

11

AN OLD HEARTTHROB ARRIVES, ROTH'S MANSION — SUNDAY

Roth had figured out why the nocturnal thieves had stolen those two specific photographs off McDonald's farmhouse wall. With her shoulders back and her chin high, she leaned back in her desk chair and glared at me, challenging me to explain how she knew.

My natural reaction was to show my boss an open-mouth shock, but that would have swelled her ego, which I didn't want. Roth is my hero, but she is insufferable—sneering, head shaking, and mocking—when she yanks one of her Eurekas out of the blue. I remained calm, relaxing the muscles in my shoulder and holding my eyes on her arrangement of the maps. The photos across my boss's desktop were in chronological order, from oldest to most recent. What had she seen? I slowed my breathing and skimmed the gross similarities and differences of the photos. Then I saw what Roth had spotted: Nature relocated the pond's location farther downstream over the years. The burglars were trying to figure out where the fishpond lay in 1838. "The pond—"

Roth gave me a smug grin. Maybe she believed I was showing promise. "Do you believe they have the map showing the jewel's location?" she asked.

I grinned back. "Maybe."

Roth lowered her eyebrows and wrinkled the skin between her brows. "What did Waya and Ian sketch on their map? Think."

I turned to Roth. "I don't know. I haven't seen it."

Roth gave a dismissive wave of her hand. "Use your brain. It's a diagram."

Darn, was she trying to embarrass me? Maybe she just wanted me to reason out the answer? "A map guides—by physical features," I said aloud to myself. "What features would Waya and Ian have used?"

She nodded, grinned again. "Go on. Say what you're thinking."

"A tree, maybe, distance from a tree maybe, a mountain peak, or . . . a pond."

Roth pointed to one of the earliest photos. "The pond would be in different locations on the map over the years. I think it was near the front of the farmhouse in 1838. But it isn't in that location any longer."

Roth kept pushing me, keeping firm eye contact. "I presume the pond constantly silted over and reformed downriver and away from the building."

"Reformed downriver?" I asked.

"I watched a science program on TV that declared each stream in a drainage system flows into a drainage basin area. Over time, ponds in that stream may fill up with silt, and the water settles into a new location further downstream."

I didn't say anything at first but eventually probed Roth with a query. "How does a pond move?"

Roth, a gleam in her eyes, explained. "The excretion of fowls on the surface can fill the pond with waste. The trees may take water directly from the pond as they grow. Debris travels from upstream and settles in the bottom of the pond."

I had another look at the photographs. "The pond moved. Obvious in hindsight."

Roth continued. "Pond location is important if Waya and Ian drew one on their map in 1838."

My mind paused, pondering about what Roth had said. "You've got me thinking Waya and Ian drew the pond on the map."

Roth rewarded me with a crisp nod and eased back in her chair. "Now, I'm ready for a glass." She buzzed our cook, Taylor, on the house intercom to ask for a glass of the cabernet sauvignon, which bottle remained half full of wine after last night's meal. Next, she buzzed Bruce in the computer room. "I need you and your maps of the farm."

Upon entering the office, he said, "Yes, Boss."

Roth sketched out her theory: The 1838 map used physical features on the farm at that time. "Where was the pond originally? Also, was there a dominant tree, a tree taller and thicker than all the others?"

Bruce jiggled his feet as if unsure what she wanted him to do.

Roth began again. "Graph the farmhouse and land over the years."

"Graph?"

"Estimate the position of trees and the pond and mountain peaks in 1838, when Waya and Ian buried the gem. Also, we need graphics for 1890, the year of the pictures stolen by the thieves."

He scribbled down her instructions. "There're a lot of oaks around de farm now."

Roth adjusted the collar of her dark tunic. "Search for an oak old enough to have been fully grown in 1838."

Bruce scribbled some more. "You want a series of landscape diagrams?"

"Make trips to eyeball the farm. Examine records at the library, the county courthouse, and computer databases as needed. Present your findings in a series of graphs of the farmhouse over time."

Bruce paused his pen over his notepad. "Why am I doing this?"

"To put an *X* on the graph where they buried the emerald."

Bruce glanced from Roth to me. "Anything else?"

Roth tasted her wine and seemed to consider his question. "That's all for now."

Bruce left the room and Angela took her leave and returned home.

After Bruce and Angela left, I pondered Roth's pond thesis. I found nothing wrong with her logic, but where did it get us? A dead end. I glanced up.

She stared at me. "What's wrong?"

"Even when Bruce finishes the topographical diagrams, we still need Ian's map."

She sighed heavily. "I know. Find it."

# # #

Leaving Roth, who'd immediately picked up a novel, I walked into the mansion's hallway and headed toward the stairs up to my room. As I passed the front door, I noticed the windowpanes needed a cleaning outside, as a film of grime diffused the light making its way into the room.

When the doorbell rang, I was stumped, my brain wrestling with how to find a missing map, and I didn't peek through the front door until I had opened it.

I was affected by the familiar, refreshing smell of a rose scent, which flowed from the doorway and spilled over me. Good grief, I had missed that fragrance. Her smile hit me, teeth showing in a wide grin. A long-lost feeling from childhood saturated my senses, that euphoric feeling of seeing presents under the Christmas tree.

"Close your mouth, Don. I'm happy to see you too."

She slipped off her blue trench coat and hung it on the clothes tree alongside the front door. Her outfit shimmered brightly: blue dress with a yellow hem, yellow straw hat with a wide brim, and a stretched vest over her dress. The late-morning sun coming through the open front door behind her framed her dazzlingly in her spring-like outfit.

Taylor and Roth came running when they heard Carla in the hallway. They surrounded her on a couch in the TV room, our media room, exchanging rapid-fire information as women do well. Having paid the taxi driver and brought in her luggage, I sat at the edge of the group and listened in.

"Tell us what happened," Taylor said.

She wiped tears and had everyone's attention. "When I ran away from Asheville six months ago, I stayed at my parents' home in Ohio. For weeks, I bundled up in my old, high-school clothes and walked in the snow and the dark. Thought and thought and over-thought what could, what should happen next."

Taylor nodded her head. "You did right to leave. You'ns would have been miserable if you had married that man."

I had fancied Carla myself, but I hadn't chased her properly. My rival swooped in and proposed to her. She'd accepted. The engagement didn't work out, and she left us after returning his ring.

"You seemed to have regained your equilibrium," Roth said to Carla.

She dried her eyes. "For months, I nursed a shattered dream. Then, one day, I was on my parents' couch early in the morning, reading the local paper. An intruder killed a small-time drug dealer in his apartment."

Taylor acted as if she was taken aback by Carla's tale of the newspaper article, keeping steady eye contact with her. "Were it someone you'ns knew?"

"No. Just an everyday crime report." Carla lapsed into a hush.

Roth broke the silence. "This story of crime. What did the police find?"

"The police had a suspect and were on the lookout for him."

Carla fiddled with her brown ponytail. "It got worse: two women, who lived in the same apartment complex as the suspect, went missing. I just knew the three had been after drugs together."

Roth bobbed her head in agreement. "On subsequent mornings, you found yourself grabbing the paper to follow the case?"

A flush spread across Carla's face. I recalled she had always been a fan of the Nancy Drew adventures. Or, as one of Roth's aphorisms says, "Always sleuth for the truth."

Roth persisted. "You followed each snippet in the newspaper and on TV, unraveling the case?"

I stood up and brought Carla a glass of water. Bruce and Mickey, who had been working elsewhere in the mansion, heard the discussion and wandered into the room.

Carla wiped her eyes again. "The police found the women's car deserted alongside a river—I just knew the two women were dead, dumped in the river. Divers searched the water, finally finding them. The police caught the suspect trying to flee Ohio."

She went quiet and next said, "I missed you all."

Roth glanced out the windows along one wall. "What did you miss?"

"The good that Roth Security does. I want to come back here, to you and the group."

Taylor broke in. "I want you'ns back, too."

Carla stopped to drink water. "My fiancé is gone, buried in a time slice of my past."

Taylor leaned forward from her seat on the couch. "You a-plannin' to stay with us?"

"When I left you, Ms. Roth said she'd take me back."

Roth raised her chin. "You're an instinctive hunter. I want you back. Your first assignment will be to help Don find a man with a map."

Taylor got up and passed me on her way to the kitchen. "Don't you'ns blow it with Carla this time."

"I won't. Bet on it."

The gathering broke up. I told Carla, "I'll carry your luggage up to your old room."

She gave me her big toothy, mischievous grin. "Thank you."

I placed her bags in her room.

She was a hot babe, poking out in all the desirable locations. "Welcome back. It's great to see you."

As I walked back downstairs, I hummed the lyrics to an old Poe poem:

"she lived with no other thought
Than to love and be loved by me."

12

TOO MANY DIGGERS, GRANDMA'S FARM — MONDAY

Carla was up early, eager to hunt Jeremiah in his 1990 Ford Ranger pickup. Though she had dressed for countryside work, wearing a blue trench coat, blue jeans, and black Doc Martins boots, I couldn't keep my eyes off her. In an ever-widening circle around the old McDonald farmhouse through the morning, she and I entered many drab gas stations and convenience stores, showing Jeremiah's picture to clerks and customers. At the same time, I scanned for old pickups in their parking lots.

Gas stations and grocery stores in the high Appalachia were a medley of architecture. "All these gas stations are as unalike as resins and watermelons," Carla said.

"My personal favorite is the simple one-story, single-room structure with white, weather-beaten, clapboard siding, and an attached, built-on shed," I said. "It's a gas station. It has a pump in front of the building."

"My favorite is the modern, glass-fronted food market where the clerk at the counter controls the outside pumps."

I nodded at her. "The pinnacle design is what I called the industrial age factory, where the cinder-block walls are painted white.

A one-room office is on one side with a limited choice of snacks. The rest of the building had paneled, roll-up doors in front of two or three bays for car repairs."

Using an old Mobil Gas map and tracking our way through a web of two-lane roads, we sought out Jeremiah and his diagram—displaying the way to the hidden gem—among all these stations and stores. Carla chatted with employees and customers at the stations while I checked the parked vehicles.

Back in my Mustang, I told Carla, "People like you."

She smirked but kept her head down, studying the map. "I could always talk."

"We'll quit at lunchtime."

She frowned. "I can't believe no one saw Jeremiah."

I shrugged. "He might've changed . . . grown a beard."

"The Ford Ranger?"

"Too common. No one notices it."

After lunch, I steered to McDonald's farm, parked on the side of the two-lane road, and walked through the woods to their house.

"What's in the bag?" Carla asked.

I raised my eyebrows to appear shifty. "Moonshine nectar."

She cocked her head at me.

When we got to the farmhouse, the grandson banged open the door. "I put up No Trespassing signs."

"Won't keep the diggers out," I said. "Carla, this is Ashley McDonald."

He leered at her. "Pleasure to meet you'ns."

Grandma McDonald appeared behind Ashley. "When you gonna stop them diggers?"

"Tonight," I said.

Grandma moved close to me and squinted. "How?"

I could smell wine on her breath. "Mickey, Bruce, and I are coming back at dusk."

"And?"

"We'll be up a tree, watching from a hunter's blind."

Grandma shook her head. "Lord, save us. You'ns as likely to fall out of de tree as catch a digger."

Carla pulled on my sleeve. "I'm coming along."

"No. Roth would kill me if a digger hit you with a shovel."

She pouted. "It's an opportunity to learn."

I shook my head. "I'm more scared of Roth."

She pouted. "Show me the woods."

I led Carla to the copse of oaks, with dug-out holes scattered about the area. We walked around the pond, circling two geese feeding on grass and a third goose, the guard, eyeing us suspiciously. Carla strode energetically ahead of me. "Wait," I said. "You don't know where we're going. Let me lead." I watched the woods for intruders as I headed toward the trailer in the stream.

When I heard the *snap . . . whee*, I turned.

His white Van Dyke and dusty-black, porkpie hat conspicuous, Connor Sandford leaned against a tree, holding the wooden match he had just lit. He held it over the bowl of his pipe. When he had the briar pipe going, his eyes drifted up and down over Carla's shapely figure. "Better-looking partner."

I glanced at his rifle, strapped over his shoulder. "Sandford. Didn't see you."

He chuckled. "I'm a mountain man. You're a city boy."

He took the bag I handed him and admired the bottle of Defiant Whiskey. "Nice." He turned to Carla. "What do you'ns think of our woods, little lady?"

Carla paused to admire several flowers with white petals circling a yolk-yellow stamen. "What's their name?

"Bloodroot," Sandford said. "I done seen dem all over North Carolina."

I interrupted. "The guys you saw in the woods—"

"What about them?" Sandford asked.

"My partner tried to talk to them."

"Tried?"

"They stabbed holes in his tires."

He pulled on his brier pipe, leaned against a tree, and blew smoke out through his mouth and nostrils. "Your partner came in from the south."

"And?"

"Crossed the woods in front of those two guys."

"You're sure?"

"The men who dug the holes always come in from the west."

Our mountain man began walking toward his trailer house.

I trailed him. "Which way do I enter the woods if I want to catch them?"

"Come in from the east."

As we followed the stream, Carla spotted his trailer house on stilts in the water. "Is that your home?"

"Yep."

"What happened here?" she asked.

He paused to pull on his pipe. "A levee broke upstream."

"And the water flooded here?"

"Yep. Flood insurance people said dis are in a floodplain."

He got in his boat. I shouted after him, "I have more questions."

He tipped his porkpie hat to Carla and began paddling to his stilt house. "Keep the moonshine nectar coming."

I led the way back up the stream. "Harmless old codger?"

"I'm not sure about your mountain man. How long have you known him?"

"I recently met him. What is it about him you don't like?"

"That eccentric mountain man is crafty. He wears a disguise, a mask."

Her intuition told me something I hadn't seen.

# # #

While still daylight, Bruce parked his Jeep, outfitted with new tires, along the two-lane road near the McDonald farm. Carla had talked me into believing she would be safe if she stayed with Bruce in the vehicle. Mickey, Roth's third operative, had followed in his black Ford Explorer. I stood outside the Jeep and zipped up my leather bomber jacket. Mickey, at a beefy two hundred and ten pounds, buttoned up his dark pea coat.

Carla came up beside me. "Remember Bruce's new tires. Be careful."

"Mickey's coming with me."

She grasped my hand and kissed me. "That's for good luck," she said. When I understood she had shown unmistakable warmth toward me in front of Bruce and Mickey, a hot, tingly sensation ran up my spine.

Mickey and I picked up boards and a wooden ladder, with cables connected to the rungs. We entered the woods and approached the McDonald field from the east. Once we got near the region where the intruders had dug up the ground, we fixed the stepladder against a tree and laid boards over two high limbs to form a platform, securing the panels in place with duct tape and wrapping the cables around the tree. To camouflage the hunter's blind, we hung camo strips from the stepladder and platform.

At dusk, Mickey and I climbed up to the platform and sat. Being big guys, we were jammed together, back-to-back, on the horizontal boards. The quarter moon gave partial illumination for seeing. I breathed in the sweet smell of blooming violets.

We waited.

I handed Mickey a package of creamy donuts, which I had brought especially for him.

"Thank you. Can we wrap up the case tonight?"

"If we catch Jeremiah, I reckon we've got a high probability of getting the map. Easy-peasy."

I heard the noise of a shovel and a dim light off in the distance. Showtime!

I climbed down and followed Mickey. Getting close to the picking and shoveling noises, I identified three people bending over the ground. A small electric lantern shed light on the group. I saw a chubby, young man in a light-brown parka; a thin woman in a beige trench coat; and a girl, in a fleece-lined, pink jacket, about ten years old. The child stood beside the woman and cried, "Mamma." Not Jeremiah and Talk.

I framed them in my flashlight beam. "Freeze! You're trespassing."

The man and woman held up their hands, and the girl held on to her mom. "Mamma, they have guns." I saw my chance of finishing the case this night slipping away, feeling a tightness in my chest and stiffness in my throat. Who were these people?

Mickey tapped my shoulder and pointed away from us. "We have different people digging off to the left."

I glanced at a twosome, who were both young, hewing at the ground.

I spun in a circle, identifying other digging sounds.

"What the hell?" I let out a soft groan of disbelief. "We're going to be untangling this?"

13

HUNT FOR JEREMIAH, MACON COUNTY – TUESDAY

The chaos and confusion of the hole diggers reminded me of pooches running and romping around a neighborhood park. With reinforcements—Bruce, Carla, and the grandson—I gathered up our unexpected visitors, coaxing the diggers to the farmhouse where we could question them and find out what was happening. Ashley got on the phone to the dispatcher at the sheriff's office and pleaded with her to send Corporal Hallowell to the farmhouse.

"You have intruders?" the dispatcher asked. "How many?"

Ashley turned around to count people. "About fifteen."

After he hung up, I studied the visitors. Most were young, dressed casually in jeans and jerseys or light jackets. No one resembled the sixty-year-old Jeremiah.

Grandma Ross, in a pink bathrobe, studied the group.

I didn't want Grandma to confuse an already chaotic situation. "They got caught digging holes."

"Dey don't look like criminals." She went into the kitchen and made iced tea for all.

Corporal Hallowell arrived and—finding we had seven different groups of intruders—questioned each group separately in the kitchen. He began with the first group Mickey and I had found: the Browns with their ten-year-old daughter. "Why come here?"

"This old man told us there was a treasure," Mr. Brown said. "Are we going to jail?"

Hallowell locked eyes with me for a moment and then turned back to Brown. "What did he tell you about this farm?"

"He knew the location of a valuable gem, but he needed youngsters to dig it up."

"Where is this old man?"

"I met him at the convenience store near our home."

Hallowell shifted his holster on his utility belt.

Brown rubbed the back of his neck. "It was okay to help him, right? We're not in trouble?"

Hallowell stared at me. "You believe him?"

Brown had a sheepish expression. "He had a map."

"Describe it," Hallowell said.

"Like old paper—parchment."

"Describe him," Hallowell said.

"Maybe sixtyish with a white beard and mustache."

"What did this bearded man drive?"

"Didn't see his car."

I wrote white beard and mustache on my notepad. Hallowell finished his writing and nodded at Brown to continue. "The old man told us to park on that nearby county road at night. Walk into the woods and stop when we got to lots of holes in the ground."

"Then what?"

"Dig."

Hallowell gave Brown a skeptical glance. "Did this bearded man tell you what you were digging for?"

"A cask with a big green gem inside."

"What were you to do when you found it?"

"Share our find with the bearded man. Can we go now?"

After the Browns, we queried Larry and Weldon, two young men just out of high school, who gave the same story: they met a bearded man at a gas station. To each group, we showed the picture of a clean-shaven Jeremiah McDonald. They couldn't confirm the man they talked with as the one in the sketch. Hallowell and I got a better description of the facial growth: bushy white beard, full white mustache, bald on top.

Bruce spoke up. "I know enough ta modify Jeremiah's picture an' show him as he appears now."

Corporal Hallowell released the intruders.

"I bet Jeremiah came in tonight," I said, "hid among this crowd, and dug his hole."

"I had the same idea," the corporal said. "And then he slipped away."

Hallowell told me the BOLO alert had yet to turn up Jeremiah or his 1990 Ford Ranger pickup. Before driving away, our corporal said, "You remember I cover a wide part of this country? Can't keep coming to a single farm."

# # #

Back in Asheville, I hit the sack and slept. Up in the morning, without much sleep, I moved slower than a corpse. In Roth's office, I told her about our previous night's adventure. Sipping coffee, I waited for her reply.

She slowly bobbed her head up and down. "Interesting gambit by Jeremiah. At night when the young treasure hunters fill the woods, he moves about with impunity."

Taylor stuck her head in the door. "You'ns looks whupped, Don. Isn't you a-goin' back to bed?"

I yawned and waved at her. She left.

Roth cupped her chin in hand. "If we prohibit entrance to the farm, we miss an opportunity to catch Jeremiah and shake the map out of him."

She drew in a deep breath. "Conversely, if we allow people into the woods each night—and search for him among those people—he might dig up the gem and elude us."

She waited, staring at me emotionless, like a sphinx, as if weighing options. "We'll search for Jeremiah at night and during the day."

"What do you mean?"

"At night, Bruce and Mickey will study the farm's nocturnal visitors hunting for Jeremiah and his friend, Talk. During the day, you and Carla will search for the pickup truck and show Jeremiah's picture."

She pushed the intercom button on her desk. "Bruce, bring me your sketches of the bearded Jeremiah."

Shortly, Bruce appeared, sat before her desk, and showed three pictures of Jeremiah with different face-hair thatches.

"That one," I said, pointing to a sneaky-looking individual.

Bruce appeared pleased. "Done. I'll make a hundred copies to distribute."

Roth continued studying the picture of Jeremiah with the beard for a moment. "The quality of his portrait is gratifying."

She switched her gaze to Bruce. "What about your plots of the farm from 1838 through today?"

Bruce unfolded more papers on her desk. "I've been to the farm twice, and I've studied the photographs. Best I can tell, de pond moved at least once. De original pond silted up sometime after eighteen-thirty-eight and before the eighteen-nineties."

"All the photographs show the pond in its present location?" Roth asked.

"They do, Boss."

"Where was the original pond?"

Bruce pinched his lips together as if Roth pushed him for what he couldn't deliver. "Hard ta figure, Boss."

Roth stared at the ceiling as if considering ways to locate a long-dead pond. "What else did you find?"

Bruce shuffled through his papers. "I identified four older oak trees across de stream from the farmhouse. These four are taller and thicker than the others." He indicated their position on the initial versions of his graphical diagrams.

"And?"

"My guess is they were small or nonexistent in 1838."

She studied Bruce's rough graphs.

"Am I done?" he asked.

"Keep working," Roth said. "Ask our historian, Angela, how to find an antediluvian, dried-up pond."

My head jerked up. *Anti-what?*

Bruce let out a satisfied breath and left. I picked up Jeremiah's picture and knocked on Carla's door and told her we were day searchers.

# # #

My morning drive with Carla to Macon County, North Carolina, was a fairyland moment. Azure blue above, vividly green forest to the sides, clear air wafted all around. When Carla had got into my car, I stared at her black stretch pants clinging to a well-defined rear end, and her rose-colored tee shirt stretched to bursting. Once back in the area around the McDonald farm, we pulled into gas stations and convenience stores to search for Jeremiah.

Carla mesmerized the men, used her bubbly personality to sweet-talk the women, and passed out prints of Jeremiah with a beard. I followed in her wake, watched for a small pickup, and felt the frustration of turning up too few leads.

As we departed a convenience store, Carla glanced up from her notepad—which I think she used because she considered all cool detectives used them—and asked, "Are you frustrated?"

"I am."

"Ms. Roth told me to keep watching you work a case. You are persistent, a bulldog with a bone."

"Don't look for quick solutions. It'll only make you wretched."

"I know," she said.

Carla had talent. She wanted to get better.

"How are you doing?"

She gave me her sunlight-bright smile. "I'm fine. I might stay here this time."

As I drove along, I kept my eyes peeled for a white pickup. "You fit in nicely with our group."

Carla turned in her seat. "I hope, with time, I can learn how you solve cases."

I just nodded.

"Eventually, maybe I can help you work them out."

I drove in silence to our next gas station. Some people are comfortable to be around. She was one of them. "I'm sure you will."

Carla lowered the Mobile Oil Road Atlas to her lap and seemed to be worrying over something. "You figure Jeremiah is a major suspect, but—"

Uh-oh, had I missed something? "Not just me. Grandma, Angela, and I found him."

"But, did you stop allowing for other suspects—I mean, once you found this guy in California?"

Up ahead, the next gas station came into view. Pulling into a parking space, I began to understand Carla had an absorbing interest in our mystery. "You mean, did I suspect someone else?"

Carla tilted her head toward me. "The old man in the porkpie hat, Connor Sandford. He acts like your friend, but I don't think he is."

Did I have a blind spot? "Why Sandford?"

"From what you've told me, he's always sneaking about. He seems to know the thieves."

Thinking back to my chitchats with our mountain man, he knew when and where the intruders came into the woods. Either he excelled at woodcraft, or he worked with them. "You're right. He needs watching."

I started the Mustang and backed out of our parking space.

She glanced at me with raised eyebrows. "We're not going into that gas station?"

"Nope."

"Where're you going?"

Two cars drove in front of us on a tight two-lane road and one car followed behind us. Several vehicles approached in the other lane. "We're going to see Grandma McDonald about our woodsman, Sandford."

My consciousness zinged me. A white Ford Ranger drove at the head of the string of cars coming toward us. "There's a pickup like we're watching for."

The vehicle sped past us in the opposite direction.

"What year is it?" Carla asked.

I turned on my right turn signal and pulled onto the grassy shoulder. "A ninety-something-year model."

I made a quick u-turn into the same lane as the pickup. Speeding up, I reached the two cars behind the small truck and passed them. I glimpsed the pickup half a mile ahead. It disappeared around a wooded bend.

My pursuit ended at a four-way intersection where I lost the vehicle. "Do you see the pickup?"

Carla scanned out her side of the car. "It's not there."

At random, I took the road to the right and sped down it. The way was empty.

"Was it Jeremiah?" Carla asked.

I pulled onto the shoulder, banging on the steering wheel rim with my palms. "Can't be sure. Got to keep searching."

We continued to the farmhouse.

# # #

Grandma McDonald enjoyed her constant wine on this mild day in the screened-in porch on the side of her farmhouse. The bottle Grandma poured from was a brand my estate-reserve boss probably had never heard of. She offered us wine, but we took iced tea. Carla and Grandma became fast friends and chatted about the intruders.

Carla sat beside Grandma. "Who do you think did the break-in?"

"It's Jeremiah."

"Are you sure?"

Grandma stared at Carla. "I think he done it."

Carla took her time before responding. "He lives across the country in California?"

"He did."

"Could someone local have done the robbery?"

Grandma answered in a soft voice. "Maybe. Who?"

"The guy in the stilt house—"

"Our mountain man?"

"Has he asked you about a buried gem?"

Grandma wrinkled her forehead. "Connor Sandford never asked me 'bout de hidden jewel."

Carla didn't respond but waited.

Grandma continued. "Everyone in de neighborhood, including him, knows dat old tale."

Carla pulled on her ponytail and nodded at Grandma. "Have you known him to be dishonest?"

"Ain't no one ever proved anything, but items do walk off when he's around."

"Sandford claims he sees the intruders without them seeing him," Carla said. "Is he that good a woodsman?"

Grandma took a moment to drink her wine. "I never sees him except he's in de woods wid his rifle. Sometimes at night, I hears a gunshot."

Before Carla and I left, I told Grandma to expect Bruce and Mickey at the farm just when it got dark. We were determined to find Jeremiah.

What I couldn't have known was that Carla and I would soon form a bond in the least likely of places.

14

MOUNT PISGAH, NORTH CAROLINA – TUESDAY

Carla and I left the McDonald farm and drove back to Asheville. I wanted to hit it off with her, but she stared at the green forest sliding past our windows as if enjoying the tree's dense growth like a kid eating watermelon on a hot day. "Nature can be gorgeous," she said.

"It's a pretty country," I said.

"Do you hike?"

"Growing up, I walked a lot at summer camp."

When I glanced over at her, she showed the smile I recognized as the mischievous grin. "Why do you ask?"

"Do you have a camping tent?"

My brain flashed to my old-fashioned tent kept in the Roth Security storage facility, keeper of our extra equipment. "I do. It's an old-style A-frame, with two steel poles, and its nylon." I hesitated. "Why do you ask?"

Carla flipped her ponytail and turned to me. "Do me a favor?"

There was a long pause while I stared at her. "How can I help?"

"I didn't know how soon I'd be working,"—she reached across the console and touched my arm, and electricity caused me to shudder—"so I reserved a camping site for a night at Mount Pisgah on the Blue Ridge Parkway."

I was unsure about how to continue and brushed my cowlick back. "I know the campsite. Nice hike up to the peak of the mountain."

"Could I borrow your camping gear?"

"Have you hiked and camped before?"

"This is my first time."

I'd need to retrieve the tent and make sure she had comfortable boots and would be warm for the night. "It's up high, about five thousand feet. What day did you reserve?"

She forced a smile. "Tonight."

I was of two minds: My left hemisphere said, *We can't be ready in time*. My right hemisphere cried, *I want to go with Carla.*

"I'm willing to go with you."

Excited, she bumped my shoulder with her fist. "I invite you."

"We'll need to hurry."

"Doing what?" she asked.

"Once we gather tent, flashlights, sleeping bags together, it'll take an hour to drive up to Pisgah," I said. "From the parking area, we hike up a winding trail to Mount Pisgah's top."

"I'll bring wine," Carla said.

As I turned to face her, I caught the tail end of her wink.

# # #

Later, back at the mansion, I packed clothes and equipment for Mount Pisgah. Before leaving, I reported to Roth our sighting and fruitless chase of Jeremiah's pickup in Macon County and told her Carla and I planned to camp out that night.

My boss smiled. "Stay safe and have fun. Where are you going?"

"Mount Pisgah."

"Oh, you better hurry."

I turned and had reached her office door when she asked, "How many tents are you setting up?"

"One."

She gave me an annoyed expression, pressing her lips tight. "Hmm . . ."

# # #

Carla's camping-site reservation came with a parking space. Two hours later, I put my car there, leaving us with almost three hours of sunlight. At her bubbly insistence, we set off for the top of Mount Pisgah, skipping the tent setup until later.

Carla might be pint-sized, but she scampered up the trail, mostly a dirt and rocky pathway. As she darted over smooth rocky outcrops, I climbed behind her to catch her if she fell but couldn't help but admire the motion beneath her stretch pants. Was it love? Was it lust? I didn't care.

Eating chocolate along the way for energy, she struggled steadily past the low-lying bushes and small trees along the trail, stopping when the path gave a panoramic view of the neighboring mountains.

She rested to catch her breath. "We'll have wine and cheese and a fabulous time around tonight's fire."

I gazed at her.

She giggled at me, flashing what I termed her mega-bright smile, which always made my skin tingle.

She spoke over her shoulder as we continued walking. "Are there bears along the Blue Ridge Parkway?"

"Black bear."

"Dangerous?"

"They avoid people."

"Have you met one?"

"Not up close. Any bear must have heard and avoided me."

Carla lunged past a gnarly oak on the ground. "How big?"

"A male might weigh two hundred pounds," I said, "and a female a hundred."

Carla charged onto the top of Mount Pisgah, with a TV tower, a separate wooden observation deck, and spectacular views. She ran around the crowded deck, ate chocolate from her backpack, and gushed about the beauty of the wilderness. My partner stopped to observe the mountains, and I reached down to slide my arm around her waist. She leaned against me.

About five years old, a small boy became a nuisance, pushing past Carla and me, grabbing the railing in front of us. Where were his parents? The little monster stood on top of the barrier and lost his balance. I had to release her and grab him before he tumbled off the rail. Carla grinned and said, "My hero."

"Carla, day's ending."

"I don't want to leave."

"We need to hike down while it's still light."

"The air is fresh. The view goes forever."

"I'm leaving, going back to the camping site."

"Why?"

"Have to set up the tent."

I got her moving down the path. "Do you still have candies in your pack?"

She slowed. "I do. Want some?"

"No. Leave the backpack in the car's trunk. Otherwise, animals will sniff it out tonight."

# # #

Dusk came, turned to darkness, and the stars spread out bright and plentiful. Using flashlights, we lit up the tent pad, a section of ground inside a low wood frame, and assembled the tent. Because Carla knew little about erecting a tent, she opened the first bottle for us. Shortly, she giggled, sipped wine, and hummed melodious tunes.

"Spread the nylon tarp on the ground," I said.

She spread the groundsheet, stood up, jarred her hip against me, and said, "How's that?"

I bumped her rump.

"How do we stand it up?" she asked with a smirk.

I had Carla steady the steel pole while I hammered it in the ground.

"I hold the rope—what you call the guy line—here on the ground?" she asked.

I nodded at her. "That's it. Drive the wooden stake to hold the end of the line."

She beamed at our standing-upright A-frame tent. "That was fun."

With the tent erect, I gathered some wood and built a fire while Carla laid out the two bottles of merlot wine and cheese. The warm day was well into its makeover into a chilly evening. Carla snuggled closer to me. "Good thing we built a fire."

I glanced up. "The stars are clear."

Her breath on my ear startled me. I felt her body's warmth as she breathed in my ear. "We're so bad. About to drain our last bottle."

She poured the remnants of the wine into our glasses and squeezed up against my chest. "It's getting cold. I need some warming up." She lowered her glass and pulled my head down. Her lips pressed against my mouth. I tasted the merlot.

When she lowered her glass, she pulled my head down and kissed me.

I tossed my wine glass away. "Let's warm up in our sleeping bags."

I untangled from Carla, got us settled side-by-side in the tent, and fastened the tent's front flap. We were snug as two dogs on a frigid night. "You're so warm."

She wriggled her bedroll closer to me. "I'm freezing. Hold me."

Ever dutiful, I unzipped the side of her sleeping bag and climbed on top of her to give her maximum warmth.

She was warm to my touch. Her dark brown eyes blazed with an urge, orbs glowing white in the dim inside the tent.

I kissed her lips, her cheek. *Oh, God,* I thought.

Her tongue caressed my lips. I heard a purr, like a big kitten.

She raised her arms.

I pulled up her sweater and found tantalizing breasts beckoned me. I rotated over her legs. She groaned and bucked up, strong for her short stature.

My left leg jerked in my excitement and drove into the front pole, yanking out the front stake anchoring the guy line.

The tent collapsed.

I cursed myself, blundered onto my flashlight, and shoved the crumpled tent aside. The cold air hit me.

15

GRANDMA'S FARM — WEDNESDAY

The black cocoon of the sky covered us, muted light falling on us from multiple pinholes of starlight. I turned on my flashlight, its beam illuminating a medium-size bear, also black. A single sound engulfed me. Carla screamed, attaining a piercing frequency I didn't know a grown woman could still achieve. Until I could shake free, my sleeping bag wrapped around my right foot. I stood up and away from the fallen tent and the bear with a backpack.

As I held my breath, gulping breaths to stay calm, how-to-stay-alive suggestions surged forth into my mind: *Make yourself appear big. Slowly move away. Don't stare the bear in the eyes.*

I stood as tall as I could. "Carla, look big!"

She had positioned herself behind me. "I-I-I can't. I'm short."

"Stand beside me, so the bear sees a big group," I said.

"I'm keeping you between the bear and me."

I moved sideways toward the car with Carla preceding me. "Don't stare it in the eyes."

"What—close my eyes?"

We shuffled closer to the Mustang, a form in the darkness.

The bear ignored us and clawed at Carla's backpack.

"What'll we do?"

"Hope he stays a vegetarian . . . and we get in the car." We reached the vehicle. I pushed her inside and got in the driver's side.

The black bear watched, with ears relaxed in an up position.

Eventually, the bear seemed to yawn, got up on four legs, and swayed away with a shredded backpack.

I had been holding my breath. Sweat drenched my clothes.

"Take me home," Carla said.

I turned on the headlights to light up the camping site, threw our camping equipment into my trunk, and drove back to Asheville. She didn't say a word until we were halfway down the mountain. "I forgot to put the backpack in the trunk," she said.

I recalled Taylor's words to me: *Don't you'ns blow it this time.* "I should have checked we had locked all food away," I said. "My bad led to a hungry black bear visiting us."

"Sure you're not angry with me?" she asked.

"Nope. I hope we go camping again soon." Taylor would be pleased with me.

# # #

When we arrived back at the mansion, Carla pulled my head down, kissed me, and went upstairs to her room.

I went to my room and dreamed:

> Where am I? I'm at college again. In a dorm room. I don't recognize it—bare walls, no roommate, clear desks, austere. Math examination this morning. Grab my backpack—go out the front door, which I don't recognize. Has the test already started? What if I'm late—so embarrassing going into a room with everyone at their desk taking the

exam—all eyes watching me. Walking over brick pathways and grass—where is the exam building? I can't remember. Did I miss the other classes? I don't know where to go. I don't know what I studied. I feel so vulnerable, so miserable.

I woke from my dream, my nightmare. My subconscious often suffered hallucinations of helplessness when I was screwing up a job, shirking my responsibility. I got up and dressed at midmorning and went downstairs and seated myself at the breakfast table.

Roth, Mickey, and Bruce drank their after-breakfast coffee. Seeing me, they raised their brows. I greeted them and busied myself, reaching for the platter of scrambled eggs and grits.

"Heared you done went camping with Carla," Taylor said. She poured coffee for me.

Encircled by my friends, I related the bare-bones account of our travels to Mount Pisgah.

"Why not take her ta a zip-line course if you wants to scare her?" Bruce asked. "A black bear is a bit much."

"Are she a-willin' to go out with you again?" Taylor asked.

I spooned grits into my mouth. "We're just friends. We went camping and met a bear."

Carla entered the kitchen-dining room, greeted everyone, and kissed me on the cheek. Sitting down, she turned to Taylor. "Any grits left?"

Taylor smirked at me.

I changed topics. "What happened to you guys last night?"

"We searched for Jeremiah," Mickey said. "Didn't find him."

"Did you spot the other fellow? The one in the porkpie hat."

Mickey shook his head.

Bruce slammed his palm down on the table. "De people doing the digging won't help us. Too busy searchin' fer a treasure."

"Offer a reward to locate Jeremiah," Roth said, "Get the diggers to be your eyes—for a thousand dollars."

She pushed back from the table, picked up her cup of coffee, and started for the office. "We'll meet at one o'clock to discuss the case. Bruce will update us on mapping the area in front of the farmhouse."

# # #

We gathered facing Roth's desk. Bruce spread out papers to show an overlay of ground features around the farm: farmhouse, pond, ancient oak trees. And a cluster of holes recently dug on the McDonald property.

I studied his plots. The house, center of the pond, and center of the dug-up holes formed a triangle. They did not lie on a straight line. I couldn't make out a pattern that said, "Dig here."

Tapping her fingers on her desk, Roth raised her eyebrows at Bruce.

"Don't know the location of the pond in 1838," Bruce said. "No record anywhere of a plat drawing. No family photograph of the front of the house before the 1880s."

"Historians have found ancient things," Roth said. "Remember to tell Angela we want to talk with her."

"I already phoned an' left a message, Boss."

"Are there distinct peaks on the mountain range near the farm?" Roth asked.

"There're high peaks in de distance."

"In the future, indicate such peaks on your map."

Bruce jotted a comment in his notepad.

"Ask Grandma if Ian had a transit," Roth said to me.

"What's a transit?" Carla asked.

Roth pinched her chin as if putting together an answer. "It's an instrument to measure angles. Colonial Americans used it back in the eighteen-hundreds. Check if Grandma has antiques on the farmhouse wall along with those family photographs."

Carla seemed puzzled. "Do you have a picture of one, Ms. Roth?"

Roth leaned back in her chair, perhaps recalling the parts of a transit. "Looks like an ancient brass telescope mounted on a base with inscribed angles—and perhaps a tripod to hold the base."

I had seen pictures of the object Roth wanted us to seek. I'd never used one.

"When you are talking with Grandma," Roth said to me, "find how Ian and Waya encased the gem before they buried it?"

Bruce coughed for attention. "I didn't find a plat of the McDonald land at the county courthouse, but I found two people had gone through the county records ahead of me."

Roth waited. "Who were they?"

"First was Jeremiah McDonald of Coloma, California." Bruce paused as if for effect. "Second was Mr. Connor Sandford."

Carla and I exchanged glances. Again, we had bumped into our mountain man in the porkpie hat.

# # #

Early afternoon, I drove Carla to the farmhouse. On the way, she chatted away about how nice it was to be back and how she and Taylor were going shopping.

I wondered if she had gotten over the sudden appearance of a bear. "Have you recovered from last night?"

She turned with her naughty grin. "The bear? I'm over that."

I smirked back. "I enjoyed you, but not the bear."

At the farmhouse, Grandma fussed and fumed at her grandson. "I'd find Jeremiah quicker than dem big buffoons ever will—stumbling around in de dark."

I thought, Big buffoon. That's harsh.

Grandma cleaned her glasses as she yapped at Ashley. "If you'ns can't stop intruders, make 'em pay. Sell tickets—collect fifty dollars from each person diggin'."

"Grandma, that's a ridiculous idea."

"What's nonsensical? They're all over de place at night. Charge them."

The grandson raised his voice. "What if the diggers stumble on the gem? We'd lose millions of dollars to gain eight hundred dollars a night minus labor costs—bad idea."

The debate didn't appear to be at a stopping point. Catching Carla's eye, I moved to the den-dining room, scanning the objects mounted on the adjacent wall. "If you spot something like a telescope, tell me."

Carla studied the far wall with photographs and colonial antiques: a flintlock rifle, a washbasin, and an oil lamp. "What's this?"

I turned to find her pointing to a brass telescope on a round base. "That's a transit."

I took it down and returned to the front room, finding Grandma now alone. "Was this Ian's?"

Grandma squinted at it. "Dat's a transit. My grandmother done told me it belonged to Ian."

"Grandma, did your old family history say how Waya and Ian wrapped the Cherokee Emerald for burying?" Carla asked.

"Placed it in a small wooden cask and covered in a coating of coal-tar pitch."

Grandma paused to sip her wine. "What are you doing about Jeremiah? Where is he?"

It was easy to like her. She wouldn't take crap off anyone. "We need to find Jeremiah. We're offering a reward of a thousand dollars for his location. Can I post notices on your farm?"

Grandma agreed without fussing.

Carla and I left her and walked toward Sandford's trailer house. We found him seated on his roof, smoking his pipe. The wind blew toward us, allowing me to sniff cherry. We waved, and he waved back. I took a bottle of Defiant Whiskey out of a brown paper bag and held it up for Connor to see. He signaled me to leave it on the ground.

I considered the water flooding the area around his trailer, with several evergreen trees sticking up above the water. I shook my head and waved for him to come over to get the single malt. He held his hand down low—place it on the ground.

"We're leaving," Carla said in a shout, "with the bottle."

I strolled toward the farmhouse back up the stream. "Yeah. With the bottle."

The mountain man shouted back at us, climbed down off the roof, and rowed across the stream to his docking point on the bank.

I greeted him and handed him the moonshine nectar. "Why are you playing hard to get?"

He took the bottle. "What do you want?"

"You keep an eye on Jeremiah McDonald. Why?"

Sandford gave me a steely-eyed stare. "Who's he?"

"The man with the beard," I said. "He comes onto McDonald's farm at night."

"I seen him. I don't know him."

I continued in a soft voice. "You went to the county courthouse to learn about the McDonald property, didn't you?"

He drew on his briar pipe, sneered, and spoke not a word.

My brain popped out a thought, a shot in the dark. "You're following Jeremiah to catch him with the map, aren't you?"

The mountain man turned and walked back to his boat. "He only carries a pick and shovel, no map."

"Are you searching for the gem?"

He chuckled. "What's wrong with hunting for a lost gem? Finders keepers!"

I shadowed him to his boat. "Where does Jeremiah McDonald hide during the day?"

Sandford began rowing toward his house on stilts, puffing on his briar pipe. "Don't know. He's not here."

# # #

Carla and I left the farm and drove to the mansion to report to Roth. On the ride back, I called Corporal Hallowell on the number he had given me. "Corporal, this is Don Gannon. Remember, I'm working on security for the McDonald farm."

"I remember you. Nothing to report on the BOLO for Jeremiah McDonald."

I turned up the audio volume on my mobile, so Carla could hear what Hallowell told me.

"On a road near the farm, I saw a white Ranger pickup—going the other direction," I said. "By the time I turned around, it had slipped away."

"We'll keep looking," Hallowell said.

"While I have you, what do you know about a Connor Sandford? Lives downstream from the McDonald farm."

"Lots of complaints about him. But no jail time. Why do you ask?"

"Would he be likely to team up with Jeremiah McDonald?"

"Doubt it. The mountain man is his own man."

Carla had been listening to Hallowell. "Just petty theft? Nothing else?"

He paused for several beats and said, "Our mountains are generally clear of gang activity. But someone is distributing cocaine, and we're focused on kids eighteen to twenty-five years old."

"Do you suspect Sandford is involved?" Carla asked.

"He spends time with them. I've got to go." Hallowell broke the connection.

"Our situation just got a little out of hand," I said to Carla. "A large emerald and now drugs."

16

JEREMIAH EVADES CAPTURE, GRANDMA'S FARM — THURSDAY

Roth, clad in a toga-like dress with long sleeves, glanced around her office, made dark by the outside morning rain. "Where's Mickey?"

"He's sleeping," I said. "Last three nights, he searched for Jeremiah at McDonald's farm, and he's going again tonight."

Roth nodded and turned to Angela, whom she had summoned. "My conjecture is the thieves stole the photographs to track down the original location of the pond. How does one find a pond long gone?"

Angela smiled and absentmindedly fiddled with a strand of her Afro before responding. "To examine strata over time, scientists take cores, plugs, over an area. We know ducks and other fowls settled on the pond. The cores along the side of the stream with the most duck droppings identify the original pond."

Roth frowned and slammed her hand on her desk, shaking a book onto the floor. "That's going to be expensive. Think. Isn't there an easier way?"

"Not any method, I know," Angela said.

"Let's try a slightly different puzzle," Roth said. "What if—hypothetically—we have zeroed in on an area where Waya and Ian could have buried the wooden cask. How would we locate that cask?"

At that point, Taylor came into the office, bringing hot tea and coffee. While Angela waited for her tea to cool, she answered Roth. "The farm's land has rich soil and isn't rocky. A search using ground penetration radar could make out a cask."

"How do you use this method?" my boss asked.

"Isolate a small area where you expect to find the cask," Angela said. "And then hire a contractor for a day."

"Do we have ground penetration radar contractors near us?" Carla asked.

Angela sipped her tea and nodded at Carla. "Most communities have contractors with such equipment."

Roth pushed the palm of her left hand against the palm of her right hand and moved them up and down. After a minute, she gave directions. "I'll have Mickey sign up a contractor to take ground cores and a contractor to use ground penetration radar."

I interrupted. "Hold on, Boss. We'll spend more money on the ground penetration radar than the gem is worth—and we don't know if it exists."

Roth turned to Angela to confirm or contradict the truth of what I had said.

"Buying our equipment and training our personnel would be expensive," Angela said. "But hiring a contractor is cost-effective."

My boss gave me a cocky smile. "I told you so. You must find Jeremiah and get the map. If I have the map and know where the pond was in eighteen-thirty-eight, I'll know where to find the gem."

She closed the meeting.

# # #

The rain cleared off, and Mickey and I drove to the McDonald farm at dusk and put up signs offering a thousand dollars for information leading to the bearded Jeremiah location. As the night grew dark in the scattered light provided by the visible moon, we saw diggers begin to appear with flashlights, like fireflies in a backyard. Once the excavators settled in, Mickey and I planned to hunt for Jeremiah in the groups and ask the diggers if they had seen the bearded man shown on the reward notices.

Grandma waited with us in the den-dining room. "Can't get no sleep. They're out there digging away. Why can't you get up and chase them off?" Next, she began talking to herself in a muffled voice.

I wished we had brought Carla along with us, as she had the gift to calm Grandma. "We're going out to look for Jeremiah shortly," I said. "If the diggers see him, we'll reward them for their information."

To avoid arguing with Grandma about chasing off the intruders, Mickey and I left the farmhouse and set out to find Jeremiah. Following the lights, we stalked him by talking with the diggers.

The weather grew a tad chilly once the sun went down. My druthers were to be back at the mansion, sucking beers with Bruce and watching a ball game. But another part of me imagined catching Jeremiah and wrapping up the case. Mickey and I strolled toward the field of holes. I heard voices and the *swoosh* of shovels and the *thud* of pickaxes as we approached closer. So many dirt mounds reminded me of a dog who buried lots of objects in his front yard. Why were these people, mostly young but a few old, digging away? Must have been like solving a puzzle. I talked with each group but compared each male with my vision of Jeremiah.

While I explained the terms of the reward to one group, I heard a cry for help. Rushing toward the sound, I found a youth on the ground, bleeding from his head onto his shirt, appearing madder than injured. "Who hit you?" I asked.

"I had the bearded man in the picture. I tried to hold him. Another guy came out of the trees and hit me on the head with a shovel."

"What happened then?"

"They ran. The bearded man wore a red-and-white checkered shirt."

"Which way?"

The bloody-headed youth pointed toward the south. "That way. You can catch him."

Mickey shined his flashlight in the direction Jeremiah had taken, revealing a faint path, leading us down the trail at a modest pace. "Don't run," Mickey said. "See if we can sneak upon him."

We picked our way down the trail, occasionally snapping a flashlight on and off to find our way. As we stepped forward, I listened. Finally, I heard the clang of metal ahead of us. We slowed our pace, brushing aside tree branches, seeing poorly by the light of the stars. I made out the sound of a pickax striking earth.

Mickey crouched down and held a palm up, telling me to stop. I halted and slipped my Wilson Combat M1911 pistol out of my belt holster.

Edging forward on tiptoes, we crept up on a light in a clearing.

As he reached down to pick up a cream-colored duffle bag, a bearded man in a red-and-white checkered shirt held a pickaxe in one hand. An electric lantern on the ground illuminated the clearing.

I stepped into the clearing with my pistol. "Freeze!"

A figure who reminded me of Jeremiah dropped his shovel and pickax, raising his hands into the air.

He sneered through his white beard. "What do you want?"

The man wasn't scared; it might prove challenging to get information out of him. Why wasn't he afraid? He didn't know what we were capable of, and we had guns. "Sit," I said.

After he sat, I told him, "Grip your hands behind your back." I bound his hands with a zip tie and picked up his duffle bag. "Didn't store the map in here, did you?" The bag contained gloves, a spare flashlight, and a small hammer, but no map. My captive remained calm.

I needed to get him inside the farmhouse to pull information out of him: Where had he stayed during the day? Where was the map?

"Jeremiah, you're coming with us back to the farmhouse where—"

Wearing a bathrobe with her feet stuffed in boots, Grandma charged into the clearing. The light from Jeremiah's lantern reflected off her glasses. "There he is. I knew it wasn't that hard to find him."

Hell's Bells! What was she doing here?

A man appeared behind Grandma, grabbed her, and put what looked like a military knife to her throat. "Drop your guns . . . lie flat on the ground . . . free Jeremiah's hands—"

Grandma's assailant, a short man, chattered continuously, hopping from foot to foot. I wouldn't feel comfortable turning my gun over to this guy.

Jeremiah started to rise. "Sit," I said. He stayed where he was.

Mickey began moving clockwise, and I moved counterclockwise, circling the man with the knife.

Jeremiah saw our maneuver. "Talk. They're flanking you."

"Let me go," Grandma said.

"Stop squirming. I'll cut you."

The man holding Grandma had a wild expression, dark brown, unblinking eyes, an expressionless mouth, and a salt and pepper Vandyke beard. "Stand back. I'm not joking."

As I moved to the side of the man, I saw Jeremiah stand up. "Sit. Or I'll shoot you in the leg." He sat back down.

From back in the woods, a rifle shot rang out—*Pow*!—hurling a bullet into the ground behind me, sending up a spray of dirt and pebbles.

A second shot followed immediately—*Pow*!—striking the lantern and plummeting the clearing into darkness.

17

GRANDMA'S FARM — FRIDAY

The lamp shattered, and its sudden ruin threw the landscape into a deep dark. I dropped and hugged the ground. My brain was confused, racing, and searching for answers. The two suspects—Jeremiah and Talk—were here in the clearing. Who was shooting?

Around me, I heard shouting, running, and the swishing of tree branches. The diggers were scattering for their lives, everyone but me. Where was Grandma? Had Talk let her go? With my nose kissing the dirt, holding my unlit flashlight in one hand and pistol in the other, I crawled toward where I heard the old lady mumbling and where I had last seen her. No more shots.

When I found her, she was sitting on the ground, cranky and mad. "Damn them! Dig up my farm. Attack an old woman."

I didn't see Talk and put my palm over her mouth. "Quiet."

Mickey crawled, noiselessly for an immense man, to crouch beside me. Sweet Jeez, we had to find cover. By shoving my partner's shoulder toward a nearby tree evident in the starlight, I aimed us toward the shelter. Staying low and pulling Grandma, we got her there.

Beside us, Grandma McDonald squirmed. "Shoot 'em. You've got a gun—"

Mickey and I dragged her next to the tree trunk. "Hush," I said.

At first, everything stayed quiet. I waited. My ears picked up the returning *whir* of the crickets. My eyes adjusted to the dark but didn't see motion. Where was the shooter?

A motorcycle rumbled in the distance.

Mickey raised his head. "Shooting's stopped."

I listened a while longer. "I think you're right." Using the moonlight, I studied the turn in the path through the brush. "I think the shots came from the left side."

Mickey nodded. "They're gone. Let's see."

We crept through the bushes alongside the path. "Someone pressed the bushes down," Mickey said.

I searched for ejected shell casings but found none. "Whoever it was, they took the time to collect the brass."

Mickey took a last glance at the ground. "They left no evidence. They're clever."

"Let's get Grandma back to the farmhouse," I said.

By the time Mickey and I shepherded her to her house, an ambulance stood in front, and EMS technicians had patched up the kid struck on the head.

"You need to come with us," a paramedic said. "The doc will want to observe you."

"No, I don't." The bandaged youngster walked away.

In the den-living room, Grandma McDonald and her grandson shouted back and forth. "Why did you go out in de dark?" he asked. "You done put everyone in danger."

She growled at her grandson. "I caught Jeremiah! Told you I would!"

"Stop shouting at me."

"Ain't shouting at you! Helping you hear!"

While they argued, I sat on a couch in the living room. *Who shot at us? Do they work for Jeremiah?* I faced Mickey. "Hell's bells. What happened?"

"Don't know. I'm hungry."

I felt shocked, a heavy sensation in my stomach, and tingling skin. Damn, someone shot at me. A simple burglary had turned violent. Jeremiah had another cohort. What had I missed? Whoever they were, they were a skilled shot. The second bullet hit the lantern dead-on. Their weapon was a rifle, not a pistol.

The ambulance drove off, passing Corporal Hallowell, who had pulled into the farm. I walked outside, and he got out of his sheriff's car and stood before me. "What happened?"

I took an instant to organize my words. "We caught Jeremiah McDonald. Someone shot at us. He got away."

Hallowell pulled out a notepad and scribbled. "Did you shoot back?"

"Too busy dropping for cover."

Hallowell put his notepad away. "Our crime scene investigation unit is coming. Help me tape off the crime area."

Additional deputies arrived, and we went with Hallowell. Except for a discarded pick and clumps of dirt, the clearing was empty. Using our flashlights, we searched the wooded area—from where someone shot at us—uncovering zilch, neither shells nor impressions in the ground.

Hallowell blew out his cheeks. "Doesn't Sandford live nearby?"

Why did he ask about the mountain man? I was puzzled. I nodded.

"Show me," the deputy said.

We walked to the spot on the stream bank opposite Sandford's house, arriving around two o'clock in the morning. Why were we here? Was Hallowell interested in the shooting or another activity? I saw Sandford's boat tied up next to the door of the trailer house. "His lights are off."

"Our detective will want to talk with him tomorrow," Hallowell said.

He confided in me as we went back to the farmhouse. "You didn't hear this from me—"

I glanced nearby. No one listened. "My lips are locked tight."

"Tomorrow, you'll meet our prima donna, Lieutenant James Hound, aka Hound."

"Is he a good detective?"

"A talented bootlicker and fawner."

"Will he cooperate with me?"

"Not unless he thinks he can use you."

"You don't respect him?"

"He treats us deputies like filth and grovels before everyone above him."

"Thanks for the warning."

"What warning?" He winked. "Good luck." He got back in his patrol car and left.

The farm grew silent again, and Mickey and I drove back to Asheville.

# # #

After three hours of sleep back at the mansion, I reported to Roth in her office.

She put down her book, *Skipping Christmas* by John Grisham, and considered me. "You look terrible."

"My eyelids droop like this when I get exhausted."

"Go back to bed."

"No, ma'am."

"I don't think that's wise. Get some rest."

"About now, Macon County is sending its lead investigator to the McDonald farmhouse. I want to be there."

Roth shook her head. "Take Carla with you. She can drive if you're too tired."

I rose to my feet and went to get Carla. How awful could Hallowell's detective be?

18

MOTORCYCLE GANG, FRANKLIN, MACON COUNTY – SATURDAY

A spanking new, black-and-white Ford Crown Victoria, with Macon County Sheriff painted on the sides, parked in front of the farmhouse. In the living room, a wound-up Grandma argued with a calm sheriff's detective. About six feet tall and wearing an immaculate, black uniform, the man stood with his thumbs in his belt and watched her with an unblinking stare. "You caused trouble," he said with a plodding, crawling cadence. "Because you didn't call the authorities."

She thrust her jaw forward and squeezed her eyebrows together. "Fiddlesticks. Our so-called private investigators weren't doing well. They needed a grandmother."

Grandma turned and walked away from the detective. "Where do you think you're going?" he said in an unruffled voice. She left the room.

The detective turned to Carla and me. "Who're you?"

Hallowell stood to the side and introduced us. "This is Don Gannon, a private dick. McDonald's family hired him. His aide is Carla Diaz."

The corporal raised his hand toward the man in the black uniform. "Lieutenant James Hound, a senior detective in the Sheriff's Office."

Hound continued the unblinking stare. He was in fight mode and did not take his eyes off me. Instinctively, forewarned, I recognized him as an alpha-type male. I reasoned I would need to choose one of three ways to work with this aggressive man: fight, flight, or apple-polish. This arrogant man wouldn't share information with me if I fought with him or avoided him.

He crossed his arms over his chest. "You can stick around. But I must have total cooperation from you."

I had made my choice: apple polisher. "Lieutenant Hound, how can I assist you?"

"Assist?"

"Follow your leadership—support you in your investigation." I felt a gagging sensation.

"I'm the face of this investigation."

Did he really say that? I lowered my head to him. "Your sheriff's office gets full credit."

Hound's mouth shifted from frown to slight smile. He would use me, either as toady or as a scapegoat, if he failed to find the shooter. "Okay, Gannon. I need to interview Mr. Sandford. The hillbilly sneaking around at night with a rifle."

Turning to his deputy, Hound said, "Corporal, I'll take over now."

As he walked to his patrol car to leave, Hallowell leaned in my direction and whispered, "Good luck."

Carla and I escorted the lieutenant toward the trailer house. I expected this confab would be a deadlock between the aggressor, Hound, and the enigma, Sandford. At the house on stilts, a glance confirmed our mountain man had tied his rowboat to a hook just below his front door. Lieutenant Hound stood on the bank of the stream and shouted. "Hello, the house." During the next several minutes, he repeatedly yelled at maximum volume.

Sandford, dressed in white underwear, fitted with buttons down the front and with legs reaching to the ankles and long sleeves, pushed open his front door. He viewed Hound across the stream and stroked his shaggy white Vandyke. Seeing Carla with us, he said, "Hello, lovely lady."

Carla waved.

"I'm Lieutenant James Hound. Of the Macon County Sheriff's Office. You are to row over to me."

Scratching at his underwear, Sandford asked, "Got a warrant?"

Hound rubbed his forehead under his black, wide-brimmed campaign hat and puffed up his chest in his tailored uniform. "If you don't. Let me interview you. You'll—"

Our mountain man proffered an offensive gesture with his fingers on one hand and closed his door.

Hound's previously unruffled countenance turned crimson. He kept staring at the house on stilts. In a slow voice, he uttered his inner thoughts. "Wish I was a buzzard. I'd fly over the stream. And crap on his head." With his brown eyes staring intently at Sandford's door, Hound appeared to hate him.

"What's next?" I asked. "Get a warrant and bring our rowboat?"

He took off his hat, ran his hand over his buzz-cut hair, and spoke in his fractured discourse. "I think I'll go at this. Another way. I'm going to check something out."

We walked back to the farmhouse. Before leaving, he turned to me and said, "I'll call you."

As I watched, he steered his car out toward the two-lane road going past the farm. Carla, in tight black slacks and white long-sleeved jersey, flashed her mega smile at me. "How did you get that obnoxious man to like you?"

I smiled back. "He likes me because he thinks I'm a sycophant, easy to step on. Didn't know you had such keen insight."

"Where'd they get Hound? What kind of accent is that? He speaks in sharply disconnected phrases."

"Who knows? Watch his lips as he talks."

Carla chuckled to herself. "Thanks for the tip." She adjusted a baseball cap around her ponytail and walked to the Mustang. "What do we do now?"

I frowned as I thought, *where is Jeremiah hiding*? "We go back to stopping at gas stations and grocery stores, looking for Jeremiah's hiding place."

# # #

Throughout the early afternoon, we showed the image of the bearded Jeremiah along the rural roads near the McDonald farm. One woman had seen a man who looked like the picture, but she didn't know where he lived. Not a solid lead. After several hours of hunting, my mobile rang. "Gannon, this is Lieutenant Hound. Meet me at the courthouse in Franklin."

# # #

Carla and I met Hound, and he drove us through the light traffic in the town of Franklin, past two-story buildings along the street, with an unbroken extent of mountains in the background. I sat in the front seat with him. "Where're we going?"

He sat ramrod straight as he drove and spoke slowly, pausing after every few words. "I'm going to get a warrant. To bust in on Sandford. The visit we're making now. Is my way to get it."

All through the town, we passed under a covering of trees, but as we left the central section, the buildings became one-story and stood by themselves.

Carla spoke from the back seat. "What's the population?"

"Almost four thousand," Hound said.

He turned onto a two-lane gravel road and, shortly after that, pulled off onto a parking area of dirt and patches of shaggy grass. He stopped beside a motorcycle, a red and white Honda XR650L. The parking area lay next to a slope down to a dilapidated one-story building.

Hound stepped out of his vehicle and started down the slope of an uneven path to the building.

I didn't understand why we had come here; furthermore, I saw no way this jaunt would help us find Jeremiah or the map. "Lieutenant, what are we doing?"

He slowed his walk. "I need a warrant. To get into Sandford's trailer."

"How does this place get us a warrant?"

He continued down the slope. "Powdered cocaine has come to the mountains."

What was he talking about? I wanted to get Jeremiah, but I didn't see how this store helped me. "Cocaine?"

"Comes in from Mexico. And several states bordering Mexico."

"This store is bringing drugs into North Carolina?"

Hound glanced over his shoulder at me. "I'm pretty sure high-school dropouts, like the ones you'll meet here. Are moving the drug into our region."

Carla had been listening, and now she pointed at the shabby house. "The kids in the gang hang out in that building?"

"Maybe," Hound said. "Can't know if hornets are in the nest. Until you poke it."

How did a gang of high-school kids have anything to do with the McDonald farm and the Cherokee Emerald? "And you believe Sandford and the gang work together?"

Hound continued walking. "Buzzards of a feather flock together."

I picked up my pace to stay with him. "What am I supposed to do?"

"In the shack. Find something connected to Mr. Connor Sandford."

"Then what?"

"I get a warrant for our mountain man. Based on suspected drug trafficking."

On a bench in front of the shack with its peeling white paint, a youth glowered at us. He wore a dark-gray hoodie over a blue sweatshirt, slouching under a sign saying, Motorcycle Repair. As we reached him, the kid straightened, pulled his hood over the red bandana around his head. "What'd you want?"

Our lieutenant stood with his thumbs looped around the belt of his trousers. "Eric, how wonderful. You're here. Let's talk."

Before responding, the kid chewed his gum and glared. "Can't. I'm working."

"Gannon, this degenerate excuse for a human. Is named Eric Weisel," Hound said in a slow voice. "Eric, Mr. Gannon is a private eye."

Eric didn't glance at me. He kept his hate-filled eyes pinned on the lieutenant. "Private property. Go away."

Hound kept a bland expression and headed straight for the open door of the shack. "This is a public building, Eric. Motorcycle repairs. Don't need a warrant."

The kid sprang off the bench and dashed to the door as if to shut it, but Hound slipped past the closing door. "I'm thinking about getting a motorcycle."

Carla and I followed them into the house. Hound began reading papers on the counters. "Like your sign, 'We don't cash checks.' "

The kid yanked the counter papers back from the lieutenant's prying fingers.

Hound's lips made a slight upturn at the corner of his mouth. "My favorite store sign is, 'Children left unattended will be given espresso and a free puppy.' "

"Get your hands off our papers," Eric said.

The lieutenant moved to a cluttered desk in the back. "Has your friend, Connor Sandford. Come around lately?"

Eric's arms were full of papers he had snatched from the counter. "Don't know him."

While Eric struggled to keep Lieutenant Hound from reading through papers on the desk, Carla and I flipped through the few documents left on the counter at the front of the store.

Carla whispered to me. "I wish our detective would talk faster."

I snickered. "Not all bad. Recall, haste makes waste."

Carla read through a handful of papers. "Uh, we're rummaging for a paper with Connor Sandford's name?"

I frowned. "Yeah, sort of like searching for coins in a woman's purse."

After sticking out her tongue at me, she said, "Eureka," and held up a canceled check stapled to an invoice and made out to Connor Sandford.

I held the payment up in the air and called out. "Is this what we're searching for?"

Hound took the invoice and smiled while he read it.

Eric lunched and snatched at the invoice in his hands.

The lieutenant pulled a leather-wrapped blackjack from his pocket and prepared to hit Eric, who pulled back, holding his arms over his face. "Boy. I'll hurt you bad."

His change, from methodical slow-drawl investigator to steely-eyed punisher, had taken an instant. He wanted to hurt. I thought, *Sociopath.*

Hound put the check into a plastic evidence bag. "Eric Weisel, I'm taking this document. Which I found in plain sight. Your establishment had. Dealings with Sandford."

We left Eric inside the shop with his eyes of hate. The Lieutenant dropped us off at the courthouse, saying he would phone when he was ready to serve a warrant at Sandford's house.

As Carla and I walked down an empty street to my Mustang, she put her arm around my back, and I placed my arm over her shoulder. Unbidden, my heart drummed a tad faster. We got in the car and began our drive back to the mansion. Carla asked the question I was chewing over. "How is investigating a group of teenagers going to help us find a lost emerald?"

I headed back to Asheville along I-26 West and US 74 West. "I don't know. Maybe there's a connection. Only time will tell."

19

GRANDMA'S POND — SUNDAY

The next morning, Carla and I drove to Macon County and crisscrossed rural roads around the farm, passing out leaflets with Jeremiah's bearded picture. She could get the clerks and store owners to view his image. Going into the afternoon, we found a few people who had seen our quarry, but they didn't know from whence he came or where he went. And so we struck out.

The fascination of stalking a lawbreaker depends significantly on whether they are easy to find or not. By early evening, my energy level had dropped to a zombie's. We should have gone on seeking, but my stomach started to growl. "Treat you to a pizza?" I asked.

She turned the Big Smile on me. "Donnell, are you inviting me out? Where?"

Carla and pizza. Couldn't get better than that. "Asheville Pizzas and Brews. Have you been there?"

She giggled and landed a soft bump on my shoulder. "First time. Let's go."

We left for North Asheville, arrived as dusk started, and stepped through the front facade: boulders on the pavement in front, blue awning over the windows, two silos to the side, and TVs over the bar. The bartender, short with black, slicked-back hair and slight stubble, served drinks and food and brewed the crafted beer at other times.

She parked on one of the bar stools. "I was promised a pizza."

"I'm ordering a flight of beers and the Carolina Daydreaming pizza," I said. "Topped with mushrooms, feta cheese, tomatoes."

"A flight?"

"A sampling of several beers."

She did a mini happy dance sitting on her tall chair. "My taste buds rejoice."

She always appeared attractive to me, but with each additional beer, she grew more enticing. Her outfit—a black jacket falling to her hip, a gray blouse, black pull-on pants, and black running shoes—was snug.

We drank beers until the sky grew dark. Leaving the tavern, I said, "There're roads that lead up to the mountains near here."

"Can you see the lights from up there?"

"Scenic views."

"Show me."

We drove up the nearby mountain, Sunset Mountain, passing over narrow roads crisscrossing back and forth. We saw few cars and the moon occasionally appeared through tree branches.

One hidden, narrow trail—that I knew—lay off a road. As I squeezed onto the path, trees brushed the car's sides and blocked moonlight.

Nervousness pulsated within me, with my breath coming short and fast. "This is a quiet place where we can talk."

I could barely see her face, but I judged by her deepening voice that her feelings were fluttering. "It's quiet," she said. "And dark."

I squeezed her hand and got a squeeze back. I had second thoughts, feeling uncertain and flustered by a less than ideal situation. "Carla."

She inclined her head up.

"Maybe this is insensitive. You spent time with your parents and canceled your engagement. I ought to take you back to the mansion, don't you think?"

She leaned sideways until our shoulders met. "Shh. Don't speak."

I slid my arm over her shoulder.

She leaned closer to me. "Hmm, there's a console between us."

I didn't know what to do. I sat like a mute, with my mouth open.

She turned sideways and tumbled into the rear seat, passing between the two bucket seats. Lord, she was agile.

"No console back here," she said.

My heart thumped as a pneumatic drill.

"Come on back."

I may get tongue-tied around women, but I scrambled out of the front seat and joined her. My chest rose and fell with hurried gulps because I was alone with this magnificent creature. We squeezed each other and kissed. The rear bench seat of a Mustang is cramped.

Afterward, I held Carla and tried to see through the car windows, which had steamed over. Her ponytail had a glowing sheen, her scent retained a refreshing smell of her rose perfume and she had me shivering with delight. I had become obsessed with this smart, bodacious woman. After a little more time had passed, we dressed and climbed back into the front seat, and I backed the car out of the tight path onto the road, with branches scraping against the sides as I exited.

Going down the mountain, I steered the Mustang back and forth, following the zigzagging lane.

Carla leaned toward me. "Put your arm around me."

I held on to the steering wheel. "Wait. I need to focus. Winding road." The road corkscrewed and tilted downhill.

"Can you talk while you steer?"

Oops. I sensed something intimidating in Carla's voice. "Sure."

She paused as if unsure of how to start. "Responsibility scares you."

My heart, which earlier had pounded, froze. I kept my eyes on the road. "Oh. Who told you that?"

"Friends who care about you."

That would be Taylor and possibly Mickey. I didn't respond, and she continued. "Don't be scared of bonding."

I turned through another sharp curve, reducing speed to stay on the mountain road. "I'm not."

"Accept we get along. Let me help you do your job."

I slowed as the winding road straightened and pulled up to a stop sign. Seeing no headlights, I pulled onto the crossroad and continued down onto the plateau underpinning Asheville.

"A basis for romance can be a partnership," she said. "You coach me in sleuthing, and I'll be your fact-finding partner."

I reflected a moment and then dipped my head at her. Carla read me like a simple road sign. In a rare torrent of insight, my mind concluded our relationship would wind about like a mountain road. And I wasn't the driver.

# # #

At the breakfast table the next morning, my boss had invited Angela to the mansion. Along with Roth, and Mickey, she listened to my report on Lieutenant Hound. I portrayed him as aggressive and mean. He might catch the individual who shot at Mickey and me in the woods—but I wouldn't bet on it.

"You need research," Roth said to me. "Dig deeper. You keep bringing me questions without answers."

I felt disappointment, a feeling of worthlessness. "I bring you questions without answers?"

She frowned. "Questions like who shot at you?"

I thought it best not to argue, and I nodded.

"Who are they? Jeremiah's collaborators or a second, unidentified group?"

I kept nodding.

"Did they mean to injure you?"

"I don't know."

"Not good enough."

Mickey cleared his throat. "Don't know what group they belong to, but they shot at the lantern, not at Don or me."

How was I supposed to know? I was the one getting shot at.

Roth resumed. "What is Hound's game? Is he hunting banned drugs as he says? Why does he suspect Sandford?"

I didn't answer but glared at her. Roth glared back.

She switched tack and quizzed Angela about the pond's location in 1838 when Ian and Waya buried the Cherokee Emerald. Angela repeated she didn't know where the pond had been at that time and the wise approach would be to take core samples along the banks of the stream. My boss folded her arms. "How deep would you sink the coring?"

"I'd drop the cylinder two feet," Angela said.

"What would be the diameter of the cylinder?

"Three inches."

"And Grandma has agreed to let us core out soil along the banks of her stream?" Roth asked.

"She agreed," Angela said.

Roth rocked to and fro for a minute and next instructed Mickey. "Have our coring contractor follow Angela's suggestions."

# # #

Hound called later that morning and told me to meet him at the stream running past Sandford's house. When I arrived, he had an aluminum rowboat, a warrant to serve, and two sheriff deputies. We carried the boat along the bank of the stream to a spot across from the trailer house. The mountain man sat in a lawn chair on his roof, smoking his briar pipe, from which the cherry aroma of his tobacco carried to me on a slight breeze.

Carla wore her trench coat and Doc Martens boots. I wore my black bomber jacket and blue jeans. "We're here to observe," I said to her. "We'll be seen but not heard."

She gave a slight dip of her head and stared at me from under her eyebrows.

Hound shouted across the stream at Sandford, "I'm serving you. With a warrant." The lieutenant held papers above his black wide-brimmed hat.

Sandford pulled on his pipe and glanced across the stream. "Let me see that warrant." He rose and walked on the roof to the front of the house. Then he descended a ladder and entered his trailer house through a window.

Hound and his two deputies rowed across the stream, stopped at the front door, and showed the warrant. One deputy rowed across the water again and picked up Carla and me.

I found the mountain man's first room large and arranged in a masculine style. It had a row of bookcases loaded with books, two locked cabinets with guns, and numerous animal heads mounted on the wall: black bear, deer, bobcat, gray fox, and wild boar. The trailer was dark and cluttered.

While the deputies searched for evidence of cocaine smuggling, Sandford and Hound faced each other, with identical expressions of authority, a wrinkled nose, and lowered eyebrows. They sounded similar when they talked. The mountain man was a little harsher, and our lieutenant was a little reedier, but they had the same cadence, slow and soft, in their voice. And neither showed a fondness for the other, both flaunting pained expressions to the other.

"What do you mean? You didn't hear two rifle shots last night," the lieutenant asked in his disjointed phrasing.

The mountain man pulled on his pipe. "I sleep soundly to avoid annoyance."

Our lieutenant frowned as if annoyed. "Which rifle do you hunt with?"

Sandford pointed toward his rifles arranged in a locked cabinet. "A Remington Model 798, with the .30-6 cartridge. Shot it a week ago."

"I'm taking it. For our laboratory to examine. You sure you didn't. Shoot it last night?"

"A week ago. Don't call me a liar."

Carla and I stood back and watched while the two men argued, and the deputies searched.

Lieutenant Hound tried to open the gun cabinet, but the mountain man said, "Stop, you'll break the lock."

After Sandford unlocked the cabinet, Hound reached in to grab a Model 798. "Interfere with my search. An' I'll slap you in lockup." He made a show of sniffing the chamber and barrel of the rifle.

When I had seen the rifle before, it had had a worn and scuffed strap. On this rifle, the belt appeared brand new.

"Sniff away. I told you I didn't fire the rifle last night."

Hound looked up from the Model 798 he held. "Is this the only Remington. You have?"

Sandford drew in a deep breath and rolled his eyes. "My other rifles are not Remingtons."

"I'm taking this rifle for testing."

"Leave a chit."

The lieutenant gathered the items to be tested and had his group row back across the stream. He stomped through the woods. "He's lying."

While helping the deputies carry the boat, I glanced across at him. "Why?"

He stared back at me. "When I asked if he shot the rifle last night. And if he had another Remington. He yakked a lot. An innocent man would say a simple, 'No.' "

We were getting nearer to locating Jeremiah. What I didn't know was I wasn't the only one trying to find him.

20

CLOSING IN ON JEREMIAH — MONDAY

Later in the afternoon, Carla and I returned to our task of searching for Jeremiah at service stations and convenience stores. Carla had changed to blue jeans, a long-sleeve light-green shirt, and a baseball cap with her ponytail sticking out the back. She had her eyes closed and bobbed her head to the beat of "All for You" by Janet Jackson. We had already been in six filling stations and one grocery store. I relaxed and enjoyed the breeze through the open window.

When the Ford Ranger passed, going in the opposite direction, I had just exited the sixth gas station. "Did you see that?"

Carla had stopped bobbing her head to the music and turned around to watch the white pickup. "Follow it!"

"Turning around now."

I drove faster. "There it is. Use the binoculars in the glove box. What's the license number?"

She focused on the pickup ahead of us. "Yes—it's a California license plate. Uh, that's him, Jeremiah."

I tailed the vehicle at a cautious distance.

Carla leaned forward in her passenger seat. "Won't he see us?"

"We aren't right behind him."

We followed the pickup, sometimes tracking with it visible and sometimes out of sight. Carla tried to phone Bruce and Mickey. "I can't get backup for us—no mobile signal."

When dusk started, I reduced the distance between us and the truck. I drove faster but didn't see the pickup. "I've lost it."

Carla glanced around us. "I remember a turnoff. Half a mile behind us."

I switched on the headlights, turned the Mustang around, and went back.

By the light from the instrument panel, I saw Carla pointing. "There's a secondary road."

In the settling dusk, I made out the turnoff—more trail than road. As I was afraid someone might see the headlight illumination, I switched to the parking lights.

"Can you follow the path?"

"Try to."

Moving along the trail in starts and stops, we found the small truck, pulled off onto a slight clearing. I looked at my mobile phone—still no signal. "Can you make a call?"

She punched buttons on her mobile phone. "Uh, no."

I got out of the car and pulled my M1911 pistol and two flashlights from the trunk.

Carla squeezed my arm and whispered, "Who's that?"

The moon provided some light, and I glanced in the direction she pointed. "What did you see?"

She hesitated. "Whatever it was, it's not there now."

I picked up no movement. "What do you think you saw?"

"In the clearing, I thought I saw a man."

I headed toward the woods to the side of the open space. "I want to investigate where the clearing goes. You stay here with the car."

She followed me.

Hugging the edge of the woods, we went up the open space on a slope. The only sound was the crickets, and my eyes spotted no motion. I thought I saw a solitary mass in the clearing. Holding my pistol in one hand, I flicked on the flashlight to light up the dark object.

Carla squealed.

21

JEREMIAH FOUND AND MAP STOLEN – MONDAY

My torch illuminated a crumpled body. What the hell. Was it Jeremiah McDonald? He lay in a supine position with his bearded face turned up and toward me—an expression matching his appearance in the fliers we had been distributing.

Carla startled me by digging her fingers into my left arm. "He's hurt!"

I killed my flashlight, grabbed her arm, and dragged her back the way we'd approached. I had seen Jeremiah's vacuous eyes and the dark liquid pooled on the ground surrounding his neck. "He's dead."

I crouched down and pushed through the tree branches, fleeing an unknown risk. Carla pulled on my shoulder as if she wanted me to stay and then stood. "We can't leave him there."

I yanked her off her feet into a crouch and hauled her behind me. "Leave him. He's dead."

Whoever had killed Jeremiah might still be around. I hustled my partner into the Mustang, maneuvered it around in the dark, and tore back up the trail. "Is your phone getting a signal?"

Carla scanned her mobile phone. "No coverage."

I drove a little farther, reaching the two-lane road.

"Now! I have a signal."

I pulled off to the side of the paved drive and had her call Roth. My boss answered on the second ring. "Speak."

I paused to control my hurried breathing. "Carla and I found Jeremiah's body in the woods."

"Where are you now?"

"I grabbed Carla and hightailed it out of there."

"Stand down. Call the sheriff's office."

"Let me return with the cavalry."

My boss was silent. She must have been considering my request. "No one shot at you?"

I glanced at Carla. "Not at us."

"Why return?"

"Hunt for the map."

The line remained mute for a full minute. Next, I realized Roth had talked to others at her end of the line. "I'm sending Bruce and Mickey. They're armed."

I turned to Carla studying her travel atlas of the roads. "Where are we?"

After Carla relayed our location, Roth responded, "Do not take Carla into the woods. Use your judgment as to how soon you inform the authorities."

# # #

While we waited, no one came or went on the path leading to the clearing with Jeremiah's body. Following Carla's directions, Bruce and Mickey arrived at the side of the road to join us. Both dressed in dark clothing and reached in the back of Mickey's Jeep for weapons, two Remington 870 shotguns. I explained my plan. "We'll search around the area where we found Jeremiah, and afterward call the sheriff's office."

"Look around first?" Bruce asked.

I confirmed. "Then tell the cops."

I told Carla, "Stay with the Mustang. A killer may remain in the woods. The rest of us will take the Jeep."

"Take me. You owe me. I saw the turnoff used by Jeremiah's pickup."

Bruce, Mickey, and I stared down at her and shook our heads. With an annoyed expression, she climbed into the Mustang to wait for our return. I grabbed latex gloves, slip-over shoe covers, and other items from the trunk of my car.

# # #

"Don't contaminate the crime site," I said. "Put on gloves and shoe covers."

We were ready. "Mickey, you stay a little behind us. Bruce, let's check out Jeremiah's body."

Three of us walked up the path and turned in on the clearing. Bruce carried his shotgun in one hand and a modified flashlight in the other. His special flashlight sent its beam through a strip of photographic film, cutting out visible light but transmitting infrared, invisible to the naked eye. Anyone watching wouldn't spot his light. Bruce would see the infrared's glow by viewing through a digital camera that didn't have an infrared filter.

We went through the forest to the side of the clearing, stopping when we reached Jeremiah. Bruce kneeled beside the body. "Two wounds. He was shot through the throat and . . . let me see . . . the side of his head."

"Are those contusions on his face?" I asked, trying to see by the moonlight.

"Yeah. Somebody's been hitting him in the face."

I scanned the area. "Must be Jeremiah's pistol off to his right side."

My partner picked up the gun with his gloved fingers and sniffed the barrel. He returned the weapon as he had found it. "It's been fired."

Bruce withdrew back to the cover of the forest. I began to sense a gun battle had occurred here. With watchfulness, we crept farther up the slope, which funneled into a path through the woods. Shining his flashlight on the ground, Bruce found a fishing line. "It's a security wire. Ain't active—no tension in de cable."

Feeling with my fingers, I followed the wire to the left across the path, finding one end connected to a tree. Reversing my way back along the cable, I found the other end of the wire attached to a keychain alarm, which someone had unfastened from a tree, releasing the tension in the line.

If an intruder's foot yanked the cable and pulled out the pin in the keychain alarm, the buzzer would alert the camp. Moving farther up the path, we found a second security system: a fishing line connected to tin cans.

Beyond the security arrangements, we found Jeremiah's camp.

Bruce stopped and raised a hand in the air. "Guys! Two tents up ahead."

By the moonshine, I recognized objects on the ground. "What a mess. Paper and gear scattered everywhere."

Bruce and I waited, prone among the trees. Mickey remained behind us, watching.

"This be Jeremiah's hideaway," Bruce said in a whisper, "but who attacked him?"

I could hardly see Bruce with his black outfit and dark skin. "Didn't know there was another group. How did they find his camp?"

"De same way you did," Bruce said. "Followed de pickup."

He took in a deep breath. "All dem papers scattered on de ground. What was this other group searching for?"

I listened for the sound of any intruder but heard only the katydids. "We're here for the McDonald map. Maybe the attackers wanted the same thing."

Bruce rose. "Let's see if de map is still here." He circled behind one of the tents. "Guys, we got another body."

I moved around the tent and stood beside Bruce. The man on the ground lay face down. The jacket on his back had jerked up, and his white tee shirt was red with blood. A rifle rested in the dirt near the body.

"Who?" Mickey asked.

To see the face, Bruce rolled the body over. "I know who he is. Dat's Jeremiah's army buddy."

I remembered Bruce had searched for known acquaintances of Jeremiah Johnson and found this man. "He had an unusual nickname. What was it?"

"Talk." Bruce went back to scanning the ground with his infrared flashlight.

Mickey had moved over to the second tent. "Blood on the ground. It trails through the brush."

I began glancing at the paper scattered about the camp—searching for Ian's map. "Mickey and Bruce, could you see where the trail of blood leads?"

They moved off, tracking the blood spatter. Wearing the latex gloves and using my infrared flashlight, I searched every paper, failing to find the map leading to the emerald. I hurried my search but left the documents where I found them.

My examination concluded, and Mickey and Bruce returned from tracking blood traces through the woods.

"Guys, dis blood splatter goes through the woods and out to the trail where Jeremiah's pickup is parked."

Mickey added. "Body dragged through the woods."

I felt frustrated. "Didn't find a map."

We stood for a moment, studying the area around the tents.

"Guys, what happened here?"

I stood off to the side of the clearing among the red spruces, surrounded by the chirping sound of crickets. Bruce's question seemed a logical place to start. "Lots of footprints. A group—maybe three or four—snuck up on the camp."

"A gunfight broke out," Mickey said. "Jeremiah and Talk died in the firefight."

"Maybe, da attackers wounded Jeremiah," Bruce said, "and beat him to get what dey were looking for."

Must have been the emerald map they sought. "Okay, but did they get it?"

We stared at each other until Mickey spoke. "An intruder got shot."

"Could be the attack hadn't been a total surprise," Bruce said. "After all, Jeremiah and Talk be armed."

Mickey pushed the safety button on his shotgun and sat on a fallen trunk. "They did reconnaissance. Knew where the trip wires were."

I thought they were audacious and took a risk with bold action. "Who are these people? They're dangerous."

Bruce and Mickey shrugged their shoulders.

I considered the bodies, the empty tents, and the debris. "Might have happened the way we think." As I scanned a final time around the camp, my eyes found a stack of shovels, picks, and a lantern. Jeremiah and Talk had been the ones digging up the McDonald farmland.

"What we do now, oh great gumshoe?" Bruce asked.

"Let's get the law in here."

We headed back to the Jeep. When we got there, we didn't have coverage to make a mobile phone call. We drove until we had a reception and called the sheriff's office to report the deaths. Corporal Hallowell had the day off, but the sheriff's office dispatched Lieutenant Hound. We went back to the trail leading into Jeremiah's camp and waited for him.

I closed my eyes. I was confused, my body feeling overheated, my mind racing for answers. Where's Ian's damn map? I've made a mess. I need Roth.

22

DETENTION CENTER, MACON COUNTY – TUESDAY

The Sheriff's Department's deputies and crime scene technicians arrived first and scampered into the woods to investigate. Lieutenant Hound pulled up half an hour later in his black-and-white squad car. With his chin jutting and back straight as an I-beam, he stepped slowly out in his pressed black uniform. Walking around the car, he retrieved a black campaign hat from the shotgun seat and adjusted it on his head ever so slowly.

With his hands positioned on his hips, the lieutenant peered over his nose at bystanders until he found me. "What did you think? You were doing?"

Into the icy torrent of his glare, I grinned in return. "I found a crime. Phoned it in. Stood down."

Hound massaged his forehead. "Dispatch said, 'Three individuals shot.' How could you know? Without scattering your trace elements over my crime scene?"

I suspected Hound's first step was to pick a scapegoat, so he could avoid blame if his investigation went poorly. "We walked in. Found two bodies and marks of a battle."

"Then what?"

"Backed out and called the sheriff's office."

Hound massaged his head again, maybe a nervous tic to gain time to think. "If I find you fouled my site. You're going to jail."

"Lieutenant, neither our fingerprints nor our footprints soil your site."

"Maybe you're. Mistaken?"

Yeah, some individuals see their life as a TV program. For our lieutenant, his role was thinking big, thinking positive, and cloaking an innate creepiness. Before I could block it, a sneer contorted my mouth. "I don't make mistakes. Oh, wait, I can't carry a tune."

Hound's neck turned red.

When he finally addressed one of his deputies, his voice was a whisper. "Take Mr. Gannon. To the detention center." Turning back to me, he said, "I'm arresting you. For interfering with my investigation."

Beside me, Carla had opened her mouth to object. I shook my head and tossed her my car keys. She closed her mouth. I whispered to Mickey and Bruce, standing at my side, that Hound had streaks of aggressiveness and meanness. The deputy stuck me in the rear seat of a patrol car, and we drove away.

# # #

Recently built, the detention center in Macon County was one of a few pleasant places to be incarcerated. I recalled one of Roth's aphorisms, which says, "A worthy PI follows their hunches and will—from time to time—spend a spell in jail." As the deputy checked me into a cell at the detention center, I asked, "Am I free to go?"

"Hound said to detain you."

"For what?"

"Question you about the murder scene."

"Does he have reasonable suspicion or probable cause to keep me?"

The deputy said in a low voice, "Talk to the Hound," and left. Several hours passed, during which time the center staff served breakfast, which tasted hunky-dory. A deputy woke me from a doze and took me to Hound's office. As I sat in front of his desk, he ignored me and pored over some paperwork. Next, he raised his head to stare hard at me; in truth, he had perfected his tough-guy persona. I was reminded of Hollywood gangster movies from the 1930s.

He interrupted his soundless glaring and fired a charge at me. "You broke the law. Tramping through my crime scene."

I launched my deer-in-the-headlights gawk in return. "Lieutenant, am I free to go?"

"Umm. Admit it. You rifled through the tents."

"Why detain me? Do you have likely cause or reasonable suspicion?"

Just as Hound's neck began its rosy tint again, a gentle tap sounded from his office door. "Come in. What is it?"

A deputy stood in the doorway. "Gannon's lawyer is here."

My, or rather Roth's, attorney wobbled into the room. Otis Quayle, a pudgy man in a cheap, blue suit, barked at Hound. "You have detained my client for five hours. Plenty of time to question him. Yet, he's still here."

"I will question him. If I want. As long as I want."

Quayle snickered. "Mr. Gannon is entitled to speedy legal action, which means a prosecutor decides within seventy-two hours to file charges or not."

Hound's neck and face changed to deep red. Jeezus Cripes, he was going to blow. "Out. Get out!"

In a motion that bunched his ill-fitting suit around his middle, Quayle held up his hands as if to ward off Hound's fury. "Be reasonable. Gannon's not going to answer questions. I know you have zero evidence—no fingerprints, shoe tracks, nor DNA—corroborating Mr. Gannon scoured through the murder site."

Hound and Quayle each turned a scornful scowl on the other.

"If Gannon doesn't confess. I'll inform the state board in Raleigh. And get his license pulled."

"I don't think so. Raleigh will ask what actual evidence you have. You've got zilch." My lawyer continued his mocking snarls for another instant. "Let my client go."

Hound shouted for a deputy, and—when the deputy arrived—said, "Release Gannon."

Quayle left. As the lieutenant chilled down, his head returned to its standard color.

"Did the gunshot residue test on my hands come back? Did it show I didn't fire my pistol?

"Tests came back. You. Are in the clear."

Hound massaged his forehead again and switched his questions. "Corporal Hallowell said you've been. Searching for a parchment."

"A map. The fellow who originally owned the McDonald farm hid something valuable."

The lieutenant waited.

"Did your deputies come across a map?"

"Nope," he said. "Did you?"

By his expression, I could tell he still thought I had gone through the murder site. "Lieutenant, I reported the crime at once."

"What did you handle?"

"Didn't touch anything."

He shook his head from side to side. "Yeah. Well, we. Found thirty-aught-six shell casings on the ground. Somebody shot a rifle."

I considered the caliber and absent-mindedly touched the scar on my cheek. "Same rifle Sandford uses."

"Same gun. Lots of people use it."

"Jeremiah and his partner, Talk, had guns."

"Yeah. A third person. Got shot. Attackers. Carried away a wounded individual."

"Did a hospital treat a gunshot wound?"

"No one with that trauma. Went to a hospital in the western part of North Carolina or eastern Tennessee. The assailant's either dead. Or engaged in amateur hour."

"Did you interview Sandford?" I asked.

"He says he went to bed early. Slept all night. Didn't have a gunshot wound."

# # #

Because I planned to take Carla for drinks at the Sky-High Bar, I wanted to impress her, wearing a dark blue blazer made from fine Italian wool. My chest showed off a light khaki, long-sleeve cotton shirt. I finished my ensemble with light blue chino dress slacks and black dress loafer shoes. As I waited for her to get ready, I snuck a peek at myself in the hall mirror and I resembled a modern-day Adonis. I had even slicked down my cowlick.

An hour before sunset, we got to the bar, located on the top three floors of an eight-story building on a fire escape and balcony area. An antique elevator and friendly operator whisked us up to the top floor of the downtown Asheville building, with formal seating and views from terraces looking out over the city and the Smoky Mountains. The decks were metal fire escapes.

Carla had switched from her jeans and long-sleeved shirt into a clinging blue dress. Angela Lightfoot—who had called to get an update on the case—agreed to meet us at the bar.

After a server had seated us and taken our order, and we placed our coats on the spare chair, Carla said, "We're back to where we began—no map."

I told Angela our tale of following Jeremiah's pickup and finding two dead men at the camp in the woods.

She blanched and gaped at Carla and me. "Worse off. No map and two people—maybe three—shot to death. Why kill these men?"

"They had something the killers wanted," I said. "Nothing personal."

Angela nodded her Afro at me. "How can you find the map now?"

I shrugged in frustration. "Got to solve the two murders. The killers must have it."

We settled into silence until our drinks arrived. At first, Carla sipped at her gin and tonic but then started to quiz Angela. "Were there originally two maps?"

Our professor got comfortable and began to fill in answers. "Two. Based on my readings of Ian McDonald's diaries."

"Waya and Ian each had a copy?"

"That's right."

"And Jeremiah stumbled across Ian's copy."

Angela glanced at me and next turned back to Carla. "My guess is Jeremiah got one of the drawings showing the hiding place."

Carla stared off at the mountains as if thinking. "Where is Waya's map?"

Angela gave a dismissive wiggle of her right index finger. "No one has seen it for over a hundred years."

Carla appeared puzzled. "Lost?"

Angela's facial features were downturned. "Must be. Waya never came back to his mountains."

Both Carla and Angela were motionless as if lost in reflection. Angela continued. "Thousands perished on that terrible march to Oklahoma. Waya and his wife vanished, along with his map."

Carla rubbed her arms as if cold. "If Waya had lived, would he have come back to North Carolina?"

Angela nodded. "To the Eastern Band of the Cherokees."

"How did this Eastern Band remain behind?"

Angela sipped her drink and gazed at the mountains. "Several hundred Indians slipped away to hide in the thick forest in the mountains."

"How many Cherokees on the reservation today?"

"In North Carolina? About ten thousand."

Dusk settled around us on the balcony of the Sky-High Bar, and the city lit up around and below us. Carla wrinkled her brow.

"What's the matter?" I asked.

"Curiosity. The Cherokee Indians who trudged to Oklahoma—"

Angela responded. "What about them?"

"What happened to them?"

"Currently, the Cherokee Nation is one of the biggest tribes in the US. They live within northeastern Oklahoma."

A chill followed the sinking sun, and I grabbed my coat. "How is your hunt for the earliest pond on the farm going?" I asked Angela.

Before responding to the new subject, Angela appeared to collect her thoughts. "Mickey and I started coring—down to bedrock—with no sign of the original pond yet."

"Any difficulty?" Carla asked.

"No. I'm following a prearranged grid as we remove the cylindrical samples of earth."

We all three sipped and admired the vista of mountain peaks beyond the balcony.

“I talked with Grandma McDonald,” Angela said. “No one dug at the farm last night.”

Maybe the deaths scared off the diggers—word spreads fast.

My mobile phone rang; it was my boss. I listened for a minute and, when she disconnected, leaned back in my chair. “Grandma McDonald is hysterical as a mother who lost her baby. A lawyer contacted Ashley—offered to buy the family farm.”

Who wants the farm? Find that person, and I’ll know who has the map. Sure, that dog will hunt.

23

AN OFFER TO BUY GRANDMA'S FARM — WEDNESDAY

With Carla close behind me, I pushed through the door into Roth's office. "Is it definite? Someone wants to buy the farm?"

She raised her head, with her pale face and white hair nestled behind a black veil. "I don't know the name of the buyer. A lawyer represents the purchaser."

The person wanting to buy the farm must have the map. "Whoever buys the farm can dig anytime they want."

Roth nodded. "Grandma called the lawyer back, but he wouldn't identify the buyer." She leaned back in her chair and buzzed Taylor to bring the Biltmore Estate Merlot that she served at the evening meal.

"Can't we request the lawyer tell us?" Carla asked. "Get the identity of the buyer."

I shook my head. "They won't tell us anything. When I hire a lawyer, they'll tell me what I want to know. But we didn't hire this lawyer."

Carla persisted. "But can't you ask?"

For a moment, I considered sending Carla to query the lawyer as she seemed to get anyone to talk about anything. "We'll check the attorney. Worth a try. I'll ask Otis Quayle, our lawyer, for help."

Taylor brought a half-filled bottle of the remaining red wine and a glass. Roth took a sip and turned to Carla. "Ask Bruce to bring his maps of the farm."

Bruce entered the office carrying sheets of paper. "Evening, Boss. What you need?"

"On my desk, spread your creations of the farm's topology."

Carla, Roth, and I looked at Bruce's map. "This exhibits the farm today?" Roth asked.

"Yes, Boss."

Roth placed her finger on the cluster of *Xs*, marking the dug-up holes. "These are the original holes before that mob began digging everywhere?"

"The first holes."

Roth took a simple protractor out of her desk drawer and stared at Bruce's diagram.

"What're you looking for?" Bruce asked.

"Support for a hunch."

"A hunch?"

Roth began to slide the protractor over the paper map. "I'm following an insight."

"What insight?"

"Can't say yet. I'm still developing it."

Bruce focused on one section of his map. "Where're you looking?"

"I'm studying the cluster of pits, which I'm guessing Jeremiah dug to extract the emerald. Where are they relative to physical structures and natural objects located about the farm?"

Bruce began to gather up his papers. "Guys, ya need me anymore?"

Roth continued to pore over the map and gave a dismissive wave to Bruce.

"Keep the map, Boss. Cuz, I have another copy."

He left the office.

She glanced up from the map. "Grandma and Ashley are coming to talk about their options. They'll arrive tomorrow afternoon."

"Options?" Carla asked.

Roth switched her eyes back to the map. "Grandma needs the money from selling the farm but doesn't want to lose the family home."

Roth looked up again. "Also, we'd be without a salvage agreement for the emerald if she sells the farm."

She was right. Without the farm, we didn't have a case. How deeply did Grandma feel about keeping the family farm?

# # #

The following afternoon, Carla and I waited for Ashley and Grandma to turn up. When their maroon 1985 Dodge Caravan drove down the mansion's driveway, I went out of the front hallway and opened the van door for the old lady.

She got out and viewed Roth's building with an expression of sorrow. "What I had a long time ago is gone. Only I'm left to remember it."

Carla and I led her and her grandson back to the shade garden and Roth, who stood to receive Grandma. "I commiserate with the loss of your cousin, Jeremiah."

The old lady sat in one of the brown wicker chairs with white cushions. "Does the sheriff's office know who done killed Jeremiah?"

Roth resumed her seat on a wicker couch. "We don't know. Don and Carla found Jeremiah's hideaway, but Lieutenant Hound of the sheriff's office is investigating."

Grandma removed her clear-plastic-rimmed glasses, wiped her tears, and turned to me. "You went ta the camp—searched through it?"

I nodded. "Combed the area. No map. Jeremiah and his friend Talk killed."

Grandma began talking to herself, "We plum can't find the map. We lost Jeremiah."

No one spoke for a minute, and then I said to Ashley, "How much digging did you see last night at the farm?"

"Digging stopped last night after the deaths. Bad news don't go slow."

Grandma dried her blubbering tears. "I ain't seen Jeremiah for many years. I didn't want to look at the body. The deputies sent a photograph of his face to Gertrude, my cousin."

Carla piped up. "Did you speak with Gertrude?"

Grandma lowered her head and muttered to herself. Presently, she answered. "I jawed wid her—it were nasty. She blamed me fer Jeremiah's murder. Said I planned to steal de emerald from her all along."

Roth shook her head. "I hope her rantings didn't upset you."

Grandma looked woebegone. I stood and walked around on the pea gravel to a side table, getting the bottle of red wine and glasses from Taylor. Back in my chair, I poured Grandma a full glass.

"Oh, thank you, Sonny."

After acquiring her glass, Roth asked the old lady to continue.

"Once, many years past, ma kinfolk were a pioneer family." Grandma began weeping. "They brung civilization to de mountains and kept our native heritage alive. Now all is slipping away. Our wealth gone—vanished."

Grandma's tears continued down her cheeks, and her nose began to run. "I feel like a frog in a rain barrel. Every time we'un make progress gettin' the emerald, something bad happens to put me in a worse situation than at de get-go." She blew her nose. "I eye de splendor of your'ns two-story structure and longed for the McDonald Farm of yesteryear. I'm going to die havin' failed my family's honor. I done lost my soul."

Roth had a sad expression. "I can't possibly understand the strain you are going through now. You seem devastated at not finding the map. Why is that?"

"I done had my family's ancient heritage handed to me at birth. The emerald would have given me back my family's old house and its grounds. Now I gotta sell de farm."

Roth stared at Grandma with a stern visage. "My advice is not to let the farm go. We could not have anticipated this new situation, but now we are searching for the map and the killers. I think it unlikely the offer to buy the farm will go away anytime soon."

The old lady kept wiping her face. "I'll tell de lawyer I need time to consider the offer. Tough choice. We're running out of money."

Shortly afterward, Grandma and her grandson left the mansion. I figured she had decided to take a chance on us solving the killings and locating the map. Saying *no* to the lawyer showed her courage.

I had a small window opening to catch who wanted the farm. I planned to work my way back from the lawyer to that person.

24

DRUG GANG IN THE MOUNTAINS, ASHEVILLE — THURSDAY

Grandma wouldn't sell her farm just now. I could speak to the lawyer, who might lose control of his mouth and blab the name of his client seeking to buy the farm. That would be dumb luck, but low probability events happen. From Ashley, I got the name of the lawyer, Dave Patski. Before seeing him, I would examine his personal history. In defense of detectives, we don't snoop; we practice awareness. I went to see Roth's lawyer, Otis Quayle, because greasy lawyers know other slippery lawyers.

# # #

Quayle hung his shingle in a suburban shopping center, his office nestling among similar spaces for attorneys, realtor agents, and insurance salespeople. His office contained bookcases of law books, his desk, and two chairs for clients. He had thick hair brushed to his right, which at a distance looked like a black bicycle helmet tipped to his side.

"Otis, I have a question."

He smirked. "Sweet Jeezus. Are you back in the Macon County Detention Center?"

"Need to ask about a colleague of yours, Dave Patski."

Quayle emitted a low grating laugh. "That talentless cretin isn't my colleague. I hear he's been defending drug traffickers."

"You don't think much of your fellow lawyer?"

"Far as I can see, his sole skill in law is smooching the judges' backsides."

"You say he represents drug dealers?"

Quayle leaned forward and took on a grim expression, his mouth opening slightly and his eyes squinting quizzically. "Sounds extreme. Is this query connected to the two killings in the high mountains?"

"Yeah."

"Patski has defended teenagers up on drug charges."

"Were they part of an organized gang?"

Quayle took his time answering. "So far, Asheville hasn't seen much gang activity."

"But could they be connected to other felonies?"

"You could call them a gang."

"Tell me about these teenagers."

Quayle raised one eyebrow higher than the other. "Aren't you friends with Harry Goodman in the Buncombe County Sheriff's Office?"

"Yeah."

"He'll know. Or he'll bring in someone from their drug squad."

# # #

I called Dave Patski, made an appointment, and drove to his workplace at an industrial park on Sweeten Creek Road in Asheville. A receptionist pointed Carla and me to the lawyer's office, where he sat at his desk, speaking on the phone. As we entered the room, Patski turned his back on me and continued to talk. Even sitting at his desk, he appeared tall and lanky with a long face and a withered left arm.

The lawyer hung up his phone and turned to us. "You're here about the offer on the McDonald farm?"

I paid no attention to his expression, which appeared to be a sneer. "Do you represent a buyer proposing to buy a farm from Evelyn McDonald?"

He changed from a sneer to a blank expression. "I can't talk with you about a confidential negotiation." He gave out a quiet laugh, resembling a neigh.

"What is the name of your client?"

"Oh, the identity of the buyer is confidential," he said with the same neighing laugh.

"Grandma McDonald is fond of her farm," Carla said. "How does the buyer plan to use the farm?"

The phone rang. The lawyer turned and talked for a few minutes before turning back to us. "I assume they'll farm. It's a farm." His face kept its neutral expression.

We conversed with Patski for another fifteen minutes, reaping more drab evasion.

As Carla and I left, I saw the receptionist had left her desk. I tugged on Carla's arm and turned down the hall. "Where're we going?" she whispered. "The entrance is the other way."

I stopped at the end of the corridor, where a door led out to the rear parking lot, pulled a roll of black electric tape out of my pocket, and cut off a strip using my Swiss Army knife. I pressed the tape over the strike plate of the doorjamb, so that the door opened and closed, but was unlocked. We walked out to the parking lot and around to the front where I had parked my Mustang.

# # #

I called Chief Deputy Goodman to arrange a late lunch and meeting at the Tavern on the Square near the County Courthouse and the City Building. When I arrived at the Tavern, Goodman, in a long-sleeved maroon shirt and tan corduroy trousers, was seated at a wooden table guzzling a beer. He put down his glass, pulled at his white goatee, and motioned for me to sit. "Guess you want to pick my tired old brain?"

Goodman was showing his age. His bread and goatee had turned a purer white since I had last seen him. "Harry, thanks for seeing me."

"I don't think I know anything that'll help you."

I grinned at him. "My friend, your brain has always been a fountain of information."

He rolled his eyes upward. "Haven't seen you since I helped you solve your death-head case."

"Our next scheduled collaboration is now."

Harry signaled for the waitress and then looked at me. "Please don't use that term when speaking to the honorable Sheriff, my boss." When the waitress arrived, Harry ordered a round of beers. "Mr. Gannon requests all charges go on his tab."

I ordered the Mt. Pisgah BLT and settled down to drinking beers with Goodman.

After asking about everyone at Roth Security, Goodman said, "What am I to gush forth for you? Whatever it is, you'll owe me."

"Tell me about drug trafficking in the mountains."

The Chief Deputy stared intently at me as he gulped at the beer. "Odd request. When did Roth start investigating drugs?"

"Have you heard about the two killings up in Macon County?"

As I waited for the Chief Deputy to answer, I caught the whiff of his old man's aftershave, his familiar Aqua Velva. "We suspect teenage dropouts from the town of Franklin are running drugs into the

Asheville area," Goodman said. "You think that group did the murders?"

"Maybe they branched out to murder and jewelry—a Cherokee emerald."

He pulled at his beer. "Lieutenant Hound is leading the murder investigation in Macon County. Have you met him?"

"Yeah. I've had the honor."

Goodman pulled out a notepad and began writing on it. "I'll talk with the deputies in drug enforcement and get a list of names with prior convictions. I'm told these teenagers gather at a motorcycle shop in Franklin."

"I know the shop. I've been there."

We ate lunch, switched topics to the Asheville Tourists Baseball Team, and parted in the early afternoon. I had two new clues. The group digging the holes were trying to buy Grandma's farm—who else could want the farm? Carla and I might identify the group through their lawyer, Patski. Goodman verified a nascent drug network in the mountains. I didn't see the connection from emeralds to cocaine, but you don't need to know all the answers when you have instinct. And my instinct told me to check out that trail.

# # #

Carla and I drove to the motorcycle shop in Franklin. I parked off the two-lane road going past the store. We could see the parking area, composed of dirt and scraggly grass, situated above the structure. Carla and I waited, scrutinizing the shabby one-story shop.

An hour later, Hound drove up beside us in his Crown Victoria, staring as if to say, "What are you doing here?" He went past, parked with his deputy, and walked down to the motorcycle shop.

Hound spent half an hour in the bike repair shop. Carla and I heard shouting between the deputy and the teenagers in the store.

When Hound came out and drove off, his deputy carried what appeared to be evidence boxes.

I started my Mustang and readied to leave. "This is where we begin our surveillance," I said to Carla. "We'll pick up here tomorrow."

"Where are we going now?"

"We pay a visit to Mr. Patski tonight."

Carla didn't flinch, only gave me an excited glance. "All right. Splendid."

# # #

That night, I planned to burglarize Patski's empty building. Carla insisted she go with me because—she said—I had the responsibility to teach her the gumshoe's trade. Rather than lose in a drawn-out argument, I agreed.

Mickey, who had consented to be our wheelman, listened but had only one comment, "Where do I drop you?"

"Drive by the front." As we passed the building, it was dark except for a single light in the front parking lot, and there was no visible security. "Go back around and park in the dark along the curb."

I sat in Mickey's black Ford Explorer for fifteen minutes, watching. "Let's get started."

Carla and I stepped into the darkness and turned into the lot surrounding Patski's office building. We crept along the wooden fence around the lot and—after checking for any movement—strolled to the back door. Carla scurried ahead of me, placed one hand on the doorknob, and crossed two fingers on the other hand for good luck. She pulled on the door, and it opened.

The hallway was coal-mine dark. I couldn't distinguish Carla in her dark clothes until I switched on my flashlight with its covering to filter out visible light. Next, I glanced through the screen of a digital camera—the one without an infrared filter—to view the infrared illumination from my modified flashlight. We reached the outer door to the suite of offices, which was locked.

"What do we do?" Carla asked.

My hand clasped two small, flat metal tools, a tension wrench, and a feeler pick. "Don't drop them," I said.

She took them to figure out their shape. "How does a lock work?"

"The door lock has five pins. A key pushes the pins up so the cylinder can turn and withdraw the deadbolt."

"Show me how the tension wrench and feeler pick work."

With my left hand, I slid the first tool in where the key would go. "You slide the tension wrench to apply tension to the cylinder—to turn the cylinder."

She held my flashlight and watched closely.

"With my right hand, I slid the pick inside the lock and pushed each of the five pins up, one by one." The cylinder turned, retracting the deadbolt from the doorjamb. "See."

"It's too dark."

"I'll show you better back at the mansion."

The door to the lawyer's office wasn't locked. Was that a portent that valuable documents weren't in his office?

Carla stood beside me. In a whisper, I asked her to close the blinds, and I went to the freestanding file cabinet. "Text Mickey we are in the office, and we're leaving when ten minutes have passed."

"Ten minutes?"

"We spend no more than ten minutes in this room. You are the sentry for us. I'll search for the McDonald file."

The file cabinet contained few files and nothing about Grandma and the farm. Also, the desk drawers had no Rolodex or scratch papers with names. Wherever Patski kept his business files, they weren't in his office. Patski had outsmarted me.

"Don, ten minutes have passed."

"Nothing of value. We're out of here."

We made it back to the Explorer without incident. Mickey had the engine running and drove off. "Find who wants the farm?"

"Found zilch," Carla said. "What's next? Burglarize Patski's home?"

I settled back in a rear passenger seat. "My intuition is telling me we should converge on the motorcycle shop."

She rotated her body to stare at me from the front passenger seat, her palms raised in a "why me" gesture. "Why're we dropping Patski?"

"My intuition says switch to the emerald to cocaine connection, and I'm stuck with it."

She shook her head. "We've begun following the lawyer. Don't stop."

I began a slow burn, my body tensing. My prideful brain wanted to do it my way. But she had proved to be smart and helpful, and I didn't want to piss her off. "Okay, Nancy Drew, only one fair way to settle this. Let's flip."

She nodded and then flipped a coin. I called heads, and the coin landed heads. We were embarking on a new and more dangerous path: searching for a drug connection to the slaying of Jeremiah and Talk.

25

SURVEILLANCE OF MOTORCYCLE GANG, MACON COUNTY — FRIDAY

I rose early, jogged around the mansion grounds, and grabbed a cup of Taylor's coffee as I passed through the kitchen.

Taylor stood over the center island with its black granite countertop. She wore a white chef's hat that spread out at the top and covered her red hair. "Ain't you'ns going to eat breakfast? We a-havin' eggs an' grits."

"Nope. Carla and I are off to pick up the ugly car."

"What fer?"

"Stakeout. You're a dear to have coffee ready."

Carla and I drove the Mustang along the Hendersonville Road to the storage compound. We pulled into the newly-built facility where Roth Security stored investigative equipment between use. I punched in a combination on the keypad beside the front gate, entered the complex, and drove to a one-story building of storage cubicles. The facility had compartments of different sizes, including a large room opened from the outside by sliding up a red, corrugated door.

I entered the space and drove out in a dark green Dodge Omni with a corroded paint finish—an old, commonplace car Roth Security used for tailing suspects.

Carla shook her head. "Poor thing is hideous. What year is it?"

"The 1980 model. It doesn't stand out."

Carla held her nose. "Depends on what you mean by *stand out.*"

# # #

We dropped off my Mustang back at the mansion; picked up my stakeout bag of items like napkins, water bottles, and spoons; and drove to the motorcycle shop in Franklin. I parked the Omni so the front faced away from the shop, but its mirrors—after a little adjustment—held images of the store.

Carla glanced over her shoulder. "If we stare directly at the store, the teenagers would see our faces eyeing them?"

"Yeah."

She turned to adjust the rearview mirror. "Parked like we are with the building below and behind us, I can watch them in the rearview mirror."

"Using the mirror, you can take photographs of the teenagers."

"If the teens gaze up from the store, they'll see the back of our headrests."

I settled down to watch. The scene around the clapboard shack was desolate: sparse patches of grass, a dirt slope down to the store, and two red-and-white motorcycles parked in the lot at the top of the hill. At first, the early morning air cooled the car, but then the sun heated it, and I lowered the driver's side window. Carla, wearing blue jeans and a magenta jersey, was confident we would succeed, smiling with a playful grin and a sparkle in her eyes. I had on a black wool blazer and blue chino pants and was more doubtful about the day, hoping and praying our surveillance would work out.

We experienced time dragging by; Carla glanced at her watch every five minutes. She didn't doze but kept watching the shack. Our pull-off was among thirty- to forty-feet tall trees. Carla noticed the tree with its bright orange fruit. "What are these deciduous trees?"

"Persimmon." I stepped out of the Omni and picked two ripe-looking persimmons for her and scooped out the seeds.

She ate the inside with a spoon. "It's sweet."

"They taste best starting in early fall."

Half an hour passed; still, no movement. At the hour mark, a man drove up in a pickup, took what appeared to be part of a motorcycle engine into the shop, and left.

"I'm, um, not sure why we're here," Carla said.

I felt conflicted, weighing the pros and cons of what to tell her. "We're going to answer Roth's questions."

"Which questions?"

"Who shot at Mickey and me and later killed Jeremiah and Talk to take the map?"

Carla raised her chin and stared at me. "You're saying the same group did both attacks?"

"Start with a shooting and grow into murders," I said.

"But why investigate drug guys?"

"I'm turning over stones. Looking for the bad guys."

"Why start here?"

"I think Sandford is connected to the killings because he found out about the emerald hunt. And the teenagers are his gang, his gunmen."

"You don't know they're all connected."

"That's like a question. To know is an answer. Roth wants answers."

She hadn't said anything for a while, and then she started talking. "Stakeout is different from my vision of a dynamic PI as a shoot 'em-up hero—a lone ranger. Uh, what do you do when you have to go?"

It took me a second to realize what Carla had asked. "Pee?"

She flashed a lopsided grin, with the right side lower than the other. "Yes."

"Hmm, I usually carry a wee bottle—empty soda bottles or maybe a tennis-ball can."

She waited.

"Early on, I tried to lug a toilet-like apparatus, but not now." She appeared to memorize everything I said.

"Now, I leave the vigil and find a restroom. Hope nothing happens while I'm gone."

"Do you see yourself as an ethical investigator?" she asked. "I mean, you went through the site of Jeremiah's murder, but you told the sheriff's office you didn't."

Her question rattled me. I felt a flush of adrenaline. "I try to be ethical. I used to picture myself as just."

"Used to?"

"Being an ethical guy has disadvantages for a gumshoe. Occasionally I might fib but not tell Roth."

"I'm embarrassing you, aren't I? I bet you'd rather do a stakeout with Mickey. He's quiet."

"With Mickey, I have to bring a box of donuts. He makes these munching noises and gets crumbs on the upholstery."

At that moment, a teen left the store and rode away on one of the cycles.

"Let's follow him," Carla said.

I started the car and trailed the rider, hanging back out of sight at times. We followed the bike in a semi-circle around the town. The teen pulled into a restaurant to park.

As I drove past the parking lot, I made out the building was a bar called Tooey's. Carla and I pulled onto the shoulder, stopped, and observed the structure through our rearview mirrors. An hour later, the teenager left the bar and returned to the motorcycle shop.

Parking our car again at the site over the shop, we watched for a few hours more but saw nothing of interest.

I began moving the mirrors back to their usual position and started the Omni. "Let's quit and return to the mansion."

Carla adjusted the mirror on her side of the car. "What about tomorrow?" she asked. "Are we coming back to spy on the cycle store?"

"Tomorrow, we're going to put you in disguise, like Sherlock Holmes. It's the only way we can get you closer to these guys."

Carla cleared her throat. "But I'm the newbie. I'll be timid."

"Wearing a disguise, you're neither timid nor extroverted. Put on a mask, and you're someplace in the halfway point, kind of like a second-stringer on the bench."

She appeared insecure, with her eyebrows raised and drawn together. Also, her eyes had the upper white showing, but not the lower white. "You're awful in a scary sort of way."

All I had to determine was what disguise she needed to use.

# # #

Back at the mansion, I sought a Carla disguise that would be attractive to the motorcycle teenagers and, at the same time, one she had the ability and passion for pulling off. Carla could masquerade herself, but my brain wrestled with a cloak she could infuse with credibility and believability. Maybe she could pose as a teacher—

I glanced up from my laptop keyboard to find Roth scowling at me from the doorway. She wore her purple, tunic-like dress with the long sleeves, which she saves for the few times she ventures forth from the mansion.

"Good afternoon," I said. I was a happy camper, with a freshly shaved face, blue jeans, a yellow polo shirt, a chain with a sun medallion, and pointed black loafers.

Roth projected her grim expression, reminding me of my mother's face back when I had to clean up my bedroom. "Carla is a bright addition to our team and is working well with you. I am giving her a welcoming dinner. We leave in twenty minutes."

"Hmm, you never take me to a meal."

"No. However, you do get to keep your job." She spun to go.

"Seriously, why are we going?"

She glanced at me impatiently, tilting her head back and gazing upward. "Carla's bedroom is austere. We're shopping at the River Art District to buy something unique to put on her wall." Roth exited the room in a billow of purple cloth, suggestive of a science fiction movie.

"We'll go to the shops to pick out a suitable landscape painting—leaving at two o'clock. I have invited Taylor to come with us."

Roth sat in the front seat as Mickey drove us to the stores. I sat in the rear area of the Explorer with Carla and Taylor. Taylor grew up in the high mountains around Asheville, where her family implanted a deep-seated appreciation for Appalachian cooking. She talked excitedly with Carla and me about the chosen restaurant. She voiced her food ideas without hesitation and continuously, her braided red hair shaking.

Mickey steered north on Hendersonville Road, a five-lane divided highway with telephone poles and lines strung along one side. With a cloudless, blue sky and humidity at a comfortable level, we went past two-story office buildings, small one-story shops, churches, one-story restaurants, and numerous small trees. An undeveloped tree-covered land alternated with the developed lots. Closer to Asheville, the developed lots changed to shopping malls.

He turned left off Hendersonville Road toward the French Broad River's east bank, the River Art District site, a complex of defunct factories and historical structures situated beside the river and the Norfolk Southern Corporation's train tracks. Our journey's end was this complex of artist shops, working studios, and restaurants. Mickey pulled into Depot Street and parked.

We strolled among a few cars but many pedestrians, some in reputable outfits like tourists and others in bar-hopper, casual clothing. A two-lane street ran along the river between an eclectic array of brick and cinder block buildings. The crowd, noisy and carrying shop bags, created an ambiance of art-studio disarray.

Our crowd walked into the Wedge Studios. My boss chatted with an artist and purchased his oil painting—a landscape of cars on a two-lane road with mountains in the far-off horizon—for Carla's room. She bought four watercolor paintings from a second artist, still lifes of flowers beside a mountain trail.

"Who are the flower prints for?" I asked.

Roth grew agitated, her face reddening, avoiding eye contact. "Your computer room is the ugliest area in the mansion. Why is there colored spaghetti all over the floor? You and Bruce have coated the walls with sheets of white paper, on which you've scrawled meaningless words and symbols. You've turned that once beautiful room into a large closet."

"Umm . . . it's a computer room."

"It's a messy room."

"Bruce and I have it like that—so our creative juices flow."

Roth wrinkled her nose as if smelling something foul. "Creative juices? When you consistently neglect to put items back in their assigned location, you're obliged to create innovative methods to assemble your mayhem into a compelling whole. You created a wall paneled entirely in scraps of paper."

"But all computer rooms—all over the world—look like that," I said.

"We will clean it up bit by bit," my boss said. "Today, we start with the walls." Mickey and I left the Wedge Studios carrying shopping bags.

"Originally, Asheville's industrialists built on the banks of the French Broad River next to the railroad tracks," Roth said to Carla. "In the late nineteenth century, the railroad played a major role in making the city grow." The five of us walked and peered at the artwork in the open doors and windows as we passed.

"What was manufactured next to the river and train tracks?" Carla asked.

"They made denim and soft flannel. Asheville Cotton Mills was the major factory. The mill operated from about eighteen-eighty until nineteen-fifty-three. Nearby coal mines produced coal to power the Asheville Cotton Mills factory and heat homes."

"Where'd they get workers?" I asked.

"Mostly off the farm," Roth said. "The manufacturers created a village system here with small houses and a church built on the higher ground above the factory. Like everything else, the Great Depression hurt the industry. Business picked up in World War II. After the war, global competition harmed the mills. Today, they no longer make cotton in the buildings but create many types of art."

Roth and Taylor led the way down Depot Street. They went into the Pink Dog Creation, where my boss purchased an oil painting, a landscape showing clouds rising over majestic mountaintops. For a late lunch, we went into The Junction, a farm-to-table restaurant with upscale Southern food. The one-page menu listed several offerings the chef did well, rather than a long list of food and drink. We ordered a rum-based cocktail called the 'Generation Gap.' We all had the sweet tea brined and fried chicken, a different and delicious dish. We finished with the key lime pie for dessert.

As we ate our meal, the couple at an adjacent table captured my notice. The woman was older than her date and wore an elegant black dress and high heels to his blue jeans and a polo shirt. I grasped Carla's disguise: she would be the sexy older woman to one of Sandford's teenager motorcyclists. The sexy older woman disguise.

"So, Taylor, I think you said your mother had a difficult time raising the children?" Carla asked.

"My pa were an alcoholic, always a-drinkin' his'n moonshine. Often, he were too drunk to get back home at night. Pa were mean. When he was drunk, he whups Mom an' us kids.

"My ma married when she were fourteen an' had a passel of us kids. She kept her family together. She a-plantin' da garden an' she brung da government check every month. I went to a one-room schoolhouse—lots of my school teachin' 'bout balanced farmin' and rotating crops.

"I helped ma with cookin' since I'm eight years old. Pa died when I were twelve years old. He died from a-drinkin' his moonshine. Pa tried more kick by addin' bleach an' paint thinner to da mash."

"I'm pleased that you remained optimistic despite your father's cruelty," Roth said.

"I were blessed with many good people in my hollow."

"Taylor, your family bonded like iron," I said. "The entire household protected each other."

The table grew quiet while we finished eating our chicken. I needed to contribute to the conversation but didn't want to talk about my childhood. "What I miss in the morning is the Peanuts comic strip. The last appearance was this past January, and I grieve for its loss. The Asheville paper said Charles Schulz, the creator, passed away at seventy-seven years old. I so identified with his character Charlie Brown."

"When I grew up, everyone talked about the comics," Roth said. "Now I think we discuss the comics less and less. I believe young people have begun to read daily news on the Internet instead of the hard copy newspaper. Of course, the comics and the newspaper complemented each other."

Silence settled on the table again until Taylor asked a question.

"What 'bout you, Ms. Roth? I heared you overcame a bad misfortune."

I held my breath. My boss rarely talked about her past.

Roth hesitated, smoothing her clothes and making a hmm sound in her throat. "Oh, I had a privileged childhood, and I loved to read and go to school. I graduated from Randolph-Macon Woman's College in Lynchburg, Virginia. I had much fortune and joy growing up.

"I married a remarkable man, a medical doctor by profession. We were in love and very happy together. He had a business partner, and they formed a company, doing blood testing. Their laboratory testing company picked up specimens, analyzed the blood, and rapidly returned the report to the doctor. My husband did the technical tasks: checking out the latest technology and doing pickups and analyses efficiently. His partner took on the financial and contractual side of the partnership." Roth looked uncomfortable talking about her past, continually staring at the salt-and-pepper shakers on the table.

"We were on top of the world until my husband discovered bills were overdue. The partner embezzled large sums from the company and fled the country, disappeared. My husband worked diligently to keep the company afloat. He began drinking heavily and died of alcohol poisoning.

"I became penniless. I started a credit-checking firm that evolved—a long story best kept for another discussion—into Roth Security. Over time, my firm built up a cash reserve—I will never again be poor!" Roth's expression switched from uncomfortable to determined, her lips set in a straight line over clenched teeth.

My boss turned to Mickey. "It's getting late. Next time, you can tell us about your life. Let's get back to the mansion."

Today had been a goof-off day but worthwhile. I discovered why Roth had an odd dread of poverty. All the time I had known her, she had been closed mouth about what had gone before. Until now. Tomorrow, anxiety would flourish as Carla dressed in the garb of a detective in disguise.

26

CARLA SEARCHES FOR GANG'S HIDEOUT, MACON COUNTY — SATURDAY

Carla was in disguise the next day. Her guise was her outfit: tight jeans, a khaki jacket, a close-fitting tee shirt, and a gray purse with a shoulder strap and a transmitter. She also bared a gloomy and chilly sulk, shown by her downturned mouth and vacant stare, her attitude matching our mid-morning surroundings. When Carla, Mickey, and I left the mansion, the temperature was a nippy forty degrees Fahrenheit, and the sky was clouded over. She told me, "I've got butterflies in my stomach."

She started the engine of the green Omni, blowing warmth over my legs. Our stakeout location—just off the road running past Tooey's restaurant—proved quiet and thinly peopled. A few one-story homes, built during the twenties or thirties, nestled along the side road on which the car stood.

"Cheer up," I said. "Disguise is essential. Consider Sherlock Holmes."

"Dressed up like a tart, did he?"

She wasn't buying into this masquerade. In exasperation, I raised my head and stared at the car roof. Several beats later, I turned to Carla. "You can do this. You'll attract this teenager as nectar attracts a bee."

She pressed her lips into a drawn-out frown. "Uh, whatever."

I waited a moment before resuming. "If there is danger, Mickey and I'll come running."

Carla pulled in a giant breath, and next blew air over her pursed lips, slowly, steadily. "My heart's pounding," she said. "I can't do anything about that."

I waited.

She raised her chin, shifting her expression into a determined look, which was a set jaw and alert gaze. "I'm going to start before I throw up."

I opened the passenger-side door and got out. "Turn on the transmitter in your purse."

She gave me a feeble smile and reached into her bag.

I walked behind her to Mickey's Ford SUV and got in.

In the Omni's driver seat, Carla turned to face Mickey and me in the vehicle behind her and spoke through her transmitting device, "Can you hear?" We both gave a thumbs-up gesture through the SUV's windshield.

Carla said, "Game Time," and maneuvered the Omni around the short distance to the restaurant. I saw her get out and walk to the door of Tooey's, a one-story structure with dirty, white vinyl siding.

I watched her disappear into the building. Mickey and I settled back to listen to the broadcast from the bug in her purse.

"This bar's a plain dive," Carla said faintly from inside. "Floor, chairs, and tabletops are dog-eared wood."

"Take a seat anywhere, Honey," a loud voice said.

"Thank you," Carla said.

The bug picked up, "Thump, thump, thump, screech, and thud."

I guessed Carla had taken a seat at a table.

"The voice you heard," Carla said quietly, "came from a waitress—middle-aged, in a white blouse, skirt, sneakers, and off-white apron."

"Thump, thump."

"Here's your menu. Want a beer?"

"That's the voice we heard," I said to Mickey. "The waitress."

"I want an iced tea," Carla said. "And a cheeseburger—medium."

At that moment, I heard a motorcycle and saw a bike roar past on the main road. It turned into Tooey's dirt parking lot. "That's the teen Carla and I followed yesterday," I said. Removing his World War II German-type helmet, the teenager headed for the building. He wore black thick-rimmed glasses, boots, a leather jacket, jeans, and a dirty-white tee shirt. His build was slight, maybe five feet seven inches tall and a hundred and twenty pounds.

"Carla won't have trouble spotting him," Mickey said.

Then we heard her whisper. "The teen entered. He took a booth to my left."

"He's bound to spot Carla in her tights," I said to Mickey.

"He's been studying my chest," Carla said. "We locked eyes for a moment."

"She's set her trap," Mickey said.

"He's young," Carla said.

There followed a long period while her transmitter relayed the tavern's background chatter. Those minutes were a critical interval: the window for our success or failure. I waited for our motorcycle kid to hustle to Carla as a largemouth bass hits a curly-tail-grub lure.

I heard the patter of footsteps. "Like, mind if Ah sit down?'" a male voice asked.

Carla had him. Mickey and I both grinned.

I heard another person approach the table. "Joel, why don't you leave the lady alone?" a second waitress's voice said.

"That's all right," Carla said. "Maybe he can help me find something."

I heard the noise of a chair sliding back at the table. "What can Ah do?" the kid asked.

"I don't talk to strangers," Carla said. "I'm named Rosa."

"All rite, Ah'm Joel," the kid said.

"Pleased to meet you, Joel," she said.

"Like, get you a beer?" the teenager asked.

"Why not?' Carla said. "Let me buy the beers—just got a bonus from my old job."

I heard footsteps. "Behave yourself, Joel," the woman's voice said. "Looks like you're talking to a proper lady."

"She do look prime," Joel said. "Bring us a pitcher of beer."

"I'd like a glass of white wine," Carla said.

"Clever," Mickey said from the seat in the SUV. "He drinks an entire pitcher of beer while she sips a wine."

"I warn you," Carla said, "I'm more a listener than a drinker."

"All rite with me," Joel said.

"She's got Joel's attention," I said. "Now she reels him in."

I heard a waitress bring a beer, and then someone pour a liquid, "Gurgle."

"Joel's started drinking his beer," Mickey said.

"I have an advertisement for an apartment in Franklin," Carla said. "Show me where it is on my map?"

"Here it is," the teenager said.

I heard the sliding of a chair. "Screech."

"Stop it, Joel," Carla said. "I don't want your hand on my leg."

After a few moments, she continued talking. "Where do you work?"

"Ah work at a motorcycle store."

"I see a cycle parked outside," she said. "A beautiful Honda XR650L. Is that yours?"

"Yeah," Joel said. "Like, it's one of the fastest bikes in the world. Want a ride?"

"Maybe another time," she said.

Carla and I had planned to meet the teenager, gain his trust, and then begin an in-depth interrogation later. We needed to find the headquarters of the teenagers' gang. Were they a criminal band led by Sandford, our mystery man in a porkpie hat? Once we identified their hideout's location, we would break in and search for the map.

"I should go now," she said to Joel. "Need to find that apartment. I enjoyed meeting you."

"Like, maybe we could go out together—sometime?" the kid asked.

"I'm a little old for you," Carla said. "How about we meet here Monday and discuss it?"

Twenty minutes later, Mickey and I watched the teenager exit the restaurant and leave on his motorcycle. Our queen of disguise followed him out of Tooey's and drove her car around to us. She left the Omni and got in Mickey's SUV, sitting behind me. I sat in the shotgun seat. "You did well."

She beamed, flooding me with her mega-bright smile. "I did, didn't I?"

"So the kid's interested in you?"

Carla grinned and nodded.

"When do you meet him again?" I asked.

"Monday at Tooey's"

"You think fast on your feet," I said. "A natural investigator."

"At one point, I slipped off my khaki jacket and pulled my shoulders back, emphasizing my tight tee shirt," Carla said. "I spotted drool running down Joel's chin. Been a while since I dealt with a teenage male."

"You had the kid ready to talk," I said.

"Among other things," Mickey said from the front seat.

When she'd meet with Joel Monday, she'd acquire the clue we sought: the site of Sandford's hideout. Once we knew where it was, we'd search for the map showing the emerald's burial location.

"Something came up while you were in the tavern," I said to Carla.

She flipped her ponytail back over her shoulder and waited.

"Lieutenant Hound called. He wants to know, and I quote, 'What do you think you're doing?' We see him in thirty minutes at his office."

Hound's speech was staccato, disjointed, and confusing. But my lieutenant wasn't a fool. He saw a connection between Sandford and the recent murders. Also, he was looking for something. I had to get the link and what he was trying to find.

27

THE HOUND SEARCHES FOR GANG'S HIDEOUT — SATURDAY

I drove in a drizzle with the wipers on low and Carla sitting beside me, apparently reminiscing about her starring role as a young woman acting overawed by the attentions of a scruffy teenager on a motorcycle. I chilled out by viewing the low, green vegetation in the fields along the country road. I bobbed my head to the beat of the song on the CD player, "We Gotta Get Out of This Place" by The Animals.

The low clouds appeared not to dampen Carla's spirit. Suddenly, she spoke. "Rows of plants in the fields."

"Yeah."

She sat upright. "Well? What are they, Mr. North Carolina?"

"Hard to see. I'm guessing cabbages."

"They're everywhere."

"Spring is everywhere."

She leaned back in her seat. "You can tell me again about my sterling performance at Tooey's."

I opened my mouth to chuckle aloud. "You are a master of disguise."

"Really?"

"Really. You've got the three *Bs*, beauty, brains, and *boise*."

Her eyes widened in mock fright. "You've developed a silver tongue to go with your big muscles."

"I try to be stimulating."

She uttered an unladylike snort. "You're better off with tall, dark, and handsome."

Turning into the compound of the sheriff's office, I parked next to the one-story, red-brick building. Carla reached across the center console and squeezed my arm. "I like you the way you are." And she popped out of the car.

# # #

The desk sergeant had a deputy take us to Hound's office. At his desk, the lieutenant glanced up and locked eyes on me, wrinkling his eyebrows in a frown. Eventually, he spoke coolly, "Take a seat." Showing yet again, he was a drama queen. I sat on a chair in front of his desk, and Carla took a chair near the door.

We sat in silence. Hound, in an ironed, black uniform, stared and scowled. "Are you interfering. In my murder investigation?"

I stared and scowled back. Darn if Hound wasn't going over old ground. This guy was no Goodman. "Nope."

Hound massaged his forehead. "I don't. Believe you."

"I'm looking for something missing."

"What are. You doing?" He stopped to glance at Carla. "Ms. Diaz and you. Staking out the motorcycle shop. The same shop I'm observing."

I brushed down my cowlick. "We're searching for a missing map."

He slapped his palm against his forehead. "Gannon, you're making me. Look bad."

He was so tedious. "I'm hunting for a sheet of paper."

Hound stood and stared out the windows behind his desk. "Here's what. I don't understand. How is spying on that cycle store. Connected to your search?"

"The McDonald family got an offer to sell their farm."

"I'm listening."

"An offer by a lawyer who represents a teenage gang in Franklin."

"Still don't see the map."

"I'm guessing this teenage gang has the map I'm seeking."

After I finished, he resumed staring and frowning. "You have. A major shortcoming. You grasp at straws."

Great, I had a shortcoming. This from a guy who had difficulty finishing a sentence and tripped over his words as he spoke.

"Has to be the same group," Carla said. "How many gangs are there in Macon County?"

Slanting his eyebrows downward and partially closing his eyelids in a show of frustration, Hound said, "First you told me. You would inform for me. And then you tramped through my murder scene."

"Hold on," I said. "Carla and I found the crime site and told you—informed you—right away."

Hound sat and swiveled his chair around to glance out the window again. After a dramatic pause, he turned back to me. "You report to me. The instant you stumble on a connection to my murderers."

"Agreed. If we find a link to the killings, we will notify you instantly."

Hound showed a broad smile revealing all his teeth. "Settled."

"Now that we've reached an agreement," I said, "what can you tell us about Sandford's house and the bike store?"

"On different occasions, we searched and discovered no drugs and no weapons used in the Jeremiah and Talk murders. Both Sandford's home. And the store are clean."

Carla spoke from her location near the door. "So they hid the guns someplace other than the cycle shop."

"My deputies can't find—drugs or the guns used in the murders."

"They have a hideout other than the cycle place," I said, thinking aloud.

Hound nodded. "Has to be—but they're careful not to give its location away."

Perhaps buoyed up by her triumph with the teenager at Tooey's, Carla's voice took on a cynical tone. "You took them too lightly."

"Didn't," Hound said. "They're cleverer than I thought."

"Wait," I asked. "Why not follow the teenagers to their hideout?"

The lieutenant gazed down at his feet, rubbed his forehead, and resumed. "At times. It isn't easy to know where they go. They depart the roads and drive into the woods. On their motorcycles. My deputies in their sedans. Can't follow the cycles."

"Tracking device?" I asked.

"They discovered. Our trackers," he said in his slow intonation. "I'm guessing they have a hiding place. Somewhere south of Franklin."

"Where do they sleep?" Carla asked.

"They say. In the cycle store. But my deputies say they aren't there. At night."

Had to be a hideout. Guns and the map stashed there. "We'll both hunt for the gang's lair," I said. "If Carla and I find it, we'll inform you. If your deputies locate the hideout first, they'll search for the map stolen from the McDonald family?"

Hound rubbed his hand over his short haircut. "I agree."

I checked my watch. Carla and I had spent half an hour, reaching a deal with the lieutenant. Now, I needed to get information from him. "What did you find at the Jeremiah-Talk murder site?"

"We found no prints. Other than Jeremiah and Talk's. Blood samples existed for Jeremiah, Talk, and the blood trail out to the road."

I turned my head to gather my thoughts. "Does the forensic evidence identify who bled?"

"The location of the blood trail. Indicates it belongs to one of the attackers," Hound said. "Our laboratory is doing DNA analysis. The sample could be compared to a suspect. If the bleeder is alive. And if we find him."

Hound began going through a stack of paper files on his desk and selected one of the folders. "The recovered bullets are 30-aught-6 and 9mm. The attackers used rifles and pistols. We are sorting out. How many of which just now."

I pointed at the folders on his desk. "Any of the weapons used in a prior crime?"

"One of the pistol shells. Fired from a gun used in a drug deal gone bad," Hound said.

Carla spoke up from the door. "There's the drug connection, again."

Hound closed his folder. "Keep me informed. I'll alert my deputies. You're doing surveillance for me."

Hound lowered his head and waved his hand at Carla and me, signaling us to leave.

A few minutes later, as we sat in the Omni, my mobile rang. Roth had called. "Grandma's changed her mind. She's decided to sell the farm. Come now!"

"On our way." I disconnected.

Carla buckled her safety belt. "Why is she changing her mind?"

"One way to find out." I started the drive back to Asheville.

28

ROTH TALKS GRANDMA OUT OF SELLING FARM — SATURDAY

On that crystal-clear afternoon, I saw Grandma's grimy, maroon Dodge Caravan as it entered the drive to the mansion. As the timeworn minivan approached nearer, the old lady was visible, leaning against the door at the front passenger seat. The slump of her body told me she was sad. Her grandson, Ashley, parked at the circle before Roth's stately home. Grandma got out and admired the green lawn, raising her head to peer at the breathtaking mansion, its gray brick shining in the bright sun.

She and Ashley followed Carla and me to the office, where Roth—seated at her desk—put down her book and rose. "Sit with your grandson. Taylor, bring Grandma a glass of the Biltmore Estate Cab."

Roth waited while Taylor brought the wine to Grandma, and she had set down her glass. "You have changed your mind and now plan to sell your farm. Is that true?"

The old lady glanced at Ashley. "My grandson a-wantin' me to sell. I don't."

Ashley, holding the Mountain Dew Taylor had brought him, stiffened beside her. "But Grandma, the farm's dilapidated. We're lucky to have a reasonable bid."

She took another sip of wine. "I can't sleep. All this pressure on an old lady. Don't want to sell—don't know what to do."

Ashley shook his head. "She were like this all day yesterday. She wanted to talk with you."

Roth waited before speaking. "Don and Carla are chasing the map. I can't guarantee they'll find it, but they're on a hot lead. I counsel you to delay taking the offer for your farm."

Ashley touched his temple while closing his eyes. "You don't know who has the map—much less where it is."

Roth wiggled an index finger at Ashley. "Do not underestimate Don. I admire his talents, notably tenacity, compassion, brute muscle, attractiveness to women, and a knack for completing complex tasks using his resourcefulness."

She paused for a moment. "Let me tell you an account of Don's ability. Once, he had nearly caught a villain when this man slipped away into the Blue Ridge Mountains. If he spent time bringing in backup, Don figured the murderer would vanish, and he, my right-hand man, took up the chase alone. Don hunted the fugitive for five days on foot in rugged mountain terrain. Don finally tracked down the man and captured him in a firefight."

Ashley scrunched his face in irritation. "He don't got no idea where the map is."

My boss shook her head and gazed at Ashley with regret. "In my experience, there are two sorts of detectives. Those that go into a case and investigate the usual suspects. The other type rams their way by rotating upside-down every clue."

Ashley went silent.

Roth turned to me. "Summarize your search."

I rubbed my chin while I organized my thoughts. "We established Jeremiah found the ancient map describing the hiding place of Waya's magnificent emerald. I suspect your neighbor, Sandford, and his drug gang murdered Jeremiah and took the map. Carla and I are searching for the gang's hideout."

Ashley was in my face. "Huntin' but haven't found. Treasure maps are the stuff dreams are made of."

Grandma drained her glass and turned to Taylor, who left the office and returned with the wine bottle. The old woman whispered, "Dreams. Yes," and wept.

Her son drank his Dew and shook his head. Roth, Carla, and I waited.

Roth delayed speaking until Grandma ceased sobbing. "Dreams? What dreams?"

Grandma whispered, "Once my family lived in a charming farmhouse, a gem. We had gorgeous grounds and parties and dances in da garden. People came from as far away as Asheville."

We leaned toward the old woman, straining to hear her soft voice.

Grandma removed her glasses and—using her dress hem—wiped away tears.

Her grandson leaned back in his chair and spread his arms in a surrender gesture. "She's done been this way. Brooding and dreaming about her childhood."

Staring at the mantle over the fireplace, Grandma whispered, "Once, my family meant something. We go back—ta our Nation's birth. My ancestor came over da sea as an indentured servant.

"He worked for seven years. Then he journeyed to da Western mountains. He married a Cherokee woman at da first of the Nineteenth Century.

"He done hunted for animal skins. Traded on da frontier. Helped Cherokee Indians build houses as da white man did."

She stopped whispering. Her body shuddered.

Ashley took the opportunity to quarrel. "Can't determine our decision built on an old heritage washed away like an eroding beach."

"If I sell da farm, what will I do?" Grandma asked. "Sit in a condominium and stare out da window—waste away and die. Today, in the home I grew up in, I'm happy to dream of my childhood days and search for a map, hunt fer my hope, bringing back the old family home.

"We used to have visitors in da garden. We done got no guests now, and bushes and da house be shabby. Franklin society looked up to my grandfather, but my grandson ain't got no status. I want to hand down a grand house fer my grandson."

She discontinued murmuring to wipe her glasses.

"We're out of money," Ashley said. "Can't wait any longer. I don't believe old dreams return to watch over the living."

"Not true," Grandma said. "We can last until the end of da year. Give them time to find the map." She blubbered.

Her final bout of sobbing seemed to break her son's doggedness. "Okay, Grandma. Let's chase a farmhouse in the air. We'll tell the lawyer we need more time to consider his offer."

Grandma got up to leave with her son.

Roth tapped her wine glass with a metal spoon. "Let me ask a question. I think I know the answer."

Holding Ashley's arm and beginning to leave, Grandma turned her head back toward Roth.

"When you were a child, did anyone say the pond had silted over?"

Grandma seemed puzzled. "Yes. I remember da old folk a-sayin' the water hole used to lay nearer da house, nearer da front steps."

Roth gave a deep gratifying sigh. "Did Ian have a secret hidey-hole on the farm? Did your family search there for the diagram to the gem's site?"

"That occurred to the family, and they searched da grounds long ago. Nothing."

Grandma stopped before leaving the office. "Can you find da map?"

Roth glanced at me. "We're close to finding where the map is," I said.

"We'll see tomorrow if we know its whereabouts or not."

29

CARLA FINDS THE GANG'S HIDEOUT, MACON COUNTY — MONDAY

I stood in the rays of the bright sun approaching its midday height and watched Carla, in her disguise, steer the Dodge Omni into Tooey's dirt parking lot. She paused while a few vehicles whirred past on the road in front of the restaurant. Leaving the car, she smiled gaily as if her mood mirrored the bright sunlight; indeed, she had seemed happy since her undercover success the previous day.

A crow cawed from the solitary tree in the parking area. Before speaking to the transmitter in her purse, Carla watched the bird fly away. Mickey and I observed Carla from the side street and listened to her through her purse transmitter. "There's no motorcycle in the restaurant's lot." She walked out of my sight, going through Tooey's front door into the building with its vinyl siding.

I got in Mickey's Ford Explorer to be comfortable listening to the receiver on the front seat.

"I'm at the same table as yesterday," Carla said in a low voice. "A waitress is strolling over to me."

"Welcome back, Honey. What can I get you?"

"Iced tea. I'm waiting for someone."

I leaned back in the passenger seat beside Mickey. "Think she'll get Joel to reveal the hideout's location."

Mickey chuckled. "She dressed for success."

"Carla caught my eye with her outfit," I said. "A one-size-too-small black tee shirt, a white jersey opened at the front, and black yoga pants."

"Blue-collar workers on stools at the bar," Carla said. "A man in white overalls is at a table, and two waitresses are taking orders."

I glanced over at Mickey. "Same tavern as this past Saturday."

I heard "Thump, thump, squee," from the bug Carla carried in her pouch.

"Oh, no," Carla whispered. "The waitress is losing her tray."

I heard, "Bang, bang, bang, yowl."

"What's that noise?" Mickey asked.

"The waitress spilled the tray and its beer pitchers," Carla said, "on the man in the white overalls."

I looked over at Mickey and laughed, whooping loudly. "Spilled beer—my kind of bar."

I heard the second waitress ask, "Are you drunk?" followed by the first server. "No. My grip slipped."

The target of our scam, Joel, roared up and parked in the bar's lot. He dismounted, carried his helmet, and jogged to the entrance. He wore the same boots, leather jacket, and jeans as the previous Saturday.

"Here's Joel," Carla said.

I heard footsteps growing louder.

"Ah'm glad to see you," Joel said.

"You missed the action," she said to Joel. "The waitress dropped a tray loaded with pitchers of beer."

"Yeah, ain't they funny?" Joel said. "Hey, Marie, reckon Ah want a pitcher."

"The sound from the purse transmitter is clear as a chime," Mickey said.

"Here comes your pitcher," Carla said.

"What'll you have?" the waitress asked.

"A red wine and a cheeseburger."

"Cook it medium?"

"Yes."

"All-rite, Ah'll have a cheeseburger too," Joel said.

We needed Joel to divulge the hideout's location. I had a feeling Carla, our lady in disguise could pull off this scam.

"Did you get an apartment?" Joel asked.

"Not yet. But I'm still searching."

"Screech." I thought Joel had moved his chair closer to Carla.

"You said you'd think about us going out."

Then the only sound coming over the bug was the background noise in the bar. I heard the waitress walking to the table. "Here is your wine." She walked away.

"Will you? Go out with me?" Joel asked.

"Joel's rushing it," Mickey said to me. "In the pangs of lust."

"We've just met," Carla said. "I don't want to get hurt."

Mickey whistled, long and low. "She's a natural performer. You've created a monster."

"That woman can sleuth for the truth," I said to Mickey.

"How you get hurt?" Joel asked.

"By hurrying a relationship. I don't know enough about you."

Mickey and I sat while the bug conveyed background noise.

"Like my working this past year at a cycle shop?"

"And?" Carla asked.

"And what?" Joel asked.

"What did you do before the shop?"

"Dropped out of high school in the tenth grade," Joel said. "Got in a little trouble before settling down."

I gave Mickey a thumbs-up. "She has him chattering like an early-morning crow."

I heard a waitress stride up, "Here are your cheeseburgers," and slip away.

"What trouble?" Carla asked.

"Robbed a diner. The sheriff's men caught us."

Joel was spilling his life's story.

"You poor thing," Carla said. "What happened next?"

"Ma friend and me got sent to juvenile detention. Court pitied us because it were our first offense, and we used a knife, not a gun."

Joel ordered another pitcher of beer.

"Rob and me got out at the same time. He returned to his family and church. I don't see him much."

The teenager drank his beer, "Gulp," and dropped the glass back on the table, "Clank."

"I began work at the motorcycle shop," Joel said. "Ah, and three friends dropped out of high school and all work at the cycle store."

"I feel I'm getting to know you," Carla said to the teenager. "Who got you the job? Family or church?"

"An old guy we met after school. Mr. Sandford. He gave me and ma three friends money and helped us."

I snapped my fingers in triumph. Carla had confirmed the suspected connection between the teens on motorcycles and our mountain man.

"Wow," Carla said. "What's he like?"

"He's cool," Joel said. "He's got long white hair and a stringy goatee. He's like my substitute dad."

"Is Sandford an old Macon County name?" Carla asked.

"Naw, Sandford's mother married twice," Joel said. "The old family name was Buckho."

I gave a wild-eyed look at Mickey. Was it that easy? Had she stumbled on the hideout?

"You and this Sandford are a foster family?" she asked Joel.

"Reckon we are," Joel said. "We stay at the old family farm. Like my two friends, we sleep there."

"Where does your third friend live?" Carla asked. "Didn't you say you have three?"

"Don't know. Ain't seen him lately."

"What does Sandford get out of helping you?"

"He's just a great guy."

"Must be more than that."

"We help with some of his projects. Sandford's a go-getter. He's going to be king of Franklin."

"What projects?"

"Ah reckon you know about me. How about we go out together?"

She had undoubtedly found the gang's hideout: the old Buckho farm. She just needed to untangle from Joel and exit Tooey's.

"Uh, where would we go?" Carla asked Joel.

"We'll go to McDonald's tonight. Ah'll ride my motorcycle. An' stop at Woodlawn Cemetery and read gravestones by moonlight."

"This kid has your approach to women," Mickey said.

I gave him my Gannon dirty glance by raising my eyebrow and showing a glassy stare.

She had finished her undercover job. She needed to leave before something went wrong. The door into the tavern kept opening and closing as the lunchtime crowd began arriving. I heard a rumble out on the road. A cycle pulled up and parked next to Joel's. The newcomer pulled off his helmet. This second rider—in black boots, leather jacket, and jeans—had a red bandana around his head. He was familiar. I recognized Eric, who knew Carla as an investigator, back when Hound tore the cycle shop apart, searching for papers with Sandford's name. The newcomer went inside the tavern.

The background noise in Tooey's had increased with the midday crowd. I heard the front door slam as Eric entered.

Joel said, "Here comes ma friend, Eric."

I heard someone shift a chair. "Screech."

"This here is Eric," Joel said. "Eric, this is my woman, Rosa."

How could she avoid exposure as a fraud? Would Joel and Eric become violent once they realized who Carla was?

There was the sound of someone walking near the table. The noise of hard objects falling followed. One of the waitresses shrieked, "Hell." Tooey's crowd shouted and hooted, and furniture crashed to the floor.

"Did someone drop another tray holding beer pitchers?" I asked.

My partner turned and opened his vehicle door as if to exit. "Do we go and yank her out?" he asked.

"Wait," I said.

Abruptly, Carla rushed from the restaurant, jumped in the Dodge Omni, and charged out of the parking lot. The two young men followed her out, gesturing and yelling at her departing car.

# # #

Fifteen minutes later, she returned to the side street, where we waited for her. "Could you hear? Sandford and his gang have a family farm, Buckho."

"Yes. I heard and called Bruce. He's searching for Buckho in the real estate records for Macon County."

Carla wiped some moisture off her forehead with her palm. "How was I?"

She took a position in the rear as I sat in Mickey's Ford Explorer's front passenger seat. "You are one talented lady detective."

Mickey asked Carla, "Did the second teenager recognize you?"

"I think not. What'll we do next? I'm dying to snoop the hideout."

She wanted to rush into action. "Slow down," I said. "Explain the noise and shouting before you ran out of Tooey's."

"I recognized Eric's red bandana," she said.

"He knew you?"

"He didn't get a clear sight of me because he bent under the table to put his helmet on the floor."

"And the sudden disturbance?"

She smirked. "Marie, one of the waitresses, walked past the table carrying a tray of beer pitchers. I jumped upright, toppling the tray, dumping liquid over my head, and drenching myself.

"Turning my back in Eric's direction, I knelt on the floor and tugged my white pullover round my head to towel my hair and cover my face. I clutched my purse and scampered for the door.

"Joel shadowed me to the door, grabbing napkins out of the table dispensers as he went. He patted my head with paper to dry it and—I realized—also patted my right breast through my tee shirt. I hopped in my car and drove away."

Carla had come of age as a PI. She had uncovered a valuable clue, Sandford's hideout location. In taking our next steps into the murderers' hideaway, we would go super-cautious.

30

ROTH PLANS THE HIKE TO GANG HIDEOUT – MONDAY

I leaned back in my chair and sipped my afternoon coffee. After a lunch of cornbread, roast pork with stuffed apples, and lemon curd, Taylor began stacking plates and carried them from the patio in front of the mansion—where she had served lunch—back to the kitchen cabinets and the dishwasher. We—Carla, Bruce, Mickey, Grandma, Ashley, and I—gathered around Roth. She narrated Carla's portrayal of a woman wooing the motorcycle teenager, culminating with how she had unearthed the location of Sandford's hideout, the Buckho farm.

Grandma, holding her glass of red, was delighted. She said, "I reckon you'ns the smartest of these young'uns. You done plum good."

Carla's eyes twinkled. "I may be even trickier acting than in actual life."

Grandma clutched Carla's arm. "Now we have to be quick. Have to get the sheriff's office into de hideaway."

Roth raised one side of her mouth, ignored Grandma, and slid her plate to the side. "The purpose of our gathering is twofold: to discuss what we know about the Buckho and to formulate a strategy to approach its environs without detection."

The old lady kept talking. "Don't wait. Let's hit it at once."

My boss wrinkled her nose and turned her head toward Bruce. "What have you ascertained about the farm?"

Grandma continued. "We McDonalds go back for a long time. Thar been Buckhoes in da hills all dat time."

Roth made a coaxing motion toward Bruce with her hand.

"Boss, I've found,"—Bruce began spreading maps on the patio table—"a good bit of information on these maps."

I rose and moved toward a chair nearer the maps on the wrought-iron table. Just before I got to the chair, scrawny Grandma dashed in from my right side and took the chair.

Bruce stood and pointed at one plot. "The farm done been in the Buckho family for generations. Last Buckho died in 1990. De deed's in trust."

By bracing her arms on the table and pushing up, Grandma, being a shorty, could see the documents. "We'uns need to get in there directly."

I interrupted Bruce. "Let me guess. The trust lawyer is Dave Patski, the gang's attorney who's trying to buy the McDonald farm."

Bruce flipped through his pile of papers. "Guy, you're right. Patski done the trust."

Roth tapped her fingers on the patio's wrought iron table. Then, she spoke directly to Grandma. "Slow down. You have good instincts, but we can get into trouble rushing into this Buckho farm."

Carla spoke. "How did Sandford come to have this farm, this hideout?"

Bruce searched through his documents on the table. "Sandford's mother married a man named Buckho, who owned the land. Sandford eventually inherited it, and he put the property in the trust. Guess he didn't plan to plant crops."

After glancing around the room for questions, Bruce continued. "Guys, the farm is in the woods. Near the border between North Carolina and Georgia. There's a single driveway to the front of the house."

"Nearby neighbors?" Mickey asked.

Bruce pulled out one of the maps and stuck his finger on it. "No one. It's isolated. No wonder the sheriff's office hadn't located the gang's lair."

Grandma stood, searching for Taylor. "We'uns just jawin'. If we'uns had already told the sheriff's office, they might-could be there."

I scanned the map where Bruce pointed. The forest had reclaimed much of the farm. Proceeding to the farmhouse via the driveway would be clear-cut but alert the gang. Hiking to the hideout from the rear would be arduous but could be done in stealth. The farm backed onto a US national forest.

"I seed my farmhouse grow more wretched each year," Grandma said. "I need the map to dig up the emerald to holt back this decay. Get to da hideout now."

After five minutes of studying maps, the group turned to Roth. "Where did you get these plots?" she asked.

"They're United States Geological Survey and road-atlas maps, Boss. I went to the Macon County Register of Deeds in Franklin to get information. Thar records date back to the early 1800s."

Roth perused the documents on her desk. "How do we approach the farm, to spy on who's there? Sandford and his teenage gang could attack us if we entered by a single road. The gang could have a CCTV and a gate on the driveway—probably do."

Ashley opened his eyes wide. "Grandma's right. It doesn't matter. Let's charge straight down the road tonight and get the treasure map."

Grandma jumped up, blocking my view of everything at Roth's end of the table. "I ain't afeared. I left my gun back at the farmhouse. Give me a shooting gun, an' I'll go." Her white hair and wrinkled face bobbed up and down at those seated around the table.

Roth shook her head. "When an undisciplined man rushes in to fail, he always declares he had no time. We will plan. Show me what's in the space behind the Buckho Farm."

The old lady, slowly shaking her head, appeared disappointed Roth had ignored her counsel. She seemed to think entering the road carried a low risk. I dreaded the gang would kill one or more of my friends if we charged in the front way.

"Boss, the big area behind the farm is the Nantahala National Forest."

Roth scrutinized the maps. "Are these lines roads through the park?"

Bruce answered. "Yes, Boss."

My boss took out a magnifying glass to study the map. "The *X* is the Buckho farm?"

He nodded.

The room went quiet while she squinted at the area enclosing the Nantahala and the Buckho farm.

"There is no road from the park to the Buckho farm."

"Dat right, Boss. Likely thick forest."

Roth checked the map scales and placed a ruler on two of the maps to estimate distances. "I assess it's about four miles from the farmhouse to the park road. Approximately correct?"

After five minutes of computing distances on the maps, we agreed four miles represented a reasonable estimate.

Roth pursed her lips. "Don, how much time would it take to walk from the park road to the farm?"

Ashley gave a dismissive wave of his hand. "It's too difficult. There ain't a trail—"

"Hush," Roth barked. "I asked Don."

I brushed down my cowlick and studied the maps. "Hikers in the Smokies travel about one and a half miles an hour. They follow a trail."

My boss waited.

"Without a trail, it might take an hour to go one mile—or four hours to go the four miles."

Roth tapped on the table as if impatient. "Could we drive to the park, leave the vehicle, and approach the farm by walking in from the rear?"

Ashley objected. "To hit the Buckho farm is a success. To wait is to invite failure."

Roth appeared exasperated with a stiff posture and rigid jaw. "If the sheriff's deputies rush in and wreck everything, it'll take a miracle to find the map. Miracles are low probability events."

Mickey waved his hand to catch our attention. "Can't leave a car overnight in the park."

My boss cupped her chin with a hand. "One person drives into the park, drops off two or three hikers, and drives out. The drop-offs walk to the hideout."

I thought about her strategy. Necessary to get a park permit for overnight hiking in the backcountry. Best to begin walking in daylight and creep up on the farm at nightfall. Sunset would arrive around eight-thirty. We'd have to cross a stream—could be swollen now.

Grandma spoke up. "This are wrong. We oughta tell Lieutenant Hound."

Roth leaned back in her chair, pulled her black headscarf away from her head, and ran her hand over her shoulder-length white hair. "I'd like to know who's at the farm before we tell the sheriff's office. Once we know it's the gang's hideout, we tell the authorities."

She turned to Mickey. "What do you think?"

Mickey thought a moment. "Mobile phone might not work in the park."

She turned to Bruce. "Can you set up a way to converse in the park?"

"I'll assemble a portable Citizen Band Radio for short-range communication dat send a signal for ten miles or more. Idn' hard to take it in and out on the hike."

"Make it happen."

Bruce left the room to set up the portable CB.

"We'll meet tomorrow afternoon to review our plan and preparations," Roth said.

During the meeting, Carla had stayed quiet. Now, she began to fidget, brushing a few loose strands of her ponytail off her face. "Who hikes into the woods?"

"Mickey and Don. Bruce will drive the Jeep and monitor the CB."

Silence.

"Any questions?" Roth asked.

Carla turned to me. "Can I go with you? It'd be a beneficial experience."

I squinted at Roth. She nodded. "Yeah. You found the farm. You can come with us."

Grandma finished the wine in her glass. "I'm aimin' to go."

We all shouted, "No," at once.

My boss began to gather the maps into a single pile on her table. "Prepare. We finish preparations tomorrow and you kick-off for the Buckho farm in the afternoon."

# # #

The next morning, I worked at my desk, updating the case file with the information written in my notepad. From my days in the military police, I had learned to document my assignments. Afterward, I searched for Carla. Looking through the exercise room and the media room and finding no one, I located Taylor cooking away in the kitchen-dining area. "Hey there. Where's Carla?"

Taylor turned from her stove. "Howdy. I heared Carla a-usin' her brains yesterday. And she a-workin' with you'ns rite well."

"Yeah. She's great. Where is she?"

Taylor raised her left eyebrow, an expression of disapproval. "You'ns would've done differently."

"How so? Where's Carla?"

"You'ns would have beat that motorcyclist to a pulp and grilled him about his hideout."

I nodded and subconsciously tracked the scar on my left cheek.

"She's a little-touched cause she's fond of you. I don't know why. You'ns never grown up."

I kept nodding. "Aha. I'm looking for her."

"And don't you be a-sneakin' into Carla's room at night. Ms. Roth wants her investigators a-solvin' cases, not a-frolickin' in the hallway."

It always seemed eccentric to have this attractive woman, who was our chef, lecturing me as a mother would. "I just want to know where she is."

Taylor turned away from me. "At the pond here at the mansion." She busied herself at the stove as I headed for the patio door to the outside. "Don't be deef to me. Be good to her."

"Umm, *deef*?

"You know, means you ain't a-hearin' me."

# # #

On the pond's bank, I found Carla reclining on a blanket. In blue stretch pants and a white tee shirt, she appeared stunning. She had chosen a place in the sun, whereas trees blocked the sun's rays on the opposite bank. The pond and stream stood behind and to the side of the mansion. While waiting on Carla to spot me, I glanced around. My eyes noted the two-story wooden guesthouse standing beyond the water. Taylor and Mickey resided in the latter structure and not the main building.

I walked up to my partner. "Hi."

Carla appeared serene and said, "Hi yourself."

"Whatcha doin'?"

"Relaxing." Carla patted a space beside her on the blanket. "I was good at Tooey's, wasn't I?"

I sat down. "You found the hideout."

She lay back on the blanket. "We make a good team, don't we?"

"Yeah, you don't seem like a gruff PI. I do, and that puts people on guard. You're quick as a lizard's tongue—"

She closed her eyes. "Ugh. Please find another metaphor. May I suggest quick as a monarch butterfly?"

I beamed.

Carla leaned against me. "Tell me. Does Ms. Roth approve mixing work and play?"

Where was this female's mind heading? Always difficult for me to figure, and especially so with this woman. "What do you mean?"

Carla smirked at me. "You know what play is. It's like when you fed me pizza and beer and lewdly dragged me up on that mountain."

I reacted as best I could. "Why does Roth have to approve? What she doesn't know won't hurt her."

Carla shook her head at a snail's pace. "She knows. Everyone in this mansion knows. Does Ms. Roth allow—how would Taylor say it—hanky-panky?"

As my Hispanic beauty locked her eyes on me, I hesitated. "What do you want me to say?"

"Will she reprimand us?"

I shut and opened my mouth and said, "PI couples succeed because they share equally in snooping for the truth in an investigation. Roth will wait and see."

My words seemed to satisfy Carla. She reached and clasped my hand. "I savor the joy of solving a mystery. I enjoy teaming up with you."

I sat beside her and nodded.

"Do you think our mentor/worker connection would break down if we fall into a relationship?"

She thought about affairs far more than I did. "We get along."

She kept dwelling on the situation. "What if we argued?"

"I may mentor you, but Roth is your boss. I quarrel with Bruce and Mickey, but disagreements pass, and we work together."

I nestled beside Carla. "I like playing with you, and—when you're investigating, you bust the bronco."

She raised her eyes to the sky in annoyance. "Don, where do you get your horrible metaphors?"

I felt hurt. "I know. You're smooth-tongued, and I'm tongue-tied."

Carla cuddled my arm. "Oh, I don't know. You can be funny." She winked.

I rolled onto petite Carla.

She glanced at the mansion. "People can see us. We look like . . . like . . . let me think. You would pick two sumo wrestlers."

She stood and gathered up her blanket. "Come with me." She walked toward the guesthouse.

I followed. "Where're we going?"

"Taylor gave me the spare key to the guesthouse." Carla gave me her mega-bright smile and mischievous grin.

I followed her into the guest cottage.

# # #

Carla sat beside me in the media room. "How do I dress for the hike tomorrow?"

I thought about where to begin. "In May in Macon County, the average high is seventy-four degrees Fahrenheit and the low forty-eight—don't expect snow. Wear layers of clothes to stay warm. Dark outer garments."

Carla grabbed her detective's notepad and began writing.

"You want a lightweight sneaker for a shoe, like a moccasin. Need leather gloves, a water bottle, and a Kukri long-blade knife. We'll get you a pair of shin guards, to protect your legs—when you bump into a tree."

She scribbled. "Do I pack a gun?"

"Mickey and I have concealed weapon permits. We'll carry pistols. Any danger, we leave, not fight."

She continued scribbling. "Won't we get lost in the night?"

"If the GPS works, we're okay. If not, we use a compass. The side of a tree with the most branches and leaves faces south, and moss, if any, grows on the north side."

She glanced at me a moment. "Do I spread black grease on my face?"

Mickey chuckled from an adjacent chair. "Makes Don look better."

"You can. Bruce, who's naturally dark, always laughs at me when I do that. You could wear a black balaclava and put your ponytail in a bun."

Carla started notes on another sheet of her notepad.

"You're light on your feet, but I'll show you a quiet-walking technique in the woods." I stretched my legs out beside her. "Bend your knees. Walk always with bent knees."

She stood and bent her knees.

I demonstrated. "Put the outer part of your forefoot down first. Slow. Rollover to the inside edge of the forefoot."

She watched my foot as I demonstrated.

"Last. Slowly drop down the heel."

Carla nodded at me. "I'll practice at the mansion. I'll walk across the room. You can tell me if I'm doing it right."

"Okay. And once you've got the soft walk, you'll have magnificent silence. Soon we'll hike into the forest to scout the farm."

"We've made a lot of assumptions, haven't we?"

"We have, and we don't know if they're right. From now on, we have to be careful and watchful."

I felt happy. My office and fellow workforce were like my home and family. The eccentric boss led well and nurtured her people. Taylor was energetic, smart, and dedicated to those around her. I adored bright Carla with her bodacious body. Bruce and Mickey were good buddies. Overall, I enjoyed working with this one-off group.

Life is good, I thought. Today had been planning and fun and games. Tomorrow we would hike through the woods and swap the known for the unknown.

31

PREPARATION FOR THE HIKE — TUESDAY

To be on the hunt is life. Waiting is chafing. The next morning in the basement, Bruce and Mickey organized equipment and clothing to scout the hideout that night. Backpacks and gear lay about the room. I watched Bruce show three portable CB radios to Roth and Carla. "Mickey and I tested dese mobile units. Guys, dey are good for about ten miles. De range be less in a valley and better on a hill."

Roth wiggled one of the sets to gauge its lightweight. "Why three?"

Bruce lay down his radio. "I'll stay at a motel with a CB. Mickey and Don will carry one as they enter the Buckho farmland, Carla will remain behind as a lookout with the third CB."

My boss gave a crisp nod. "What if the motorcycle gang also has a CB radio?"

"That far back in the woods, they probably use a satellite dish to stay in contact, not a CB radio."

Roth took in a deep breath. "Are you ready?"

Bruce ran his hand through his corkscrew curls. "Yes, Boss."

"Acceptable."

She turned to Carla, who had just returned from the national park with me. "Report."

Carla pulled a notepad out of a small courier bag. She was getting to be quite the detective. "We drove to the Nantahala National Forest. There's parking on the side of the park road at the point closest to the farm. Also, I purchased an overnight permit to stay and hike in the park."

Carla reached into her purse, drew out a plastic card, and handed it to Bruce. "We have a week's reservation at a motel near the park. Here's the card to enter the room."

Bruce spoke up. "I'll remain dere to monitor de other two CB radios and keep in contact with you, Ms. Roth."

"Acceptable." Roth turned to Mickey. "Your activities?"

"We have to cross the water. I'll wade through the stream at a shallow point. Connect a rope over water to trees—we pull ourselves across on the line."

Roth turned to Carla and next back to Mickey. "Has Carla crossed a stream on a rope?"

"No. But we won't let her drown."

Roth nodded and said to me, "Are we ready?"

"Yeah. We are."

"Acceptable." She then called Taylor on the mansion intercom. "Please bring coffee and tea to the basement." Roth cupped her hand around her chin as if considering. "Don, I assume Lieutenant Hound knows Carla and you are roaming around his county. Are you touching base with him?"

I was frustrated with waiting, holding my fists tight, and digging my fingernails into my palms. Needed to keep my feelings in check and not speak without thought, leading to regretting what I said. My boss was nervous, micromanaging everyone. Why wouldn't she stop badgering? "Hound called this morning. He wanted me to drop by the Sheriff's Office. I begged off by telling him I expected to have a substantial lead soon."

Roth tapped the top of a workbench. "You've got maybe twenty-four hours until he demands to know what you're doing." She gave me a contemplative stare. "Tell me about the fine points of hiking to the farm."

Taylor brought a refreshment tray down to the basement. Mickey grabbed a handful of cookies.

I worked to calm myself, pushing down on my cowlick and rubbing my temple. Why didn't Roth just relax? "If we come in from the rear, we'll avoid most detection devices, but not a dog. Numerous farms have a canine—"

She stopped drinking her coffee. "And."

I clasped my hands together and stared at the basement wall. "In the daytime, I'd expect breezes to blow from the valley—where the hideout is—up towards the mountains. We'd be downwind from a dog hiking in during the day. At night, I'd expect breezes to travel downhill towards the valley and the dog."

"Any dog would catch your scent at night?"

Beside me, Carla furrowed her eyebrows. "Can't you toss sausages—with a drug inside—to the dog?"

I shook my head. "Maybe, but what if the dog had been taught not to take food from a prowler? What if the canine had been fed and had a fierce loyalty to its owner?"

Carla was inquisitive. "So what do we do if they have a dog?" Her question was reasonable.

"A dog has a strong sense of smell," I said. "But it picks up scents close to the ground. When we are high on the hill behind the farm, any dog might not locate us."

"Won't the dog smell us when we go down into the valley?"

I reached down and pulled a short, basic rifle out of my backpack. "I'll carry an air rifle with a tranquilizer dart. I'll knock out a medium-sized dog in under fifteen minutes."

Carla scowled as if thinking about what I had disclosed.

I put the rifle back in my backpack. "We have three hikers, water—"

The house phone rang in the basement. Roth answered and listened for a moment. "Grandma, it's good to hear your voice. I'm putting you on speakerphone."

"Dat lawyer—Patski—called. If I sell within three days, we pick up a one-time, ten percent increase in da payment for our farm. Ashley wants to sell."

Roth locked eyes with me and spoke with Grandma. "We're ready to search for the map at the gang's hideout. Wait and see if we secure the map."

Silence.

"I want—more than anything—ta keep the farm. Dat land been my life and my parents' life."

My body was full of frustration, my jaws clenching. The old lady needed to calm down and trust us.

"Sorry, I had ta adjust my glasses. I'll wait before selling. You gotta find de map."

"We'll keep you informed," Roth said. "What's happening at your farm?"

"Dem workers drilled holes along da banks of the stream. Dug up a passel of dirt. Angela done found the first pond, from the early eighteen-hundreds."

Roth and Grandma disconnected the call. Roth kept quizzing me. Why wouldn't she stop? "What else did you do for the night hike?"

I held up a flashlight. "Mickey, Carla, and I will carry two flashlights each and extra batteries. To see at night, we'll use a filter, so the torch illuminates with infrared light. Lastly, tonight is close to a full moon, and the weather forecast calls for no rain."

"You're saying you can hike in tonight?"

I took a moment to chill, rocking back and forth, and go over a checklist in my head. "Yeah. See how far we get."

Roth gave me a thumbs-up. "You have the known down pat. Go ahead and find out about the unknown."

32

HIKE TO GANG HIDEOUT — WEDNESDAY

Riding along in the late afternoon in Bruce's Jeep, I watched the lush greenery slide past on the gentle mountain slopes stretching for miles. In my mind, I once more reviewed the inventory of equipment we carried for our excursion. We had everything. *Sandford, you took Ian's map. I'm getting it back.*

"What is this rolled-up bedding beside me?" Carla asked.

I glanced over at Carla, sitting beside me in the second row of seating. Bruce replied from the driver's seat. "Three sleeping bags. Each of you sticks one on your rucksack. The temperature's going down to forty-five degrees tonight."

She grabbed one of the rolled-up bags. "I guess we planned for everything."

My mind recalled Carla was inexperienced in some areas, as I let a broad grin form on my lips. "I remember some of my grandfather and grandmother's vacations. Preparation broke down as soon as they hit the road, and then they winged it."

Bruce drove into the Nantahala National Forest; he kept watching the odometer and pulled to the side of the park road when he estimated the farm lay directly north of us. Carla, Mickey, and I exited the vehicle and put on our rucksacks. I helped Carla adjust her straps and gear.

At five o'clock in the afternoon, Bruce started his vehicle. "Guys, I'm off to the Quality Inn and Suites Robbinsville. When you get to the farm, call me on the CB radio, and we'll coordinate."

Mickey, grasping a hiking stick, led us away from the road and into the woods. "Dusk starts at eight-thirty. We want to cross the stream by then."

Walking through the woods, I heard leaves crushing under our feet. The forest floor, littered with leaves from the past winter, lacked the quietness of a cleared path. Trees, some with thick trunks and some with narrow ones, and bushes surrounded us. Branches brushed against my goggles.

Mickey took the first position in line. After using his compass to determine the direction, he headed north. "We'll take short breaks but keep going."

I was third in line. After a while, I asked, "Carla, is the pace right for you?"

"I'm fine. Just have to take more steps than you big boys."

I checked my mobile phone and found I had no signal. I tried the CB radio. "Bruce, got your ears on?"

"Guys, I'm at the motel. Over."

"We're moving at a good pace. Over and out."

Mickey raised his right hand above his shoulder, and our line stopped. He checked his compass and slightly adjusted the direction of our hike.

Carla slid her green backpack off her shoulders. "Are we making too much noise?"

I kneeled beside her. "Not a problem. Forest animals will hear us and scamper away. We'll go quiet when we're closer to the farm."

Carla and I stood and followed Mickey, who used his Kukri long blade knife to remove a thick interlocking of branches. With the trail cleared, Mickey hammered eight-inch yellow wooden stakes in the ground to mark our path.

"How far have we gone?" Carla asked.

Mickey glanced over his shoulder. "About half a mile."

Carla turned her head toward me. "How does he know?"

I felt a low branch bang against my shin guard. "Mickey has a mechanical pedometer to count steps, to measure approximate distance."

Mickey raised his right hand, stopped the line, and turned to Carla. "Going too fast?"

Carla shook her head. "I'm keeping up. Don't pamper me."

A little later, Mickey studied his compass, pedometer, and watch. "Roughly a mile in an hour. Ready?" Off we went again into the thick greenery.

Minutes later, Carla asked, "What's making that sound?"

I listened and heard animals rustling through the brush and birds in the trees. There was a clicking, followed by a harsh—*Jaay!—Jaay!*

"That's a bird," I said. "A blue jay."

Our noiseless line stepped forward, following Mickey.

Later, Mickey held up his right hand and again checked his compass. Afterward, he continued in the same direction. "The sun's going down."

Mickey pushed ahead as if still intending to locate the stream and cross it before the last light of the day disappeared.

He hacked his way through more thicket with his knife. After another fifteen minutes, he stopped again to listen.

Carla spoke up in front of me. "I hear running water."

I heard it too. Mickey continued walking. We broke into the open along the bank of the stream.

Carla stepped up to the stream bank. "Water looks deep."

Mickey stuck his hiking staff into the stream. "Knee-deep. I can cross, but we'll keep scanning."

He tossed a tree branch in the current and, as he walked along the bank's edge, easily held even with it. "Think it's slow enough for us to cross here."

Carla pointed across the stream. "Are we going over here?"

I kept walking along the bank. "Not yet. I think Mickey wants a shallow area where the water slows and thick trees stand close to the banks on both sides of the stream."

She pointed at the stream. "I see the rocks in the water. Can't we walk across on them?"

"Could slip off and fall in the water," I said. "We want to avoid a severe sprain or a broken leg."

Mickey stopped and considered the bank on both sides. "One tree here and another directly across the stream, opposite each other. We cross here."

We grabbed rope and two pulleys out of our backpacks. I attached a pulley to a tree on our side of the stream. Mickey and I each pulled a cable out of our rucksacks. Mickey tied the end of one line to the tree on our side of the water. I ran my line through the pulley and handed the two ends of the cable to Mickey.

Mickey took off his shoes and socks, rolled up his pants, and walked across the stream leaning on his walking staff. He carried the three ends of the ropes to the other side and sat to dry his feet. I watched Mickey tie the single rope end to a tree on the stream's other side.

"Are you ready to cross?" I asked Carla.

"And why wouldn't I be?" She pulled herself over the water on top of the rope with her stomach pressing down on the cord. One of her legs hung down toward the stream; the foot on the opposite leg hooked over the top of the line. She had crossed and was dry.

Mickey attached a pulley to the second tree. We had affixed pulleys to both trees. Mickey cut and clamped both ends of the second rope, forming it into a circular cable going through the two pulleys.

I put a rucksack on the circular line. Mickey pulled the backpack over the stream and took it off the line. After we had all three packs on the opposite side of the water, I crossed on the rope tied between the two trees. We left the cables and pulleys on the two trees for our return trip to where Bruce would pick us up.

Before leaving the stream bank, I viewed the horizon and saw the blue of the sky over the top of the dark forest.

Mickey studied his compass and afterward led the way into the woods.

After a while, Carla said, "Getting dark now."

When he couldn't see where he walked, Mickey shined his flashlight with the red filter on the ground. He whispered, "Stop."

I rested while Mickey checked his pedometer and compass. He nudged Carla's shoulder and pointed. Deer had their flanks and backs turned toward us, deer with small antlers, long legs, sleek bodies, and long tails.

As we continued hiking, I noticed Carla's face getting red. "Mickey, we better slow down to let Carla get her breath."

"No, you don't. I'm all right."

I persisted. "You're getting red in the face."

"And I hear you behind me huffing and puffing. We don't need to stop."

Mickey regarded us over his shoulder and whispered to himself, "Umm."

I was rapidly becoming an expendable mentor. I shut my mouth.

"What's making that sound?" Carla asked several minutes later. The recurring katydid chorus sounded—*Katydid!*—*Katydidn't.*

"The katydid, also known as a long-horned grasshopper," I said.

Carla aimed a glare at me. "Are you joshin' me?"

My role as a wise mentor was over.

After another hour had passed, Mickey checked his compass and pedometer. "Hard to tell. Think we've gone about six miles up and down—maybe four straight-line miles like on a map."

Carla was scarlet in the face. She sat and leaned against a tree. "Where's the farm?"

Mickey rotated his head back to study the sky. "Have to find it."

"How?"

"Hopefully, it's nearby."

"And?"

"We search for a glow of light. Forest animals don't light up the woods at night."

Carla searched around. "I see dark. Don't see any blaze of brightness."

"You have to be higher up," Mickey said.

"How do we do that?" Carla asked.

Mickey glanced over Carla's shoulder at me. "Just so happens, we have a climber in our midst."

I ran my flashlight beam over the nearby deciduous trees and located a tree with branches at least half a foot in diameter. After checking for dead limbs around the trunk, I reached the lowest branch with one hand, wrapped my other arm around the tree, and climbed to the first branch. Next, I went up the tree, gripping the limbs close to the tree. I stopped near the top where the tree had shrunk to six inches in diameter. My eyes scanned over the forest treetops, watching for a light glow in the distance, and found it, which seemed below me as if the land veered downward from where we were. I relayed the direction of the glow to Mickey.

Mickey used his compass to align with the light, and we three set off. Sure enough, the ground sloped downwards. After half an hour of marching, my eyes again spied the illumination from the farmhouse ahead of us.

I tapped Carla's shoulder. "Begin silent walking."

My next move was to fire up the CB. "Bruce, got your ears on?"

"I hear you, Don. Over."

A branch smacked my goggles, and I switched the CB to my opposite hand. "We've pinpointed the farm. ETA in half an hour."

"Guys, I'll phone the boss. Over and out."

The trees ended about a soccer field distance behind the farmhouse. The farm's fields had small shrubs beginning to grow. Sheltered behind an outcropping of rock among the trees, we trained binoculars on the farmstead.

Beside me, Carla whispered. "Lights on in the house."

I crouched and stared over the rocks. "I see a doghouse and food bowl—under the overhead light back of the house."

She whispered again. "What's that grunting sound?"

Mickey raised his head to listen. "That's a pigpen. There beside the red barn."

She kept asking questions. "What's in the small white structure? Chickens?"

"Yeah," I said. "The gang's asleep now."

Carla glanced at the farmhouse. "These motorcycle guys raise chickens and hogs?"

I slipped off my backpack. "They must have grown up in a farming family. Used to raise animals. But they don't want to till any fields."

Mickey raised his head. "What's in the barn?"

I glanced over Carla's back. "I'm thinking of motorcycles."

The occupants turned off the house lights. Carla contacted Bruce to confirm our procedure. "Bruce, we observe tonight. Two of us rest in sleeping bags, and one watches. We rotate the watcher every four hours."

"Guys, I'll inform da Boss and stand by in dis motel room."

# # #

Sunrise came about six-fifteen. An hour later, a German shepherd appeared in the yard, one teenager, Joel, gathered eggs, and a second teenager, Eric, fed the dog. The hogs woke up and grunted oinks.

"The dog doesn't know we're here," Carla said.

"We're back from the house and higher and there's not much wind," Mickey said.

The two teenagers pushed motorcycles from the barn and mounted them. Sandford came out in his porkpie hat, changed his hat for a helmet, and got on the rear seat of one of the motorcycles. They drove away up the driveway at nine o'clock, leaving only the dog at home.

After a quarter-hour had passed, Mickey stepped out of the tree line and shouted at the dog. Alerted, it ran at Mickey. He scampered up onto the stone outcropping and grabbed his hiking staff. The German shepherd, snarling, attempted to clamber up the ledge. With his wooden staff, Mickey whacked the dog on the head.

I shot a dart into the dog's side. It yelped and scampered away. Ten minutes later, it was unconscious. Mickey and I put a muzzle on the dog and tied it to its doghouse.

Carla watched the road leading into the farm, ready to warn Mickey and me if a motorcycle returned.

We found the farmhouse doors locked, but the gang had left a side window ajar.

"No one here," I said. "But there're many places to hide a map." Inside the farmhouse, I went through a study exploring for a diagram to the gem—found nothing. I tried to leave objects and papers in their original positions.

Mickey went into the living room. "Monitors for a CCTV system, and"—he turned on the system—"the cameras face the driveway."

"Good to know," I said

"Been an hour," Mickey said. "Let's check the other rooms."

I entered a bedroom, explored for papers, but found none. A trashcan held bandages, with smears of dried blood.

In the kitchen, Mickey eyed donuts on a counter. I caught his eyes and said, "No."

Following two hours in the house, we left by the rear door. Mickey shook his head. "They could have hidden the map anywhere."

I nodded. "Sandford could even be carrying the map."

We circled the barn and found the happy hogs enclosed in a corral built of steel posts with steel mesh wire surrounding the border. Mud, trash, and grunting hogs jammed the inside. "Sure are happy creatures," I said, holding my nose.

Mickey remained silent and stared at one of the hogs. "What is that pig eating?"

I leaned over the fence to see better. "It's a long bone, probably an animal bone."

The object shifted in the hog's mouth. "No, that's human. Could be an arm bone."

Mickey moved around the enclosure to another hog. "The bones in this one's mouth are like fingers. Human."

"Sweet Jeezus," I said. "This farm is a death camp." I was startled, and shortly I would become panicked.

33

ROTH GIVES HIDEOUT LOCATION TO THE HOUND — THURSDAY

I stood by the pigpen, motionless, like that moment when your traffic lane abruptly stops because of a car crash farther ahead of you. I cringed, my lungs gasping for air, and my chin and lips trembling at the sight of the pig chewing on a long human bone. Someone had tossed a human body to the hogs, which spawned a horror inside that the straightforward shooting of Jeremiah and Talk had not. What savage fiends were these? I turned toward Mickey, fought back the urge to upchuck, and glanced away toward the sky and the rising sun.

"Motorcycles coming," Carla's voice screeched from my CB. I jumped. "Get out!"

Mickey and I clutched our equipment and ran away from the pen; we ran across the field, heading toward the rock outcropping in the woods. I remembered. "The dog!" Adrenalin gushed into my blood. Panic took my breath, bursting in and out, steering me to look all about, above all behind me.

We spun sideways and sprinted to the doghouse. We couldn't leave the muzzle on the dog. That would reveal we had entered the house. As we flew, I slid the air gun from over my shoulder. Mickey, muscular and hefty, ran as a rhinoceros with sturdy thuds, covering the ground at a steady pace. He grabbed the rope restraining the German shepherd and released its muzzle strap. After I shot the dog with an anesthetizing dart, it yelped and limped away.

"The dog shook the dart onto the ground," I said.

"Forget it," Mickey said. "Run."

Dashing across the field again, I heard two motorcycles nearing the house. If they saw us now, a nightmare would shower down on my head. I reached the tree line in a frenzy, taking great gulps of air and feeling sweat dribbling down my back along my spine. I found Carla lying prone behind the ledge, gazing through her binoculars at the building. She gave an impression of unruffled serenity.

Carla jerked her head up from the binoculars, whipping her ponytail around her head. "They're at the front of the house—didn't see you."

We observed the house for half an hour. The motion around the farmhouse was orderly, with sounds of lunch preparation and the sight of Eric going out to the chicken house and back. It seemed we had escaped exposure. We gathered our rucksacks and trekked back through the woods. Bruce gathered us at the park and went back to Asheville.

# # #

My mind was trashed, wanting to be in bed and not get up. The scene with the hogs had made me sick, causing me to spit, cough, and throw up. I had to find the energy to brief my boss. I couldn't sit down because I wouldn't get back up again. In her office, I summarized the hike and search of the farmhouse for Roth. She stared at the ceiling and tapped her fingers on her desk. After a few minutes, she asked, "How did Carla do?"

I felt pride for Carla. "She kept up. She's a trouper. A little bossy."

Roth adjusted a sheer charcoal scarf wrapped around her head and pursed her lips. "And you're not?"

"She talks more than I do."

Roth waited for a moment. "Shame you didn't have sisters. You'd understand women better." She continued. "How sure are you the bone shaft was human?"

"I was an MP in Desert Storm—saw human bones. What the hog had in its mouth was human. But you'd need a medical examiner to be positive."

Roth pushed up the sleeve of her maroon tunic and rubbed her arm. "You searched the farmhouse for the map? You saw many places to hide documents?"

"The drawing, showing where the emerald lies, could be anywhere in the farmhouse."

My boss cupped her chin in her hand. "Can't keep going back and searching the hideout. Eventually, they'd notice you and start shooting."

I nodded at her. "Yeah. Wind up with a hog pen full of human bones."

"You need a face-to-face with Sandford. Make him tell you where the map is."

Roth went back to ceiling staring and desk tapping. "Regardless, we have to inform Lieutenant Hound about the hideaway. Our suspicion is human body parts lie about."

She stopped drumming and switched her stare to me. "Get him on the phone."

Little good would come from calling Hound. I pulled business cards out of my pants pocket to search for his phone number. "You sure? Hound won't care if he finds Ian's map or not."

"Get him."

I dialed Hound's direct line on the house phone and handed the receiver to Roth. A loud voice came on the line. "Lieutenant Hound. Macon County Sheriff's Office."

"Good afternoon, Lieutenant Hound. I'm Harriett Roth. I run a private investigative company in Asheville—"

I heard Hound's voice. "I know who you are. What do you want? I'm busy."

She switched the house phone to speakerphone. "For our mutual benefit, I propose a trade. I offer—"

"I'm the law. I don't trade."

"Unfortunate." She waited for a beat. "I could help you clear up your two Macon County murders. Now, we'll never know." Roth severed the call. Next, she picked up a novel and began reading. Three minutes passed. The phone rang.

Hound's voice, calmer now, began. "Ms. Roth, murder is a felony. Tell me what you know."

"First, I don't know if my information is relevant. Second, I gathered my material in a confidential case for a client."

Hound was noiseless as if thinking. "Tell me what you have. I'll know. If it's significant."

Roth leaned back in her chair, maybe to settle in for a lengthy negotiation. "My client paid for this knowledge. If you allow a helpful return for my client, I will tell you what I know."

"It's murder. You must assist the law with. Knowledge about a homicide."

"I can't be sure I have evidence linked to the murder of two men."

"The Sheriff's Office doesn't trade."

"But the authorities do trade, don't they? Don't you use a confidential informant?"

Hound didn't raise his voice but continued talking in a calm, slow tempo. "I could have you arrested. For justice obstruction."

Roth rotated the chair behind her desk, taking her time to scan the semi-gloss white paint on the poplar mantel behind her and stare out the wooden French patio doors along one wall. "You could, but I wouldn't say anything. Neither would my lawyer. Easier to treat me as your CI."

"No. A CI has an agreement with a law enforcement agency. To provide information in exchange for favorable treatment in their court case."

Roth rocked her chair forward and sipped her coffee. "Nonsense. A CI is not defined in an official statute but is commonly recognized."

Silence from Hound.

"Mr. Gannon will give you the information gathered for my client. If you arrest Sandford, let me view a map he has—to solve my client's case."

We waited.

"Your case involves helping the McDonald family, right?"

Roth smiled to herself. "Yes. I'm looking for the stolen McDonald family map."

"If what you have is straightforward. Evidence or witness to a crime. No deal."

"I do not have evidence you can present in court," Roth said. "I didn't witness a crime. I have a clue you can use to solve your case."

After another minute had passed, Hound spoke, "You tell me what you know. I'll consider. Helping you with the missing document. Tell me the clue. Now."

"No, Lieutenant Hound. First, designate me a CI."

I held my breath, waiting for Hound to agree. "I appoint you. My confidential informant. What's the clue?"

"I know the location of Connor Sandford's hideout."

"Where is it?"

"I'll send Don Gannon with maps showing its location," Roth said. "It's in the deep forest."

"Just now, I'm busy following important aspects. Of my own investigation. Can't talk to Gannon today."

She straightened her chair and addressed me. "Tomorrow, take copies—of the maps showing Sandford's hideout—to the lieutenant in Franklin."

Later, as I began to make copies of the maps showing the hideaway, I wondered if Hound would take me along to serve his warrant at the hideout?

I remembered an old saying, sometimes you're the bug and sometimes the windshield. I knew Carla was stormy, fiery. Sure as shooting, she would demand to accompany me to guard the back of the hideaway. I couldn't allow her into a deadly, chaotic situation. It was going to be my time as the bug.

34

HOUND PLANS RAID ON HIDEOUT — THURSDAY

"Cease fire!"

Carla stood in front of her shooting lane, flashing intense annoyance, her face a red she had never shown me, waving a Glock 26 pistol in the air. The range master, flapping his arms in a surrender gesture and exposing a face of fright, echoed my shout at her. Carla calmed and placed her practice gun on the shelf at the front of her path to the paper target. The gun range official directed Carla to put her pistol in its carry bag and kicked us out of the shooting area and the building.

Nothing had gone smoothly that morning. I thought back to when the breakdown began, how Carla had hit me with the subtlety of the British cavalry at the Charge of the Light Brigade in the Crimea. "I'm going with you to storm the hideout."

I didn't react well. No, I hadn't been paying attention. Carla had been quiet. She had been hatching something in that pretty head. Why hadn't I foreseen the looming mayhem and gone to Roth? Instead, I sealed my fate: "You can't go."

"Why not?"

"There'll be shooting." My retort sounded weak. I had, bit by bit, learned not to use the word *you* on Carla. That only began a duel of wits, an activity in which she had an advantage.

She wrinkled her nose, signaling the start of combat. "Women can shoot."

"You're not trained."

"Am too."

"Mickey, Bruce, and I were taught by the Army. The Military Police."

"I know how."

I dug in, tightened my face, cleared my throat. "It's too dangerous."

She flanked me using the doe-eyes maneuver, her innocent, wild-eyed look with big brown eyes. "Why won't you allow me to show you what I can do?"

I grasped Roth had counseled me about what I was doing. I had shut out my partner. My boss had pleaded with me to listen to Carla. "We're going to the shooting range," I said. "Get your equipment and show me what you can do."

As I drove her to the shooting range, I sensed trouble, heralded by a gunmetal gray sky. Carla was silent as a mausoleum statue. Her face bore a stern expression set off by a worn baseball cap, with her brown ponytail flowing out the opening at its back. I drove down Sweeten Creek Road to the range and got her checked in. At her assigned lane, she placed a brown duffle bag on the shelf and pulled out earmuffs and safety glasses, which she put on. She took a Glock 26 pistol out of the carrier and laid it on the shelf. I stood six feet back of her, donned ear and eye protection, and watched her load her weapon. I observed this pistol held ten nine-millimeter rounds in a double-stack magazine and had a relatively short grip. I didn't know she had purchased it.

She fired her pistol steadily down her lane at the target, twenty-five yards away. Next, Carla ejected the magazine and set the Glock on the shelf. I heard the whirl of the pulley towing the board back up the lane to the shooter. She glanced at the marks on the corrugated cardboard and stepped back, allowing me to see how she had done. She had tightly clustered her hits in the center bull's-eye of the series of concentric circles. Crap, Carla was a deadeye shot.

My chest tightened, a foretelling of pain to come. I stepped back from the target.

She smiled as she picked up her magazine and pistol. "So I'm going with you? Right?"

"No, you can't. It's too dangerous."

That was when she shouted at me, waving the magazine and the unloaded Glock about her and the range master kicked us out.

# # #

On the way to the sheriff's office in Franklin, we stopped by Grandma's farm. Carla plastered herself to the passenger-side Mustang's door, refusing to speak to me. If she were unhappy, then obviously, I would have to share in her misery. After an hour of driving in chilly silence, the balmy day turned to late morning, and we parked to the left side of the farmhouse. I spotted Grandma through a screen.

We entered a screened-in side porch where Grandma met us, holding her usual glass of red wine. She murmured to herself, "Carla, you'ns plum pretty. Not wearin' the working outfit I seed you in last time. Now, you pert-near spring-like in your full-length blue dress—love the fluffy cowl at your neck." Grandma and Carla chitchatted.

I broke in when they faltered to take a breath. "Grandma, we're close to breaching Sandford's hideout with the Macon County Sheriff's Department."

She bubbled with excitement, flinging out her arms, sloshing a splotch of wine out of her glass. "I has ma own news. Won a two-week vacation in da Caribbean."

Wrong time. Wrong place. "You won it? How?"

"It come in de mail." Neither Carla nor I spoke, as if stunned. Grandma continued her story. "Ashley and I'm gonna be in the Caribbean fer fourteen days."

My jaw sagged. This development could be a disaster for us. To keep Grandma on the subject, I didn't ask what family.

Carla covered her eyes with a hand. "You'll be gone from your farmhouse for fourteen days?"

Grandma removed her glasses to clean them. "Yep. A surprise. Didn't enter no contest."

Maybe because we didn't share her joy, Grandma seemed puzzled, glancing around as if searching for an answer. She began to chatter. "Would you like something to drink? And Don, you'ns look all dressed up. In your black pants and shirt and brown sports coat."

I told Grandma I'd enjoy coffee. As the old lady aligned her glasses on her nose and began to get the beans out of the refrigerator, I explained my anxiety about this free island trip. "I wager a lawyer—the one trying to buy your farmland—sent the envelope. Sandford wants to get you out of the way so he can dig up your property."

"You'ns mean it's a trick ta send me away"—her expression turned sad; her lower lip dropped—"so they can dig holes in the farm?"

"Yeah."

She plopped in a chair and clasped her hands. "I won't go. I won't give up ma emerald."

Carla put the coffee beans back in the fridge and poured wine into Grandma's glass. "Cheer up. I located Sandford's hideout. We're going there to find your map."

Grandma removed her glasses to wipe away tears. "Find Ian's map soon. I pert-near out of money."

Carla hugged her. "We're on our way to tell Lieutenant Hound where Sandford's hidey-hole is. We'll swoop in with your sheriff's office and recover Ian's old drawing."

I hoped we could deliver what Carla had promised. Our mountain man struck me as a tough nut to crack if he decided to keep the gem's location a secret.

# # #

We left Grandma for the Macon County Sheriff's complex. My partner continued to glance out the passenger-side window and plaster herself to the door. However, she was cute in her blue dress. I took a chance to disrupt the silence. "Thought you worked well on our trek through the woods."

Carla turned and spoke to me. "You mentored me well. Thank you."

"Yeah? Thank you."

"I did do well, didn't I?"

"You were magnificent. You are becoming the quintessential Nancy Drew."

She glanced away and then turned back with her thin-lipped smile. "Taylor is mistaken. You aren't completely inept with women."

I didn't argue with her. Maybe Carla liked me. She had to know I wanted to protect her from a shootout at the Buckho farm. Just now, I needed to buckle my safety belts and maneuver through her wrath. "Do you think you're going to enjoy being a detective?"

Carla hesitated as if to consider my question. "Yes. What does Ms. Roth think of me as an investigator?"

"She thinks you're a natural."

We drove in quiet for a time. "Will that jerk lieutenant take us to serve his warrant?"

I had been thinking about this question. "He won't want to take us with him."

Carla left her side door for a moment. "Why not?"

"If he gives us permission and someone gets killed, he gets the blame. Hound's a *blamer*—he blames others but avoids getting blamed himself. He'll say we can't go."

I steered the Mustang into a parking space at the sheriff's office facility. A deputy escorted Carla and me to an interview room. We sat at one side of a table bolted to the floor and beneath three fluorescent lights on the ceiling. Carla began to speak. I quietened her by holding a forefinger to my lips. I figured Hound left us there to eavesdrop on us as time slipped past. It lapsed slowly. I occupied myself scanning the room, its walls an ugly brown and bare. I suspected a mirror concealed an observation room on the opposite side of the wall. The room had a slight smell of old paper. I leaned my head on my chest and closed my eyes.

Lieutenant Hound and his deputy entered by opening the door in a rush. They sat and we faced them from opposite sides of the desk. The stiff-back lieutenant ignored us and pored over a notepad. Working on his tough-guy persona, he raised his head to stare hard at me. He commenced his slow drawl of accusation. "You're on thin ice. Withholding information about the murders."

I enjoyed playing the smart-aleck with Hound. Would he take a wiseguy like me on a raid of Sandford's hideout? No, he wouldn't. It was difficult, but I had to treat the ninny with respect. "Lieutenant Hound, we work for the McDonald family, investigating intrusions on their property!"

"Don't waste my time. What's in it for me?"

I brushed my cowlick with my hand and tried to appear rattled by his tough-guy role. "On the McDonald Family case, we found the motorcycle gang's hideout."

Hound rubbed his forehead. "Where is. This hideout?"

Carla spread Bruce's documents on the table. "Our colleague marked the hiding place on these maps."

Hound studied the documents. He pointed to one of the sheets of paper and spoke slowly. "Corporal, check out this address."

After the deputy left the room, Hound resumed. "This Buckho farm. It borders the National Park?"

"Yeah," I said.

"One road—hmm. Entering the farm."

Carla turned her head to me and then back to Hound. "Lieutenant Hound, we assume Sandford has the McDonald map at this old farmstead."

He looked up, puzzled. "Map? We'll have to wait and see."

We talked until the deputy returned. "The last member of the Buckho family died a few years back. The property's in trust."

"Any record of tax irregularity. Or drug activity?" the lieutenant asked.

The deputy shook his head.

Hound rose and began to leave the interview room. "Corporal, I'm going to the district attorney's office. To get a warrant. I want to move. Rapidly on this."

I stood. "You said you'd help us find the McDonald map. I need to come with you on your raid to identify it."

He shook his head. "Sorry. Can't take civvies where there's likely. To be gunfire." He left the room.

I followed him down the hallway. "Lieutenant, we need to be there when you serve the warrant."

He spoke to his deputy. "Get them. Out of here. I have what I want."

Carla pulled on my arm. "Hope reporters at *The Franklin Press* and the *Asheville Citizen-Times* don't learn we found the gang's hideout."

Hound kept walking but glanced over his shoulder.

"And the sheriff's office wouldn't help find the missing McDonald map."

Hound turned. "Don't you dare threaten me! I'll arrest your pretty butt. For interfering with an ongoing investigation."

Carla showed a perplexed expression, which was a slack mouth and a widening of her eyes. "Didn't say I'd talk with reporters. Just hope no one does."

He stood in the hallway and rubbed his head. "I plan to raid two days from now—early. You can go with us . . . but stay behind my deputies."

Success. We would be close when the sheriff's office raided Sandford's hideaway. "I have some ideas on the best way to approach the farm."

He seemed disinterested in my aid, which he indicated by bending away from me and starting down the hallway. "I'm entering the Buckho Farm. By charging fast down their driveway."

I couldn't say I'd been in the farmhouse and seen the video equipment focused on the driveway. "Don't you think—"

Hound interrupted in his unruffled voice. "They won't know we're coming. Stay out of my way when we go in, a day away."

Carla and I left the building and drove away. Maybe a frontal attack would catch the motorcycle gang unawares, but I doubted it. The back-door path into the farmstead offered a surefire way to surprise our mountain man.

# # #

An hour later, back in Asheville, Carla squawked like a blue jay, pouring forth her frustration at being excluded from any shootout. She bounced on one foot with her ponytail whipping about and protested to Roth. "I found the hideout. I hiked there. I can shoot."

To my mind, our young detective was infuriated, determined to charge into the rear with us big boys.

Roth remained calm, yawning, and holding her novel open to the page she read. "Please sit and calm yourself. I have two pages remaining in my book."

My boss finished reading, shut the novel, and spread her hands on her desk. "The concept of Grisham's *Skipping Christmas* is the family takes no part in Xmas and spends the money saved on a ten-day Caribbean vacation."

Carla sat on her seat's edge, dying to protest to Roth. My experience was we would have to wait while our boss summarized her recent read. "The premise is pedestrian, and it lacks what all good Christmas stories have: there is no miracle," Roth said. "The book satirizes the usual holiday buying and the extreme decoration of the neighborhood, but where is the magic?"

"You read the entire thing," I said. "You must have found some value."

She leaned forward, sliding her chair closer to the desk. "The story had funny moments. On the roofs of the community, neighbors, trying not to plunge to earth, wrestled giant snowmen into an erect posture."

"You're saying it's out of character for the author, but it's funny."

"Yes, I guess I am." Then Roth faced Carla.

My boss sat with her fingers loosely clasped in her lap, her features soft, calm. "You taught yourself to shoot?"

"Yes. Took a few lessons at first."

My boss smiled. "Well done."

"Let me go with Mickey and Don?"

A long-drawn-out moment elapsed before my boss resumed. "Well, yes, you can." Roth hesitated. "But . . ."

Carla cut short the smile she had started. "But what?"

"I envisioned you shadowing Hound during the frontal raid."

"Oh."

"I want Don and Mickey behind the farmhouse during the attack. You're the only one I trust to be in front with our impetuous lieutenant."

"Trust?"

"I leave the choice to you," Roth said to Carla.

"The choice?"

"I need you to go with Lieutenant Hound. After the attack, get him to focus on finding the diagram leading to the gem."

"My choice?"

"Your choice. Either be at the rear of the Buckho farmhouse or in front where I need you."

Carla nodded. "Okay. I'll go with the deputies." Carla had her place, and the countdown began.

35

HIKE THROUGH FOREST TO HIDEOUT – FRIDAY & SATURDAY

My brain was sluggish, in deep REM sleep. A noise filled my bedroom. My head was outside the cover with an eye open on deep blackness. My eyelid closed, my tongue felt gooey, and my ears picked up the noise, a tapping. I tried to snuggle deeper under my covers. The drumming wouldn't stop. *Hell's bells, make it go away. Please go away.* I slowly went along the path to reviving. I raised my head out of the covers, and my brain settled on the bedroom door as causing the tapping. I lifted my head farther; dull pain flooded my head. I realized my companions—Bruce and Mickey—and I had sucked brews until our local bar, Blazers, shut the night before. I yearned for the noise to stop, but it kept up. The pain in my head eased, and I slid my rump off the mattress and stood. A bedside clock heralded five-thirty.

Then I wobbled to the door and got it open. Carla stood at the entrance with her knuckles raised to rap. She held a forefinger over her lips and took my arm with her other hand. "We can catch the sunrise." I was too nauseated to welcome her, dressed in a knee-length blue dress, a subdued pattern of white and orange leopard spots, low-cut in front and back, and a blue ribbon tied in her ponytail. I harmonized with her in my rumpled, blue pajamas with small teddy bears that Mother had given me. "Grab your bedspread," she said with a devilish grin.

The hallway was quiet and dark as a cave. Carla carried a tote bag of donuts and coffee while she tiptoed out to the pond. I plodded after her. Sitting on my bedspread, we watched the sunrise at six-thirty. She said, "You are ashen. How many beers did you have?"

I stayed silent and ate five donuts and afterward felt human. "Poor baby," she said.

I gargled with coffee to get the yuck taste out of my mouth and felt on the verge of recovery.

At seven, Taylor and Mickey walked from the guesthouse to the main mansion.

Carla kissed me, and I kissed her back. Then she rose and walked toward the building just vacated. "I still have Taylor's extra door key. Come." Carla had forgiven me for telling her she couldn't go to the potential shootout. I trailed after her. *Oh, happy day.*

# # #

I'm in hog's heaven. Wait! Crappy metaphor! I'm in a fish paradise. Sitting with Roth, Carla, Mickey, and Bruce at the long table in the kitchen/dining room, I dug into Taylor's yummy sautéed trout at lunch. "You'ns a-getting' cucumber salad and mushmelon."

"What's mushmelon?" Carla whispered into my ear.

"Cantaloupe," I whispered back.

Roth refilled her glass from a bottle of Biltmore Estate Red Blend. "Recall Hound unleashes his foolish frontal raid tomorrow morning."

I took the bottle from Roth and freshened my glass. "A plan without planning."

Carla took the bottle from me. "Lacks a brain."

"He has to get a warrant," I said. "And his sheriff might alter his plan."

Roth stuck a fork into her cantaloupe. "After lunch, phone Hound and confirm his timing for tomorrow."

"Yeah, ma'am."

Later, I heard his gruff voice on my mobile phone. "What do you want, Gannon?"

"What time is the raid tomorrow?"

"The sheriff nixed my plan. We're not going—in the morning."

"When do you go?"

Hound answered in his slow cadence. "I'm setting up an observation post—to confirm the gang is at the farm. Two days from today—we swarm the farm in the morning."

"How did your sheriff change things?"

"We're setting up in the woods—along the sides of the driveway. Once the men are in position—we'll send patrol cars down the drive."

Better, but still a frontal strike.

"Don't talk to the press," the lieutenant said.

He told me to be ready in two mornings and broke the connection. Roth wrinkled her forehead but didn't speak.

"What do we do?" I asked.

Roth began drumming on the table. "Are there drugs and automatic weapons at the farmhouse?"

"Yeah."

"You saw them?"

"I saw them. When I searched for the emerald map."

Her eyes narrowed as if in deep thought. "So, once Hound busts in, he'll find illicit contraband?"

"That he will."

"He'll arrest Sandford?"

"Only if the deputies can catch him."

My boss frowned. "Will he fight or surrender?"

My shoulders tightened. The answer was foreboding. "He's creepier than his reputation. He'll fight."

"He might be better off surrendering."

"Our mountain man always carries a rifle, a viper coiled to strike."

"Could Sandford escape into the woods?"

I held my glass and studied the wine's color. "He's a woodsman on a farm next to primary forest. He'd vanish."

Roth shook her head. "So, Hound's deputies go in the front. Sandford, clutching our map, skips out the back."

I nodded. "Gone like a morning mist."

Roth spoke to Mickey, who had listened in silence during the meal. "Is he too lethal for Don and you? Might you be overwhelmed?"

Mickey stopped stuffing cornbread into his mouth. "Wouldn't happen. We'd have the benefit of surprise."

She hesitated. "We could leave the capture of our mountain man to the deputies."

"I doubt they could handle him."

My boss got hold of a wine bottle and gave a half shrug when she found it empty. She gazed out the windows along one wall. "Could you wait at the rock outcropping behind the farmhouse?"

"From the rock formation, we'd see him if he left out the rear of the hideout," I said. "Plus, the solid boulders would shield us from bullets."

Roth had driven the discussion, but now she said nothing as she seemed to be considering what I had said. She issued instructions.

"I restate, when the deputies begin their raid two days from now, you must be in the woods behind the house."

That old fluttery feeling started in my stomach. "I'll be there."

"Bruce will drive Mickey and you to the National Park, drop you off, and wait back at the motel."

We would follow the same approach as on our previous hike. "Okay."

Bruce shifted his weight and folded his arms across his chest. He might have a problem with his task.

Roth continued. "On the morning of the raid, Carla will coordinate with our lieutenant. If the deputies capture Sandford, she will work with Hound to get the map back."

Bruce raised his voice. "Why can't I go wid Don and Mickey? I'm an ex-MP. I do fieldwork."

Roth, with an attentive expression, viewed him. "I know you can do fieldwork."

"L let me go with de guys."

My boss hesitated.

"I don't want to be de guy left out all de time."

Roth tapped the dining table with her left hand and raised her eyebrows in a questioning gaze. "Don, can the three of you work together to cover the rear?"

Good grief. I'll have to support Bruce, or he'll never let me hear the last of this. "Mickey and I could wait forward in the rock outcropping. Bruce could set up behind us to guard our flanks and rear."

"Anything else?"

"Yeah. Bruce places well-aimed fire on any danger he spots."

"You three would be in contact through your walkie-talkie?"

"With the walkie-talkie," I said. "Bruce could identify an enemy and tell us their number and direction."

Roth smoothed the front of her maroon tunic and tugged down her sleeves. "Okay, Bruce. You go with Mickey and Don."

Roth ended our after-meal strategy meeting. Planning for the armed hike to the hideout left me tired. We drifted away from the table, and I snuck back to bed for a short lie down. I slept like an exhausted child. In the end, there was only one team I wanted for this job, and we were all set.

# # #

Our history professor, Angela Lightfoot, arrived early afternoon. Carla, Angela, Roth, Bruce, and I met out on the patio in front of the mansion. Angela flashed a triumphant smile. "I located the first pond. The ground coring pulled up silt and bird droppings. The sediment and droppings were in an egg-shaped area directly in front of the McDonald farmhouse."

Angela spread Bruce's map of the farmstead on a wrought-iron table in front of Roth and pointed to a section. "I show the earliest pond on this map. Its location in the early eighteen-hundreds."

Roth studied the diagram. "Well done." She turned to Bruce. "Overlay the pond's location on your map together with the site of the holes dug by the intruders."

"Yes, Boss."

Bruce left the patio to merge the two maps. Angela and Carla stayed to chatter with Roth. I joined Mickey to gather our hiking equipment and knapsacks. Mickey partially disassembled the barrel from his Remington 870 shotgun and packed the weapon with his gear. By late afternoon, Mickey and I had finished preparations to hike the back way to Sandford's hideout.

# # #

A taxi drove the three of us into the Nantahala National Park. I slumped in the second row among our rucksacks. I watched the burgeoning trees flash past in the early afternoon sun and envisioned situations that might evolve if the mountain man escaped out the back of the Buckho Farm. Some circumstances wouldn't go well for us. If he—a man used to firearms—elevated a rifle toward us, I had to react. If I responded too slowly, Sandford would kill Mickey or me. If I acted first and slew him, a dead man wouldn't help me find the map.

The driver slowed and pulled his vehicle off onto the shoulder of the two-lane, asphalt road bordered by a dense curtain of trees. I ceased fretting and gathered my equipment. I placed our current park pass into one of my cargo pants pockets; we had to show the pass if we bumped into a ranger in the night. My fingers confirmed four donuts nestled in a pouch of my rucksack.

Bruce paid the cab driver. "Guys, let's do it."

I adjusted my pack and smirked at Bruce. "Yeah, let's do it."

We hiked north, toward the stream between us and the farmstead. Mostly, Mickey followed the yellow, wooden stakes, the ones he had hammered into the ground to mark our trail on the earlier hike. He stopped every fifteen minutes to view his compass and verify our path pointed toward the Buckho farm. His Kukri knife hacked through any brush.

Mickey stopped walking. "I hear the stream."

We had reached the flowing water in just under two hours. At this pace, we would arrive at the bluff behind the farmhouse as dusk descended. We searched for the ropes we had stretched over the water on the earlier hike; without them, we had to wade across.

"Which way to where we strung the lines?" I asked. "Right or left?"

Mickey studied his compass and pointed right. "Downstream."

We followed the stream and searched for the ropes hanging from the trees. "I see the cable," Mickey said.

It took fifteen minutes to pull ourselves and the rucksacks to the opposite bank. "We're all dry this time," I said.

Mickey gave a thumbs-up. "Yeah, keep walking."

By checking compass readings and locating the trail-marking stakes, Mickey kept us on track. Our path led down a mountain. Daylight faded.

"I see a glow up ahead," I said.

Mickey halted and found the illumination. "The farmhouse."

Lessening his pace, Mickey began a quiet walk. We crept into the position behind the rock formation. I couldn't spot the watchdog; it must have been in the house. As darkness descended, we settled behind the outcropping and unpacked. Mickey assembled the barrel to his shotgun. I pulled out my M1911 pistol.

I prodded Mickey's shoulder. "You did well."

"We got here."

I pulled the pastry out of my rucksack. "Because you hate to do surveillance without donuts." I handed them to my partners.

Mickey sucked down the first one. "Jelly."

"Yeah."

I had discovered two of Nature's fundamental rules: donuts for my partners and dark chocolates for the ladies led to peace and tranquility. Bruce finished his last donut, murmured his gratitude, and glanced over the outcropping. "Looks quiet."

I peered through my binoculars at the building. "Sometimes, I glimpse a person going past a window." I saw a bedroom light turn off in the house. "They're turning in for the night."

We were in position behind the boulders, waiting for morning. I tried to get comfortable. No matter how I adjusted my body, a rock nipped my hip. I took the first two-hour watch while Mickey and Bruce slept. Operating from this rock outcropping involved a tradeoff: we could spot Sandford fleeing the farmhouse, but we would be in a field of fire from weapons shooting from the front of the house. After two hours of surveillance, I woke Mickey and settled down to sleep.

My last watch finished at six o'clock. I roused Mickey. "Dawn in half an hour."

Mickey rubbed his eyes and turned to scan the main building. "Any activity?"

"Nope."

Mickey stretched his limbs. "When do the deputies strike?"

"Seven o'clock, sharp."

I kept observing. "No one's moving in the building. Hound might catch this gang sleeping after all." I waited and listened to the sound of crickets. As the sun's rays began to appear close to six-thirty, I heard the quick, whistled sounds of birds, maybe wrens.

Beside me, Mickey rose on his elbows. "Someone's in the kitchen."

I watched. A light went on in the front room where we had seen the CCTV monitors. As dawn broke, I slumped down and checked the time. Fifteen minutes to go until Hound swooped. The farmhouse blocked my view of the driveway.

Mickey inched up his binoculars to his eyes. "Two individuals in the kitchen."

The light went off in the kitchen. I saw a figure run from the house to the barn. "Oh-oh, they've seen something. They're reacting."

Bruce woke and glanced around. "Guys, what's happening?"

Mickey dropped down to face Bruce. "It's showtime. Pull back and find a sheltered spot to cover us."

He left without a sound, carrying a Remington Model 700 and seeking his firing site.

By seven o'clock, I saw no other motion and heard no sounds other than birds singing. At two minutes past seven, police sirens blared from beyond the house. I peered over the outcropping.

At first, only the sirens sounded. Next, a popping noise joined the siren wail.

Mickey stiffened beside me. "Gunshots."

I listened. Multiple guns were firing—a firefight. "Keep your head behind the rock."

Bruce called on the walkie-talkie. "Automatic rifle fire."

Mickey spoke into our walkie-talkie. "See anything?"

"Guys, nothing so far."

I peeked around the mound, scanning the outbuildings. "I see a muzzle flash. Coming from the barn."

"The pigs hear the fighting," I said. "Listen to 'em grunting."

"A man's leaving the house," Bruce said from the walkie-talkie.

Lifting my head, I spotted a figure running out the back of the farmhouse and around the henhouse. He wore a porkpie hat and had a rifle slung over his right shoulder. Mickey gave a warning. "Sandford's at twelve o'clock, coming straight at you."

36

SURPRISE ABOUT THE EMERALD MAP — SUNDAY

As the bursting of popcorn in a microwave slows before stopping, the popping sound of automatic and semiautomatic weapons slacked off. Our mountain man, in a worn, brown coat, carrying a tan duffel bag over his left shoulder and a long gun on a sling over his right shoulder, fled across the field. With his head down and shuffling gait, a vision of a muskrat darted into my head. Sandford stumbled, regained balance, and slogged on.

Mickey roused. "Should we greet him just as he makes the woods?"

"Yeah."

I left my rucksack at the outcropping and pushed the slide back to cock the hammer of my pistol. Then I scrambled, hunched over, to my left. Mickey followed me. I wanted to stop Sandford before he got into the forest, so we would have him exposed out in the open. Letting him get in among the trees had a drawback: we didn't want him to take cover behind a tree trunk.

Stillness settled over the farm. The firing of weapons had concluded, replaced by the shouts of men.

Mickey and I avoided making rustling noises. Our quarry might hear us, drop his bag, and pull his rifle off his shoulder. Our mountain man chose that time to pick up his pace. He got to the tree line ahead of us and rushed in among the trunks and bushes. Mickey and I caught him there.

I leveled my M1911 pistol at Connor, my finger on the trigger guard, so I didn't shoot him accidentally. "Freeze!"

Mickey stood to my right, holding the shotgun. A maple tree separated Mickey and me, and we stood a car's length from Sandford.

He raised his head, halted, and considered us. Deliberately, he placed his briar, his smoking pipe, between his teeth.

He raised his left hand and stroked his long, white goatee. "Well, lookee here." He took two short steps forward. "You're smart . . . for a city boy."

I didn't want him close to me. He needed to be on the ground, prone, with flex cuffs around his wrists. "I said freeze."

I scanned his body for a handgun but didn't see one. "Drop your bag. Rifle on the ground!"

I scanned his rifle. It had a strap looped over his right shoulder. The gun's muzzle pointed up, with the trigger-guard oriented to his right.

"Whatever you boys say."

A slight, bitter smell wafted past in the air. I heard a pig grunting in the distant pigpen. My head felt dizzy; my legs and knees weak. Sandford's black eyes were lifeless. Empty, open-eyed, unmoving, staring at me. Eyes without a soul and nothing but a camera lens that didn't click. His eyes were connected to a brain set to murder.

As if to drop the bag on the ground, Connor rotated his left shoulder backward, grabbing the canvas bag's strap at the same time. As the bag came forward, he took two more steps toward me.

I shouted, "Stop."

He slung the bag, striking me on my torso and head, and sprang around me, on my left side. I suddenly stood between Sandford and Mickey's shotgun.

I shifted my finger to my pistol's trigger.

Then he performed a rifle maneuver, a sudden switch, catching me flatfooted: He reached back with his left hand and grasped his rifle's barrel. While holding on to the barrel with his left hand, he dropped the sling off his right shoulder. His right hand gripped the trigger guard and pinned the butt against his right shoulder. In a smooth, swift motion—like in a Cowboy Western—he had done a quick draw with a rifle.

He would kill Mickey in a split second.

My trigger finger plucked—*Pow! Pow!*

Shocks went through my arm, and the pistol's muzzle kicked up. My heartbeat raced.

Sandford stood motionless, holding his rifle.

His weapon dropped. He crumpled forward.

Mickey pointed his shotgun at the downed man. "You hit?" he asked me.

I stared at Mickey, my two hands shaking. Sandford's motion had been so fast, over in a flash. I shook my head at my partner.

The rifle remained under Sandford's right arm. Mickey stepped on the barrel with his foot, nudged the arm off the gun, and kicked the weapon away.

Sandford had spun a quarter-way around and landed on his left side. He had two wounds: to his chest and his arm. His airway remained clear and his breath regular. He rasped at me. "Smart. Waiting out back."

Mickey cut away the bloody jersey covering his chest. Bright red blood pumped out from the wound near mid-chest.

Mickey took off his white tee shirt and tied it to a branch. "I'll wave a white flag at the deputies—get help." He walked onto the field, waving his tee shirt.

I stayed with the injured man. "We're getting EMS for you."

"It hurts. You got me good."

His heart rate was rapid, his respiration growing unsteady.

I spoke to him. "You have the map to the emerald. Don't you?"

Sandford coughed. "Yeah." He coughed again. "I had the old McDonald diagram."

"Where is it?"

He sneered and wheezed. "Gone." His respiration increased. He sweated, but his skin felt cold to my fingers.

"Gone? Where?"

"Burned"—he coughed and hacked—"to a crisp."

Was he lying? Was he making up a story? "You burned it?"

Mickey and a deputy—wearing a black Kevlar vest—arrived.

The injured man wheezed, bled, and sweated. "It's in my . . . head."

"You're saying you memorized it?" I asked.

He smirked at me and began hacking again. "You need to keep . . . me alive."

"The ambulances have arrived at the farmhouse," the deputy said. "They're doctoring the wounded."

I examined the supine man. Now he didn't speak at times, slipping in and out of consciousness. Cardiac trauma loomed over him. "Sandford, talk to me."

He didn't answer.

He wasn't going to make it much longer. "He's dying. We've got to carry him to the paramedics."

The deputy stood at Connor's calves, I waited at one of his hips, and Mickey took a position at his shoulders. Bruce came running up and took the other side of his torso. We four knelt on our knees and—at Mickey's command—raised to a squat, lifting the wounded man to our knee level. At Mickey's second command, all four of us stood, supporting him.

He didn't move or cry out.

We carried him through the field toward the farmhouse.

Two paramedics rushed up and examined Connor, but one paramedic shook his head. Sandford was dead, from the trauma to his chest. Since he was the last person knowing the location of the emerald, I felt damned dreadful about his death.

I remained in the field with Bruce and Mickey. "I don't have the map—can't find the emerald. I failed Roth."

My courage sank as I began manic pacing in a circle on the field. I clenched my jaw. *Damn!* I had lost everything; the map didn't exist, and Sandford's death had obliterated any chance of locating the emerald. Grandma had backed the wrong horse and would never again see the splendor of the McDonald family homestead. I had screwed up. It couldn't get worse.

Mickey clapped me on my shoulder. "And Lieutenant Hound has a dead deputy. He'll be selecting a scapegoat soon."

# # #

I stood beside the mountain man's body in an ambulance at the head of the driveway. Even though the day had emerged bright and the woods were lush and green, I continued to mourn his death and my screwup. The coroner, who had been busy examining other bodies, squatted beside Sandford. "Dead. Gunshot to the chest. Bag him and transport him to the morgue." Next, he strode down the driveway to view further fatalities.

Hound appeared next to me, his face wet with sweat and his black dress shirt wrinkled and dirty. He gave me a haughty stare. "You shot him behind the house?"

"Yeah."

"You alerted the gang. Before we were in position."

There's an old saying that goes; someone made an error; others will get blamed.

"No! You started the raid a couple of minutes after seven. When Sandford ran out the back at seven-thirty, the firefight was over."

Hound turned to view an EMS team carrying one of his deputies to an ambulance. "You did this. If you hadn't given us away. We'd have surprised them."

"The gang saw you coming. You were the one surprised."

Grass and dirt spattered Hound's dark trousers. He motioned to one of his deputies. "Arrest Gannon. He ruined my operation."

"Don't get involved," I whispered to my partners. "Tell Roth."

The deputy stood next to me. "What's he accused of?"

"I had things under control until Gannon. Wrecked my. Arrangements."

"What charge, Lieutenant?"

"Second-degree murder. Or voluntary manslaughter."

"I shot in self-defense."

"Add an accusation of. Interfering with an authorized sheriff's operation."

I realized Hound would accept no responsibility. "You should have surrounded the farmhouse and rushed it from all sides."

The deputy pulled his handcuffs off his belt. I turned with my hands behind me. The deputy cuffed my hands, led me to a patrol car, and drove to the Franklin Detention Center.

# # #

A sergeant charged me and led me to a holding cell at the Center. It had been built recently and had a bright appearance and smelled okay. My enclosure consisted of a bed, a desk, a toilet, and a washbasin. I had lunch courtesy of Macon County and next caught up on my sleep.

Late in the afternoon, a deputy took me from the cell to Hound's office.

As I entered, I found Roth's attorney, Otis Quayle, and our lieutenant verbally gnawing at each other. Quayle, in his cut-rate, blue suit, bombarded Hound with his lawyer bombast. "You've kept my client for eight hours. You've had many opportunities to release him. Why is he still here?"

Hound sneered back. "I interrogate him. As I need to."

They continued their lawyer-police officer mantra. Uninvited, I took a seat and settled back, observing like a spectator at a tennis match. The deputy stood against the doorjamb.

Quayle smoothed his eyebrows. "My client crouched behind the farmhouse, observed what happened. You had no deputy standing guard at the rear. Sandford ran out the back—escaping."

Hound's face grew red even as his voice stayed calm. "Gannon interfered."

"Nonsense. No deputies to interfere with behind the farm. Mr. Ploughman, Mickey, had to search to find one of your deputies."

Hound massaged his forehead. "Gannon and his men. Were armed."

Otis rolled his eyes at the ceiling. "Every human there carried a weapon."

"My deputies. Had a reason to be at the farm. Why were. Gannon and Ploughman there?"

"Hunting for a client's map," Quayle said.

Hound massaged his forehead again. "I'm not releasing him until. Seventy-two hours have passed."

Quayle jabbed his finger at Hound. "If not for Gannon, a fugitive would have vanished. Local newspapers would have blamed you for losing him."

Hound stared daggers at Otis. "Gannon killed the man."

The lawyer paused to brush his eyebrows. "Gannon tried to capture him. What should he have done when he saw Sandford? Blow kisses?"

Quayle's bluster grew in intensity like a terrier's final rush to tear a rodent out of the ground. "You found the gang's hideout through Roth Security. You caught the entire band because of Roth Security."

Hound gritted his teeth in frustration. I reckoned Quayle had convinced Hound not to shift the blame onto me.

The lawyer smiled. "Gannon shot in self-defense. If you imprison my client, it will come out you got a deputy killed and would have let the leader of the gang escape except for my client. Let my client go, and you get all the credit for wrapping up the gang."

Hound spoke to the deputy at the door. "Release Gannon."

I bowed to Quayle in gratitude. "Now, would you give me a ride to Roth's mansion?"

My efforts had failed to bring the map back, and the emerald was lost forever. I thought of a line from Shakespeare's King Richard the Second: "I can call spirits from the vasty deep." Roth solved impossible puzzles, but even she couldn't recover the burnt map. Or could she?

37

ROTH SAYS SHE CAN FIND THE EMERALD – SUNDAY

Quayle dropped me back at the mansion, where I found the rest of the band had gathered on the patio behind the estate in the garden. All but Taylor, who had started preparing dinner, frying breaded pork as she does Southern Fried Chicken. When she caught sight of me, she walked across the kitchen/dining room and hugged me. Today, our chef wore a bright white apron with a red chef's hat that fluffed out at the top. Her braided red hair hung down her back, and she was sympathetic, giving me a low soothing purr and a thoughtful look. She stepped back. "Bruce told me de map are toast. De emerald are lost forever."

I felt shame. My eyes were wet. "I'm a bum. I let Roth down. I ruined Grandma."

"That ain't what my husband, Mickey, says. He says you'ns shot a killer."

I didn't feel courageous. I couldn't remember pulling the trigger. One moment Sandford stood, and then he didn't. "It wasn't smooth. I had a bumpy ride."

I took a pitcher of iced tea from Taylor and carried it as we walked out the back into the garden set against a background of deciduous trees. The path of gray flagstones went through low-lying green plants, and afterward, the tall oaks—with their leaves budding—and next passed a small clearing, where somebody had laid gray pea gravel for the patio.

The entire band—Roth, Bruce, Carla, Mickey, Angela, Grandma, and Ashley—sat there on light-brown wicker chairs and couches with white cushions having polyester covers and filled with foam. Taylor went back and forth between the kitchen and patio, serving food and policing the dirty dishes. I sat beside Carla, who pecked me on the cheek and said, "Welcome back." Because our case involved every person present at the pea-gravel patio, I guessed Roth had arranged a meeting to apologize to Grandma for my failure. The old lady sat beside Roth on a couch and appeared to me to have moist eyes. I assumed she was in sorrow because I didn't recover the map.

I stared across the low table toward Roth. "Thanks for sending Otis to get me out of jail."

She nodded. "Bruce told me you had to shoot Sandford."

"He moved . . . fast. I didn't expect his action."

"But you kept him from killing Mickey. You did well."

But I didn't. My brain knew our mountain man had been within a split second of shooting Mickey. It was clumsy. I stared down at my hands.

The group went silent until Roth spoke. "You've seen death before? Right? In Desert Storm in 1990?"

Yeah, Desert Storm. Ten years past. Roth must have thought I'd started to clam up and she was trying to get me talking. "At first, I was in the military police in Saudi Arabia. The military moved my battalion around to guard prisons mostly. The prisons were camps in Iraq surrounded by barbed-wire fences."

Roth inhaled through her nose and pushed out breath through her mouth. "You guarded. Didn't shoot guns?"

"The army trained us in firearms."

"Did you fire at humans?"

"One night, Bruce and I directed traffic at a crossroads, and I fired at attackers. I probably hit a few of them. There were bodies in the morning."

Roth leaned in with her hands on the arms of her chair. "In the past, you fought impersonally at a distance. But Sandford was close, and you saw your bullets tear into him?"

I felt beads of sweat on my forehead. "Yeah."

"Your face is ashen. If you're agonizing, take time off and mend. Allow pain to go away."

I shook my head. "I'm okay. Want to keep working."

Taylor put a plate in front of me and took a try at cheering me up. "You'ns a-stayin' in jailhouses right much these days." I smiled at her, and she carried dirty plates to the kitchen.

I changed the subject. "What happened while I was in jail? Did you search the Buckho farm?"

Carla spoke up. "The deputies wouldn't let us in the farmhouse. Their weird lieutenant said you broke the agreement with him by firing your pistol and warning the gang."

"What did the deputies find in the house?" I asked.

"Lots," Bruce said. "Firearms and cocaine. Human bones in de pigpen."

Taylor walked down the path from the mansion and served individual trays. She gave chicken-fried pork chops to the patio people and filled coffee cups and iced tea glasses. Sweet potato biscuits and steamed green beans completed the goodies on the tray. Taylor had covered the pork chops with peppery cream gravy. I took a bit of a succulent feast and set my plate and cup on a small side table.

"Whose bones?" I asked.

"Guys, forensics ain't back yet," Bruce said. "A member of dat motorcycle gang disappeared about de time Jeremiah and Talk got killed in de woods. Deputies think de pigpen bones belong to him."

I assumed the biker's wounds formed the blood trail through the brush at Jeremiah's camp. "The gang tried to treat the wounded teenager at the hideout?"

"Yes," Bruce said. "De CSI team found bloody gauze, a tourniquet, and spent tubes of antibacterial cream. All dumped in a pit to be burned."

"Can't we sneak in and hunt for the map? Maybe Sandford lied to me."

Bruce sported a grin. "The boss told us to go into de house and rummage. When de deputies wrapped dat farm in yellow tape and left, Mickey, Carla, and I entered and searched for three hours."

"I suppose you didn't find a map. Guess Sandford did burn it."

"No map," Carla said. "We read every scrap of paper. That was a long shot, and it didn't pan out."

"You did due diligence by searching in the hideout for a copy."

I finished chewing pork and bit into the last biscuit. Taylor brought us small serving bowls with blackberry cobbler topped with vanilla ice cream.

Grandma started moaning and wringing her hands. "It's gone. The map's gone. I'll never see the emerald."

Ashley harangued his grandmother. "Hell, I told you to sell the house to that lawyer. Now, we got nothing."

Roth's expression showed sympathy as she reached out to squeeze Grandma's hand. "If the map perished with Sandford, his lawyer would withdraw the offer to buy your farm. Is the buy offer still there?"

Grandma sobbed. "My grandson called de lawyer dis morning. They done canceled dere bid."

"That worthless glass wipe wouldn't talk wid me," Ashley said.

Roth finished her cobbler. "Hmm, the lawyer doesn't have the map."

The old lady began sobbing again. "Our funds are almost gone. Soon, we'll be broke."

"We're poor people," Ashley said. "Jus' like white trash."

Roth rose, walked around the low table in the patio center, and patted Grandma's shoulder. "Where's Taylor? Grandma's wine glass is empty."

As my boss returned to her chair, all eyes followed her. "We seem to have lost our way in finding where the emerald hides. I was thinking. Did our investigation miss an opportunity?"

Taylor came up the path with a bottle of red wine. After Grandma and Roth filled their glasses, Roth continued. "Relaxing here on the patio, I suggest we have all the time in the world to think about what we did and didn't do. We should try to review every step we took in tracking down Waya's gem."

I wasn't listening to her discussion, one hand in my lap, and head down. "What does it matter? I ignored Sandford, who was hunting the gem the whole time."

"Don't blame yourself for something we all missed. You're a smart man who has a great deal to be thankful for."

"I think Sandford got on to the map to the emerald," Carla said, "when he observed Jeremiah digging holes on the farm."

Grandma interrupted wiping her glasses to comment. "Connor Sandford were always around. Familiarity breeds a cloak—an' relaxes caution. No one saw him a-comin', least of all, poor Jeremiah."

I had injured my self-worth by failing to find the emerald. "Two events didn't make sense. Why wasn't I suspicious of Sandford exploring the public records of Grandma's farm? It took me forever to notice all those many motorcycles around the McDonald farm."

"Each of us knew," Angela said to me. "Don't be so hard on yourself."

Roth narrowed her eyes and swayed from side to side as if trying to think. "We, and not just Don alone, didn't follow up on the public records and the motorcycles. I don't think a path of blame is getting us anywhere."

She put down her empty bowl. "Maybe we ought to go over other steps we took? How about the farm and the photographs Jeremiah stole?"

Beside me, Carla whispered. "What is Ms. Roth doing?"

"She's stubborn," I whispered back. "She doesn't want to admit defeat."

"How long will she continue?"

"She can go for a long time."

I turned my attention back to Roth, who was saying, "Angela and Mickey have been exploring where the ponds have lain."

"By coring along the stream's edge on Grandma's farm," Angela said to the group, "We detected the pond's location in eighteen-thirty-eight."

Roth nodded. "You know the pond's location on the night Waya and Ian buried the gem?"

Angela nodded. "A small lake lay in front of the farmhouse in the early eighteen-hundreds. Bruce outlined the original pond on one of his maps."

My boss had started to repeat herself, leading us into stuff we already knew. "How does the pond help us?"

My boss took her time to admire the tall oaks shading the garden. Individual rays from the setting sun found a way through the leaf cover. We were going to get a long story. "In their search, detectives keep on one of three routes: follow the action, follow their intuition, or follow the money."

Ashley finished his Mountain Dew and stood to interrupt Roth. "Dis are nonsense. She don't know what she's talking about. We need to leave."

Grandma had been staring at Roth as if listening intently. Now, she wiped her face with a napkin to dry it. "I'm not leaving. Let me hear what she has to say. Sit."

Roth started up again. "We followed the action. We got four people—Sandford, Jeremiah, Talk, and an unknown teenager—killed. Others died. Also, Sandford cut off our further endeavor along that path by destroying the map."

I spread my arms to my sides. "What else can we do?"

Roth answered. "You could follow a hunch, which would get you going in circles. Or you could track the money, the practical path to solving our case."

She enjoyed teasing me like I was a kitten over which she swung a shiny object. "What money? What are you talking about?"

"The holes. They show the way to the wealth, the emerald."

My brain had slowed, having increased trouble in finding precise statements. "The holes are empty. Nothing there."

My boss shook her head. "I beg to differ. Jeremiah told us something vital when he dug the holes. But only if you know what we learned from his actions."

A low buzz arose around the patio as each person tried to guess what she meant. "We learned nothing," Ashley said. "Weren't no emerald in de holes."

My boss shook her head. "We learned the gem wasn't there. And we learned what the map looked like."

Grandma made a noise in her throat like a cat when someone steps on its tail. "Do you mean dat? Can you'ns see de picture?"

"See, you ain't learned," Ashley said. "Dey don't know what were on dat map."

Roth spoke to the old lady. "Don't stress. I judge I can work out what the map depicted."

I knew Roth. She had done it again: worked her way through a knotty problem. "You think you can find the emerald, don't you?"

She held out her coffee cup to Taylor, who had returned from the mansion with a fresh pot. Roth drank from her refilled cup. "I do."

"How?"

I held my breath and waited on Roth to explain. "I had Bruce bring his maps out to the patio," she said. "I brought drawing pens, a protractor, and a compass. Let's help Taylor clear a surface on this table, and I'll explain."

And then her approach blossomed, and the clock started ticking.

38

ROTH PREDICTS THE GEM'S POSSIBLE LOCATION — SUNDAY

Bruce pulled a stack of maps out of his rucksack and placed them on the patio table. The table grew crowded as my boss crammed drafting instruments on top of the papers. Taylor helped by clearing away plates, glasses, and silverware. The perky redhead, moving around the pea gravel patio in a walk best described as a glide, carried another tray of dishes and eating utensils back to the mansion.

A hush settled over the patio. I listened as Roth, sitting to my left, spoke in a quiet voice to comfort Grandma. "When you're down, you think you can't get up again. Don't quit. We'll get your old Carolina home back." I wondered why Roth was making such a risky promise. Would she look back tomorrow and think it seemed like a good idea at this time? Grandma removed her glasses, blew her nose, and cleaned her plastic-rimmed spectacles.

"I don't think so," Ashley said. "Just like dey promised you de map but couldn't get it, dey won't find anything."

Picking through Bruce's sheets of paper, my boss said, "I propose we focus on the location of the pond in eighteen-thirty-eight—as worked out by Angela—placed into Bruce's plots." She pulled out a page showing the farmhouse, the pond existing today, and the holes dug by Jeremiah and Talk. A second sheet exhibited a similar view but replaced the present-day fishpond with the small lake as it existed back in eighteen thirty-eight. I saw the 1838 and the current ponds were in different places. But I already knew that.

Roth grabbed photographs from the ground behind her chair and laid them on the table. "To decipher where the emerald hides, we should check one other item, the historical photographs taken at the McDonald Farm."

She scanned through the old pictures. "The eighteen-ninety and the present-day pond are in different locations. Do you see that?"

Ashley interrupted. "Who cares? You done fritter away our time."

My boss took a deep satisfied breath. "Viewing the photographs, we independently confirm the stream and pond changed over the decades."

Roth waited a moment. "Now, where did Waya and Ian bury the emerald?"

"No one knows," Grandma said and glanced around the open-air patio. "Oh, would Taylor bring me a glass of wine?"

Roth waited until Taylor put the wine in front of Grandma. "What do we know about how Ian and Waya buried the gem? They set out at night, is that correct?"

Grandma swallowed half the liquid in her glass and nodded. "I remember a-readin' Ian's diary. To avoid being seen by neighbors, he hid the gem at night. My great-grandmother said dey had been drinking single barley malt before dey left the house."

I marveled at how Grandma could drink so much and stay reed-thin. She was maybe five feet, two inches tall, and weighed a hundred pounds. Yet she treated every meeting as a drinking break.

Roth pursed her lips and paused as if for dramatic effect. How could she know the emerald's whereabouts? My boss, dressed in an A-line floor-length chiffon dress in black, which set off her shoulder-length white hair, had a fair bit of ham in her. No one at the table spoke. She continued to query the old lady. "Did they wrap the gem in a case or a container?"

"My great-grandmother told me dey carried de emerald in a small wooden cask, with two metal bands reinforcing the sides. According to old family gossip, dey took a jug of single barley malt with them."

"How big was your great-great-great-grandfather?"

"How big?"

Roth turned her head as if to gather her thoughts. "People tended to be shorter in the nineteenth century. In terms of a man today, was Ian a small man, large, or average?"

Grandma took half a minute before answering. "He were a large man for his time."

"So, his stride might be similar to an average man's today?"

"I reckon so."

"Did family gossip say if Waya and Ian toiled in the darkness that night or moonlight?"

Grandma took another glass of wine from Taylor. "Great-grandmother always told de family the light from the moon shone brightly."

Taylor, smiling, turned back to gathering used plates and silverware.

Roth leaned back in her wicker chair, closed her eyes, and breathed at a steady rhythm.

Ashley rose from his chair. "She'ns through. Got nothing more to say. Let's go home."

I timed her: after three minutes and seventeen seconds, her eyes popped open. "They went out at night carrying a lantern, transit, wooden cask, jug of whiskey, paper to write on, and shovel. They had been drinking strong whiskey. To hide the emerald, I doubt they carried out an elaborate procedure that night."

She rummaged through Bruce's maps and pulled forth two. I could see both well, but those farther away around the patio got up and scurried to Roth's end. One of Bruce's ground sketches had the present-day pond while the other had Angela's early-1800s pond. My boss chose the sheet showing the McDonald house, the present-day fishpond, and the cluster of holes dug by Jeremiah and Talk.

Roth placed her forefinger on Bruce's map. She checked the scale of the page and made measurements with a ruler. "The distance from the farmhouse's front door to the group of holes is 253 feet—or about 101 steps. At an angle of twenty-nine degrees west of south."

I studied the sheet. I saw the straight line, from the door to the dug-out pits, cut through the left edge of the existing pond.

Roth took a moment to be sure our eyes were on her. "What did Jeremiah—by excavating those holes—tell us about the map drawn back on that night in eighteen-thirty-eight?"

The group at the table stared at the sheet. Yes, Roth had drawn a straight line from the farmhouse front door to the holes in the ground. But how trustworthy was the line just encountering the periphery of the present pond? Couldn't that intersection be by accident or pure luck?

Then Carla said, "Oh." We all turned to her. "Part of Ian's directions were in terms of a single distance and the pond in eighteen-thirty-eight. But Jeremiah didn't find the emerald using the current pond."

"Hold on," I said. "What if the edge of the pond expanded in the wet season and contracted in a drought? Or the walker—stepping off a straight line—had a shorter or longer stride? Big inconsistency."

Carla grinned her mega-bright smile so dear to my heart. She pointed at the cluster of pits shown on Bruce's drawing. "Jeremiah thought the same thing. He excavated lots of holes around the point two hundred and fifty feet from the door and skirting the pond's edge on the left. The gem wasn't there."

Roth picked up her narrative. "I theorized what was on the map. My first assumption was Ian's map was simple. I presumed the instructions were a distance measured in a direction from the farmhouse's front door."

"What kind of direct measurement would Ian have made?" Angela asked.

"An angle based on permanent objects, things Ian and Waya could see and measure."

"A tree?" Bruce asked.

Roth turned to Bruce. "Tell us about the trees."

"I searched, found no trace of a tree in front of the house from a time back in eighteen-thirty-eight."

"Had they been cut down?" I asked.

In reply, Angela spread photographs of the farm over the near-to-the-ground table. "In the old pictures, do you see any trees?"

I picked up several images, viewed them before passing them to others, and selected a couple more. Back in the nineteenth century, the McDonald family had cleared their farmland for planting and harvesting. The only trees were in the garden behind the farmhouse.

Grandma held up her wine glass to ask Taylor for a refill. "Great-grandmother told me de trees had all been removed for lumber and a-plantin' the land."

Roth had an unbroken line of reasoning. Ian and Waya wouldn't or couldn't have used a tree as a marker.

"If not a tree, what else could Ian have used on the diagram?" Carla asked.

Roth pointed to a mountain range on the map. "You've seen the photos. The permanent objects were the house, pond, and that distant mountain peak."

Angela picked up an early photograph, its image showing a distant peak beyond the fields of crops. "This mountain is called Standing Indian. It isn't a steep mountain but the highest point of a gradual range."

I was getting confused. I brushed my cowlick into place. "Did Ian and Waya use that mountain peak for directions in their map?"

Roth gave a slight shake of her head. "I doubt it."

She hadn't convinced me. "Why do you doubt it? Sighting on the mountain with their transit and reading an angle would have been doable."

My boss cleared her throat and turned a condescending glare on me. "My second assumption is Occam's Razor justifies my first assumption."

I knew what that was: the more assumptions one must make, the more unlikely such an explanation is correct. A straight line at an angle from the front door was the simplest assumption.

I shook my head. "But Ian and Waya could have put the mountain in their map."

"Donnell, they were drunk as skunks. The more intoxicated one is, the more motivation there is to keep it simple."

She waited, but I didn't say anything, and she went on. "My third assumption is Ian's directions used the pond's location in eighteen-thirty-eight. Because the terrain had changed, Ian's directions led to where Jeremiah dug and not to where the gem is."

Sitting up straight in my wicker chair at the patio, I said, "Because the pond's location shifted."

Roth pointed at Bruce. "Draw a line from the farmhouse door through the left border of the small lake at its eighteen-thirty-eight site. The old pond Angela found."

"Okay, Boss." Bruce studied his map and carefully drew a line. "Done, Boss."

"Measure two hundred and fifty-three feet along that line and stop. Mark where you are with an *X*."

A low buzz began among the people around the patio. As if calculating, Bruce slowed down to glance at the plants, the pink-purple-and-white, showy *Orchis*, just beginning to bloom along the path through the shade garden. Next, he crouched over his sheet with the ruler and drew the line Roth described. "Two hundred and fifty-three feet, Boss."

Roth carefully watched the drawing of the line. "I think *X* marks the spot where we'll find the barrel containing the emerald."

Bruce began to gather his maps. "But Boss, we don't know if that is what Waya and Ian did or not."

My boss had faith in her ability and conclusion, as shown by a sparkle in her eyes, a smug smile. "Angela found the pond's position back in eighteen-thirty-eight. We'll dig using the pond's eighteen-thirty-eight site and find the stone."

"Oh, please make it so," Grandma blubbered. "Let the emerald be there."

Ashley sputtered out a laugh. "Dere you go again. All she is talkin' about are assumption on assumption. She got no idea where de gem are."

Angela pointed to the map showing the 1838 pond. "At the farm, I'll drive a steel rod into the ground where Bruce placed the *X* on the map."

I had been glancing at Mickey during the discussion. He hadn't spoken but had been nodding and studying Bruce's maps.

My boss brushed her palms together to indicate a completed task. "Well done, Angela and Bruce. Mickey, see how soon you can schedule the contractor, the ground-penetrating radar guy, to be at the McDonald farm."

Mickey nodded at Roth and stepped to the edge of the patio to phone.

My head spun. "Let me see if I have this straight. We determined a line from Grandma's front door through the left border of the pond in 1838. We walk two hundred and fifty feet along the line and stop and drive a rod in the ground?"

Roth nodded. "Finally, we examine what's beneath the surface using ground-penetrating radar."

Mickey turned from speaking over his mobile phone and said, "Two o'clock tomorrow afternoon. Metal-detector contractor at the McDonald farm."

Roth grinned at Grandma. "Tomorrow, we solve the mystery."

39

ROTH HUNTS THE EMERALD — MONDAY

I couldn't sleep that night because I kept agonizing over tomorrow's dig for the emerald, flopping onto one side, staring at darkness, and then plopping onto the other flank. Eventually, the first sun rays appeared at the bottom of the window shades, the *awk-awk-awk* of ravens rang out, and I rose and showered.

Carla answered my knock from her side of the door. "Who's there?"

"Get dressed."

Silence.

"Do you know what time it is?"

"Let's go eat?"

"Hell no. I'm sleeping."

"I'm hungry."

"No."

"Please."

Silence.

I went back to my room. I had learned Carla was not a sunrise person. Ten minutes later, she knocked at my door. "This had better be good."

That morning, Carla and I got into my silver Mustang and I drove into Asheville to search for nourishment in the food truck lot at 51 Coxe Avenue. She wore a long-sleeved green shirt with unhooked top buttons and cream-colored jeans. She carried a slight pudginess, but on her, it looked fantastic. Lust is in the eye of the beholder.

An earlier drizzle had ended, revealing a dark blue sky with a few white clouds stretching like string into the distance and leaving the air with a chill. We parked near the restaurants on wheels, and I sniffed a cornucopia of food odors: frying hamburgers, French fries, and chicken, with the intensity of a recognizable smell ebbing up or down depending on which food truck was near. My ears barely picked up the little traffic noise; I heard the bang, sizzle, and crackle of kitchen pans and cooking food. One truck in the lot—a paved area, bracketed by a parking lot, a bank, and a bus station on three sides—had opened to serve cuisine. The open truck was the Crazy Creole. Both of us got a mac-an-cheese and a tasty po'boy sandwich, dried off a wooden bench with napkins, and sat.

I focused on keeping the po'boy's liquid ingredients from dripping onto my clothes. "You seem happy."

Carla wiped her mouth. "I am."

"When you were with us before, you weren't always cheerful."

She finished chewing a mouthful. "I was stupid to get engaged. Less said on that, the better."

She gathered the remnants of her meal to go in the garbage. "You're considerate. I like that in a man."

"Thank you." I picked up our refuse, stuck it in a trashcan, and returned to her. "We were all sorry to see you leave."

"I told you. I had a meltdown. Didn't know what to do."

"Now, you do?"

She flashed her jumbo smile. "Yeah. PI jobs are fun."

I grinned back at her. "And what do PIs do?"

"You and I run around, meet people, and dig up things."

I thought about her answer. It caught reality.

Carla studied her wristwatch. "We still have time until we drive out to the McDonald Farm. May I ask an awkward question?"

"What?"

"Taylor says you won't accept strong women."

Uh-oh, I sensed an opportunity to wedge my foot into my mouth. Talking with a clever woman always scared me. She thinks differently from a man and investigates things in her way. Like in that movie, a guy shows up for a knife fight but finds it's a gunfight. Maybe Carla had just shoved me into a pitfall to see if I respected her thoughts. If I disagreed, I was in trouble—time to backstroke. I planted a debonair-man-of-the-world grin on my face. "Nothing to accept. A strong woman is what she is."

She showed a stern demeanor. "So you say. Taylor tells me you avoid smart women like a cat bolting a bathtub."

I went silent for half a minute. Then I had an idea. "If this is your subtle way to ask if I accept you as a strong-willed woman, then yes. You are a scary combination of beauty, wit, and animal magnetism."

"Animal magnetism?"

"You're sexy."

She gave me an eye roll. I doubted I had fooled her. "I remain hungry," she said.

I got up and walked toward the Juicy Pig, which had just opened. "How about barbeque?"

She followed me.

We got pulled pork sandwiches and ate them in my Mustang.

"Do you like Ms. Roth? The two of you seem to quarrel a lot."

"I never quarrel with her. We debate."

Carla gave me a displeased stare, her skin clustered about her eyes. "Do you enjoy debating her?"

"She's the smartest person I know. You may have noticed—she's eccentric."

"Will she be right?" Carla asked. "Will we find the emerald where she predicts?"

"Do you doubt her?" I asked.

Carla hesitated at first, then said, "Mrs. Roth's analysis seemed sketchy."

"Did you understand what she said?"

"Not everything. Put in your words?"

I cleared my throat. "Jeremiah followed the map and didn't find the gem. Roth thinks the map was simple, uncomplicated, and he revealed the pathway to the gem. He didn't find the emerald because he used the pond's location today."

"I understood that."

"Jeremiah followed a straight line from the farm's front door for two hundred and fifty-three feet and dug. The line intersected, or touched, the left border of today's small lake."

"I see. Jeremiah would have recovered the emerald if he had used the left border of the old pond."

"And that's what Roth is doing."

"She could be wrong,"

"The thing is, Roth is almost always right," I said.

# # #

Carla and I reached the McDonald farm in the early afternoon. The morning chill had vanished, the humidity was slight, and a bright blue sky hung above with no clouds. Mickey's Ford Explorer parked to the left of the farmhouse. A white Dodge Ram 1500 pickup with the words, Ajax Ground Penetrating Radar, on its side parked next to the Explorer. I pulled in beside Mickey's Explorer.

Carla gripped my arm. "Ms. Roth is here."

I spotted Roth, Grandma, and Ashley on the farmhouse's screened-in porch. My boss and the old lady both held wine glasses. "Unusual. Roth hardly ever leaves the mansion."

Grandma and her grandson appeared to be quarreling.

Mickey, Bruce, Angela, and a contractor in grimy white overalls grouped over the pickup's hood, reviewing papers.

"What's happening?" Carla asked.

Mickey raised his head. "Studying Bruce's map. Pinpointing the location of the emerald on the field."

Hal, the contractor, was a white guy about fifty with a three-day stubble and a dusty, blue baseball cap. He greeted Carla and me and returned to studying Bruce's diagram. "A cask? Like a keg?"

Mickey nodded. 'Had metal bands around it."

Mickey and Hal walked out onto the field.

"The contractor has a lawnmower," Carla said. "Why? To mow the plants over the spot where the *X* is?"

"Looks like a lawnmower, but that's the radar scanning machine. The contractor pushes it across the ground like a mower."

Carla stared at the device that Hal maneuvered. "I see. It has a battery and not a gas engine. On the handlebars, it has a screen."

"Yeah, it's quiet."

I turned toward the screened-in porch. "Let's check in with Grandma and Roth."

Roth wore a long black tunic over a gray dress and a white headscarf. She sipped her red wine and seemed composed. Grandma jiggled her wine glass and appeared nervous with her muscles tight. The grandson, dressed in farmer overalls, walked up and reached for her wine glass. "That's enough wine for you."

Grandma jerked her glass back. "Damn it. Leave me alone." She was angry, with cold, flinty eyes.

Carla stopped in front of our boss and spoke up. "Hi, Ms. Roth. Are you anxious?"

"She's not worried," I said. "She has two chances in three."

Carla gave me a puzzled expression and Roth showed a tight-lipped grin.

"Let me explain. One chance she figured out Ian's map, a second chance she didn't figure out the map correctly, and a third chance she located the emerald by blind luck. Dumb luck counts."

Roth shook her head at me and pointed at the group, moving onto the field. "Don, please take Ashley to the worker group and find something useful for him to do."

"Ashley, go with 'em," Grandma said with protruding eyes.

Back at the pickup, Mickey and Hal argued.

"If I find an object like a small barrel, you want me to stop work while you dig it up?" the contractor asked. "A cask, you say?"

"Yes. And if the underground object is trivial, you continue scanning."

"Not going to happen. I agreed to go over a finite area, give you a film record, and leave."

"How about we pay you for the rest of the day?"

The contractor thought a second. "Okay. I stop when you tell me to, and we dig."

The contractor pushed the radar apparatus onto the field, stopping at a point a little over two hundred feet from the farmhouse's front door.

"What are those plants?" Carla asked, pointing to rows of leafy, green growth.

Ashley answered. "Soybeans. Just starting to grow."

In the field, Angela and Bruce identified a search area, which Bruce marked with line-marking paint and a football-field line-marking machine. Angela stood nearby in Wellington boots, holding a small trowel and Bruce's maps. Mickey stood back, holding a shovel. The contractor pushed the ground-penetrating-radar machine about, staying within the laid-out lines. "Here's something," Hal said.

Angela viewed the image on the screen. "Irregular shape. It's a boulder. Not the keg."

The contractor resumed scanning under the ground.

"Wouldn't the McDonald family have dug up the cask when they plowed their fields?" Carla asked.

She had asked a good question. "Ian farmed. He would have known to dig deep to keep the keg hidden."

I glanced across the field at Roth and Grandma. Roth sat relaxed in her chair, occasionally talking to Grandma. The old lady continued tense, drinking copious amounts of wine, her eyes never leaving the field exploration, sitting far forward on her chair.

Hal completed a column of the grid Angela and Bruce had laid out and started the device down the adjacent column.

Ashley, who stood beside me, squirmed. "He ain't found nothing yet."

I wanted him to be still. He was causing me to be edgy. "Hold on. It's a big field."

The contractor stopped walking. "Another object."

Angela stepped to the screen. "Yes. We've found something."

Hal was curious, raising his eyebrows and pausing to examine the screen.

"Perfect circle," Angela said. "Dig it up!"

Mickey, in white tee shirt and jeans, stepped up with his shovel and dug. The soil appeared loose. After ten minutes, I tapped Mickey's shoulder. He stepped aside, and I began excavating. After I shoveled for a spell, Bruce touched my shoulder and took the shovel.

He dug for five minutes. "Something solid."

"Let me see," Angela said. Bruce got out, and she jumped into the hole. "It's wood—crumbling wood."

Bruce shoveled more, but he collapsed the cask's sides.

"Stop shoveling," Angela said. "Let me use my trowel and fingers."

Angela got in the hole and dug with short strokes of her trowel, her Afro bobbing with the scoops of her arms. She placed her fingers over the visible wood and lifted the top off the cask. "There's a sack here, like the bags used to transport grain. The cloth is disintegrating."

I turned and saw Roth and the old lady trotting over to us. She was holding on to my boss's arm.

Angela examined the old sack wrapping and unfolded the bundle. She drew in a breath like a final rush of water sucked down a drain. "Goddamn, it's huge. It's the emerald—the Cherokee Emerald."

A gem, in its uncut, unpolished state, rested in the center of the burlap bundle. I viewed a deep, vibrant green with streaks of dirt. The gem was oblong, the size of a fist—a large natural rough emerald. I enjoy looking at plants, but this emerald was a greener green.

"Let Grandma hold her stone," Roth said. Grandma sat down on the soil in the field, holding the jewel close to her chest, sobbing without control. Her face blazed red with tears rolling down her cheeks.

Ashley gave the impression he was embarrassed with a flush across his cheeks and wincing.

"This gem's big. I'm not a lapidarist," Angela said, "but I didn't see a fault line."

Angela, Carla, and the grandson stood Grandma up, supported and led her back toward the farmhouse. She dug in her heels and shuffled back to Roth. "Thank you. Thank you. Dis didn't seem possible."

I watched Roth. She pursed her lips as if contemplating something. "I regret I took the risk Sandford would kill Don or Mickey." The diminutive Grandma hugged the solid Roth, and then my boss began walking back to Mickey's vehicle. I strode beside her. She frowned at me and muttered to herself, "A chance I'd locate the emerald by blind luck. Pfui." I have a hotdog for a boss, awe-inspiring, but what a character.

Roth had brought the long, frustrating search for the Cherokee Emerald to a successful finish. Approximately a year later, we celebrated by a final party at Grandma's farm.

40

KENTUCKY DERBY DAY, SATURDAY A YEAR LATER

The case of the Cherokee Emerald began on the day of a Kentucky Derby race. In a way, it ended a year later. I drove Carla to the McDonald Farm to celebrate the next race. A fairy-tale genie had rebuilt the farm, transmuting all woebegone vestiges of the formerly rundown farmstead. Workers had replaced the narrow dirt road into the farm with a wide asphalt driveway bordered on both sides by newly planted oak trees. Getting closer to the farmhouse, I saw a new barn equipped with the latest farm equipment. I halted in a parking area of white gravel. The old farmhouse had acquired rebirth, a fresh coat of paint, and a tasteful porch, with an architectural touch of Doric columns, built onto the front. That last bit seemed a little much.

The Cherokee Emerald, in a public auction, fetched a significant sum. Both private investors and the North Carolina Museum of Natural Sciences submitted generous bids for the gem. Roth went ecstatic, and Grandma cried in joy.

Carla raised her eyebrows. "Hmm. I'd say Grandma brought back the splendor of the bygone days of McDonald."

We walked into the living room past a maze of bridge-player tables. The women card players wore funny hats and the men dressed in sports coats and dress shirts without ties. Most card tables' ambiance appeared festive, but a few games were a fight to the death.

We went back to the newly minted garden with its network of spiffy, green hedgerows. The chest-high hedges were well-trimmed and full. Ashley, in a white polo shirt and blue sports coat, talked with a group of men. All around the garden, neighbors wore ostentatious hats, downed drinks, and chattered away.

Drinking red wine but sans a funny hat, Roth sat on a green, wrought iron chair, speaking with Grandma. Taylor, recruited for the day as a chef for Grandma's social, strolled the garden, serving cream cheese and cucumber finger sandwiches and mint juleps.

"You appear years younger," I heard Roth say to Grandma. "You were under constant strain, worrying about the old homestead."

Grandma wore a straw hat with a red rose. She wiped her eyes with a cloth napkin. "It's a dream came true. This," and here she swept both arms about the garden, "is how I remember my younger times." She sighed. "My dear departed grandmother, rest her soul, would be proud. This old house is back, stately, alive, full of people."

Roth patted Grandma's hand. "I'm happy for you."

"You made it possible," Grandma said. "You visualized the map even though Sandford had destroyed it. You found the emerald!"

Roth glanced cautiously at Grandma, with a downcast expression and sighing. "The separation of foolishness from brilliance is determined only by triumph."

My boss had streamed forth another of her endless aphorisms. If anyone thought she was indispensable, Roth did. True, she often verged on brilliant, but that didn't alter the fact she had a swelled head. Carla and I moved off to see others and grab drinks from Taylor.

In Grandma's garden, as I drank my fourth mint julep, Carla rested in a wrought-iron chair next to me. Someone had given her a wide-brimmed black hat with brown and black feathers attached to the top. In a yellow, wide-brimmed hat with pink flowers and green leaves, Angela Lightfoot had joined us. I had gotten sloshed on my drinks, but Carla had been nursing her cocktails.

"You done good, my young Nancy Drew," I said to Carla.

She sat with her legs pulled under her on the chair. "Thank you. We form a great team, don't we?"

My thinking had been growing woozy. I needed to find a sober driver to get us home. "Did a commendable job of getting the young motorcycle rider, . . . eh . . . Joel, to disclose de infer . . . infermation on the gang's hideaway."

"Ah, yes, young Joel," Carla said.

I took a sip of my drink. "Alas, he got shot and died in the shootout at the Buckho farm. As publicized, . . . the course of drew love never runs smooth."

Carla raised her hand to her mouth. "That's terrible. In a way, it's my fault."

"Don't see it dat way. Sandford's the culprit. Dat violent man."

They observed me with puzzlement. Angela's mouth fell open and Carla gave me an incredulous stare.

I posed a question to Carla and Angela. "The emerald calmed Roth's greedy nature and give Grandma back her wistful dream. But . . . but . . . weren't de driving force always de violent man, and not de gem?"

Silence surrounded me, with the party din in the background.

"You mean Sandford?" Angela asked.

I nodded. "He were the drug king, recruited dem teenagers, searched yars for the emerald, and eng . . . a . . . neered the killing of at least six individuals. I include dem three teenagers and the deputy slain in shootouts."

Carla stared at me, askance. "What's your point? Do you want to rename the case?"

I raised my empty glass to Carla. "My point, . . . my dear Diaz, . . . is we solved our first case and tracked down a brutal soc . . . sociopath."

Afterward, the horses raced, I had another julep, and my memory fogged. I vaguely recall Carla, Angela, and Taylor hoisting me into a vehicle's passenger seat and later dropping me on my bed at the mansion. As they left my bedroom, I heard Taylor say, "Needs a grownup to manage him." She has a sharp tongue but a big heart.

THE END

ABOUT THE AUTHOR

R. M. Morgan worked as an engineer in both the U.S. government and academia. In his job, he investigated mysteries like a detective, unraveling the physics of car crashes to establish how to save drivers and passengers. After years of writing articles in that world, R. M. Morgan discovered the joy of writing mystery novels. Currently, he lives in Southern California and is writing the fourth book in the Roth/Gannon series.

If you enjoy detective mysteries, give R. M. Morgan novels a read. The books that keep the reader guessing whodunit right up to the end.

Further information about R. M. Morgan is available on his website, www.rmmorgan.com.

Printed in Great Britain
by Amazon

66765674R00199